FORE THE

Young Lions

Andrew Mackay

AuthorHouse™
1663 Liberty Drive
Bloomington, IN 47403
www.authorhouse.com
Phone: 1-800-839-8640

First published by AuthorHouse 8/8/2011

ISBN: 978-1-4567-7437-0 (sc)

Printed in the United States of America

~ Dedication ~

Young Lions is dedicated to the memory of my grandfathers, John Mackay of the Seaforth Highlanders and Sheik Kassim Khan of the Hong Kong Volunteer Regiment who both fought for their country in the Second World War.

Chapter One

"We don't have a snowball's chance in hell, sir." Witherspoon shook his head as he handed the order back to Lieutenant-Colonel Hook.

"That's what the Persians said about the three hundred Spartans at Thermopylae, Roy." Hook said grimly as he folded up the order. "London needs to gather enough troops to launch a counter attack to push the Nazis back into the sea. I'll sacrifice the lives of everyman in this battalion to buy Headquarters more time. Including my own life and including yours. Especially yours, Roy." Hook continued with a twinkle in his eye.

Witherspoon laughed at Hook's black humour. "Zero chance of success, zero chance of survival," Witherspoon shrugged his shoulders, "what are we waiting for?" He grinned as his eyes lit up like a stick of dynamite. "Strength and honour, Colonel." Witherspoon stretched out his hand.

"Strength and honour, Roy." Hook smiled as he shook Witherspoon's hand. Lieutenant-Colonel Richard Hook M.C. stepped forward and gazed out over the sea of faces that made up the Third Battalion of the Royal Regiment of Fen Fusiliers (RRiFFs).

"As you know, the Germans began landing on the south east coast of England yesterday," Hook announced. "Unfortunately, we have not been able to hold them on the beaches…" murmuring broke out amongst the assembled troops and rippled through the men like a wave.

"Silence in the ranks!" Bellowed R.S.M. Witherspoon.

"Thank you, R.S.M.," Hook continued. "I have further bad news… at dawn this morning, German forces landed at King's Lynn…" The RRiFFs reacted as if they had been physically slapped across the face.

"How can they be so near?" Alan Mitchell asked his best friend Sam Roberts.

"They're less than an hour away by car," Sam answered as he felt a hot jet of urine flow down his inside leg in a torrent and form a rapidly expanding pool on the ground. As he blushed in acute shame and embarrassment he smelt a sudden waft of ammonia drift over him and he realized that he was not the only one to have pissed himself.

"The Germans are heading south towards us here at Hereward," Hook continued. "We are the only ones who can stop them from taking Cambridge. We march north towards King's Lynn immediately."

As the RRiFFs marched through the streets of Hereward Sam spotted his father and mother and his elder sister, Alice, in the crowd.

Alice thrust a flower into the upturned barrel of his rifle. "Good luck, boys. Be careful. Corporal Thompson, look after my two baby brothers for me," Alice said as she playfully ruffled their hair.

"I will, Miss Roberts," Corporal Thompson, the boys' section commander, promised as Alice planted a quick kiss on the cheeks of both boys.

"Sam, Alan, come back in one piece. I love you both." Michelle Roberts sobbed through tear stained eyes as she hugged her boy and her surrogate son, Alan, in a ferocious bear hug. Alan had spent many a happy week end and holiday with the Roberts household and was regarded as a member of the family.

Sam and Alan had to gently but firmly prise Mrs. Roberts' hands away from their necks or else the boys risked being physically ripped from the column of marching men. "Goodbye, mum," Sam shouted over his shoulder. "Don't worry: We'll be alright."

"I'll look after him, Mrs. Roberts!" Alan promised. Children cheered and ran scampering alongside the marching troops, weaving in and out of the files, threatening to trip them up.

Sam spotted his father, Alex Roberts, standing at attention with his right arm raised in salute. "I wish that I was coming with you, lads," he said as he tapped his left leg with his walking stick.

"I know, dad," Sam said. Alex Roberts had suffered a leg wound whilst serving as a Captain with the RRiFFs in the last war.

"Strength and honour, Sam," Mr. Roberts said as he shook his son's hand. Sam replied with the Fusilier motto as his father shook Alan's hand.

"Strength and honour, Mr. Roberts," Alan replied.

Alex Roberts' eyes welled up with tears as his youngest son marched off to war. "God bless you, lads," he croaked.

"This is going to be a long slog northwards," Sam said as the Fusiliers left the cheering crowds behind. He awkwardly pulled his soggy trouser leg away from his damp skin.

Alan Mitchell and Sam Roberts were fifteen year old school boys at St. John's Academy located in the medieval market town of Hereward in county Cambridgeshire. Alan

Mitchell and his younger brother David were inmates at "Cromwell" Boarding House. Sam Roberts and his older sister Alice were day pupils from an old Hereward family and had been educated at St. John's for generations. Sam's three older brothers had also attended St. John's. Both Alan and Sam were second year Officer Cadets in the St.John's Academy Officer Training Corps which had amalgamated with the hastily raised local Home Guard unit, the Royal Regiment of Fens Fusiliers (RRiFFs) 3rd Battalion (Home Guard).

Richard Hook still possessed the ramrod straight back, firm hand shake and rapid pace of walking which stood him out as having been a soldier. Hook had fought in the First World War and after he had been demobbed he had studied Chemistry at the University of Glasgow. After graduation, he trained as a teacher and was offered a position at his old school, St. John's Academy. Principal Teacher of Chemistry, Mr. Richard Hook, had been the Commanding Officer of the School O.T.C. for fifteen years and at the outbreak of the war he had been promoted to Lieutenant-Colonel and had become the C.O. of The Third Battalion The Royal Regiment of Fens Fusiliers (Home Guard).

"Hallo? What's going on?" Hook asked suddenly.

There was a commotion ahead. The troops in front had stopped marching.

"What's going on, Mr. Mason?"

"This is Sergeant Downham, sir," Captain Mason, Sam and Alan's company commander, replied. "King's Lynn Home Guard. He says that the Germans have captured the port and are at this very moment heading down this road straight towards us."

Downham came to a position of attention and reported "The Huns attacked at dawn and took us completely by surprise, sir. They've captured the port and killed or captured

4

most of the Home Guard. The survivors are streaming down the road now along with hundreds of refugees. The roads are completely clogged and blocked up with refugees. They're running away from the Huns like frightened sheep."

"Enemy forces?" Hook asked.

"From what I saw, sir, the advance guard is made up of a motorcycle battalion mounted on a mixture of motorcycles with a sidecar armed with a machine gun and single motorcycles. I don't know what else they have got, I'm afraid."

"Where are they now, Sergeant?"

"Not far up the road, Colonel. Listen, you can hear their machine guns."

Hook put his hand up to his ear and shielded his eyes from the sun as he looked up the road. "Machine guns. Yes, I can hear them. Clearing their way through the refugees. The swine." Hook clenched his teeth in sudden anger. Refugees were starting to flow down the sides of the Battalion with the Fusiliers acting as a breakwater.

"Sir, shall I clear the refugees from the road?" Witherspoon asked.

Hook thought quickly. "No, R.S.M. It's an impossible task. Get the battalion into Wake and take up the position of a snap ambush. The Huns may appear at any moment. Get me the company commanders at the double."

"Will you two simmer down in there?" Corporal Thompson shouted from the next room. "Shut up and keep your eyes peeled and your ears open for the Jerries."

"'Keep your ears open?'" Alan repeated, "I can't hear a damn thing over the racket that the refugees are making." Sam nodded his head in agreement.

There was a constant sound of babies and toddlers crying and parents cajoling and pleading with their moody broods. The refugee column weaved its way in and out of the dirt and debris left by the people who had already passed through the village of Wake like a giant wounded worm.

"Listen in," Thompson hissed. "Here they come!" A loud burst of machine gun fire tore through the air. Children started screaming, women began to cry and men grabbed their families and hurried along the road. The refugees abandoned their possessions and started running like lemmings.

The first German motorcycle combination sped towards Wake Bridge, the gunner firing his machine gun into the air above the heads of the refugees.

"Right boys, listen in," Thompson poked his head through the door into the room. "Only open fire when the whistle blows. Any questions?"

"No, Corporal!" The boys answered in unison.

"Alright lads," Thompson looked into the face of Alan and Sam in turn. "Keep your heads down and your powder dry. Strength and honour, lads."

"Strength and honour!" The boys chorused.

Alan turned around to Sam. "I'll see you when it's over."

"Not if I see you first." Sam smiled grimly. The boys shook hands with exaggerated formality.

Alan and Sam took up their positions side by side at a window. They held their rifles with the butts pressed tightly against their shoulders. Their hearts beat louder and louder as beads of sweat ran down their faces and stung their eyes. Sweat chaffed their collars and made their trousers cling to their legs.

The sudden whistle blast made the boys jump. "Rapid fire!" Bellowed Thompson. Alan found a German at the end of his foresight and squeezed the trigger. The Nazi fell backwards off his bike like a lifeless puppet.

Alan had laid out his .22 rounds on the windowsill and was frantically reloading, working the bolt action as soon as he had fired. The street was rapidly filling up with twitching and twisting dead and dying Germans, as the Fusiliers poured rapid fire into the traffic jammed enemy. Nazis lay slouched over the handlebars of the motorcycles or lay half in, half out of the sidecars. Very few Germans were managing to fire back. They had been slowed to a virtual walking pace by the wall of refugees that had continued to clog the way and by the debris on the road. But here and there, amongst the wrecked and burning motorcycles, isolated groups of Nazis were fighting back.

"Grenade!" Thompson shouted.

A German potato masher grenade cart wheeled through the air – hit the wall of the house, rebounded and exploded back in the street. "Here comes another! Take cover!" Another grenade flew through the air, and sailed through Thompson's window. The grenade blew up and shrapnel whistled through the air.

"I'm hit!" Shouted Alan as he dropped his rifle and put his hands up to his eyes. He collapsed and hit the ground as Sam hovered over him.

"Where are you hit?" Sam asked with his hands on Alan's shoulders.

"In my face. I can't see! I can't see!" Alan screamed as he sat sprawled on the floor, blood streaming from his face down his hands and arms.

"Take your hands away, Alan!" Sam ordered through the smoke, his ears ringing from the impact of the grenade explosion.

"I'm blind! I can't see! I can't see!" Alan wailed.

"Take your hands away, Al, let me look at you," Sam insisted. He gently laid his hands on Alan's and prised his shaking fingers away. "It's alright Al," Sam reassured him.

"I'm blind…" Alan moaned.

Sam knelt down and examined Alan's face. It was covered with blood. He emptied some water from his water bottle onto the corner of his sleeve and wiped away some of the blood. Sam stopped wiping and examined the wound. "It's a piece of shrapnel. It's cut you on your cheek, and it's sliced a nice clean wound. Lots of blood, but not very deep. The medics should be able to sew you up with half a dozen stitches."

"What about my eyes?" Alan asked. His black hair was matted thick with blood.

"They're fine. Your eyes were caked shut by the blood, that's all, Al," Sam reassured him.

"Oh my God!" Alan's bloody hand went to his mouth. "Corporal Thompson!"

Sam bent over and ran through to the next room, remembering to keep his head down as a brace of bullets buzzed through the open window and drilled a neat line of holes in the back wall. He bent over Thompson's silent and still form. Sam turned him over. Thompson's wide-open eyes stared back at him. "He's dead, Al."

"And Willy?" Alan asked about Thompson's partner.

Sam examined Willy, who lay on his front next to Thompson. His back looked like a bloody sieve and was still smoking. "He's a goner too."

"Christ!" Alan muttered, clutching a torn piece of his uniform shirt to his war wound. "What do we do now?"

"We keep fighting and we pay those dirty murdering Nazi bastards back for Corporal Thompson and Willy."

The boys had hardly resumed firing when they heard three long loud whistle blasts which signaled the cease fire.

"Alan, Sam – are you alright?" A bodiless voice came from upstairs.

"Yes, Lance-Corporal," Alan answered. "But Corporal Thompson and Willy are dead."

The boys heard a curse. "Bad luck. I'm taking over command of the section. Check the enemy dead. We don't want any prisoners. We'll cover you, but be careful. Don't do anything stupid. Grab any Hun weapons and ammunition that we can use."

"Yes, Lance-Corporal," Sam answered.

Alan and Sam cautiously poked their heads out of the door and slowly crept out into the street with their rifle butts pulled tight into their shoulders. Other Fusiliers were doing the same. Alan and Sam stepped over dead and dying Germans and prodded them with their rifles. Isolated shots echoed down the street as the RRiFFs administered the coup de grace to wounded enemy soldiers.

Alan returned to the house with two rifles slung over one shoulder and two sets of webbing over the other. Sam staggered into the house with several belts of ammunition draped around his neck and carrying a MG 42 machine gun in his arms.

"Blimey lads – who do you think you are, Pancho Villa? All you boys need is a sombrero and a handlebar moustache and you would look like Mexican banditos!" Lance-Corporal Vincent exclaimed as he walked down the stairs. "It looks like you've captured the arsenal of the entire Nazi army!"

Alan and Sam grinned at Vincent like a pair of Cheshire cats.

"I'll have that!" Vincent exclaimed with a triumphant look on his face, as he grabbed the machine gun.

"Hey!" Sam protested. "That's not fair! I found it! Finders keepers!" He vainly tried to hold onto it.

"Listen Sam," Vincent tried to reason with him. "Do you know how to fire it? No, I thought not, so give it here."

Sam reluctantly surrendered the weapon like a defeated general surrendering his sword.

"Good lad. Alright, lads, we're moving out immediately." The rest of the Section came down the stairs. "Let's go." Vincent and his Fusiliers filed out of the house and started threading its way through Wake High Street. The scene was that of utter carnage. There were dead Germans and crashed and burning motorcycles lying everywhere. Spent cartridges littered the ground and pools of congealed blood were already starting to attract flies in the heat. The RRiFFs trudged through the smoking and burning village towards Fairfax.

Vincent and his men reached Fairfax an hour or so after the battle of Wake ended to find the rest of the battalion already digging in. Wake Road ran straight through the village from north to south. Norwich Road was a tree lined sunken road that cut through Wake Road at right angles from west to east just before the first houses of Fairfax began. A man kneeling down on Norwich Road had cover from view as well as cover from fire from both Fairfax and from the fields on the Wake side of the road. The Fusiliers were spread and stretched out to the left and right on the road for several hundred feet and were frantically digging in with whatever came to hand. Those lucky enough to have liberated a set of German webbing made use of an entrenching tool; the others used their helmets, mess tins or their bare hands.

Oberstleutnant Christian von Schnakenberg lowered his binoculars and took off his helmet. He smoothed away his matted hair and wiped the sweat and dirt from his eyes. He was at the edge of a small forest about a quarter of a mile from the enemy positions. "Verdamnt!" He turned around to face his second in command, Major Frederich Lindau. "They're digging in. We don't have enough time to attack them before it becomes dark."

The motorcyclists had suffered over three hundred casualties in the landing, the fighting in King's Lynn and in the ambush at Wake so von Schnakenberg's regiment, The First Battalion Potsdam Grenadiers, had taken over as the spearhead. The Grenadiers had remained pinned down on the wrong side of Wake Bridge whilst the motorcyclists were being massacred and had been unable to help. Von Schnakenberg's men were chaffing at the bit and they were burning to avenge their fallen comrades. They had lost dozens of friends and comrades trying to cross the bridge and swim across the River Ouse to help the trapped soldiers of the motorcycle battalion. Devious booby traps and cowardly sniper attacks had claimed further lives. The Grenadiers were like a pack of blood thirsty dobermans straining at the leash. Von Schnakenberg doubted if he and his officers could hold them.

Von Schnakenberg turned around and faced his second in command; "Freddy," he asked, "what do we know about the enemy forces?

"We found half a dozen enemy dead in the village with the letters "H.G." on their armbands. Poorly dressed in a mixture of military and civilian clothes. No doubt they're Home Guard," Lindau explained. "We also found discarded but destroyed shotguns and .22 target shooting rifles, plus their shell cases and 0.303 rifle cartridges."

"But no machine gun shell cases?"

"No, sir."

"So," von Schnakenberg thought aloud, "poorly dressed and poorly equipped but well led. They wiped out most of a battalion after all. How are the men?"

"A Company has suffered heavy casualties but the other

companies are fine. The whole battalion is eager to attack, sir." Von Schnakenberg seemed unsure and uncertain. "Oberstleutnant, the enemy has been lucky once. But they're schoolboys and old men. They must have suffered casualties and they've probably used up most of their ammunition. They're Home Guard, Oberstleutnant. Surely the Potsdam Grenadiers are a match for them?"

"What the hell…?" Alan said. A loud explosion made Sam and Alan duck down into their foxholes like frightened rabbits.

"Take cover!" Lance-Corporal Vincent shouted. "Mortars! Heads down!"

The mortar shells landed in the field to the front of the Fusiliers' positions, in Fairfax, behind the soldiers and on top of the men themselves. Alan and Sam sat crouched down in the bottom of their shelters with their knees pulled in tightly to their chests with their hands wrapped around their heads. The earth shook continuously and mud and grass slid into the foxholes. Alan had the horrifying thought that he might be buried alive.

"Stand to! Battalion! Three hundred yards to your front. Rapid fire. Rapid fire!!!" Hook's instantly recognizable voice thundered through the Fusiliers' shelters.

Sam stuck his head out of his foxhole. German soldiers were less than three hundred yards away.

"Get stuck into them!" Vincent screamed.

Sam rapidly worked the bolt, pushing a round into the chamber. He'd hardly pulled the butt into his shoulder and brought the foresight to bear on a distant grey figure when he pulled the trigger.

"Keep it up. Keep it up!" Vincent shouted his encouragement.

The distant German figures kept on coming. They

seemed to be advancing in waves. They ran forward a few yards and then disappeared, diving into the ground. They opened fire and then popped up a few seconds later in a different position, and then kept coming.

Alan allowed himself a satisfied smile as he fired and saw a German crumple and hit the ground. He looked to his left and saw Vincent with the captured machine gun pulled up tight against his shoulder. But something was wrong: Vincent's finger was on the trigger but he was not firing. What the hell was going on?

Oberleutnant Wilhelm von Schnakenberg lay down in the grass, his face smeared with a mixture of dirt and sweat. He was sweating profusely and panting like a dog. Wilhelm was a happy man; his platoon, despite taking casualties, was fighting well. He and his men had now reached a point roughly one hundred meters from the enemy position. They were now ready to start the final attack. He smiled to himself as he remembered his big brother's shocked reaction when he announced his intention to follow in Christian's footsteps and go into the family regiment. Christian had done his best to dissuade him; but alas to no avail. Many of Wilhelm's friends and fellow officers had good-naturedly remarked that they doubted if there was enough room in the Potsdam Grenadiers for two von Schnakenbergs. He had replied that there was enough fame and glory to be won for both of them, and plenty left over to spare.

His elder brother, Christian, was the youngest Oberstleutnant in the German Army and had led the First Battalion the Potsdam Grenadiers through the fighting in Poland, Holland, Belgium and France. Wilhelm was proud of his brother, but he had a lot to live up to and he had a desperate desire to prove that he had earned his place in the regiment. He was there on his own merits as a result of what he had done and not because of who he was.

A loud whistle blast cut through the air. Wilhelm immediately leapt to his feet, "Potsdam!" He screamed at the top of his voice. The other Grenadiers leapt to their feet, "Potsdam! Potsdam!" They shouted. This is it, Wilhelm thought to himself. A final bayonet charge guaranteed to put a poorly equipped enemy to flight. The soldiers charged through the knee-high grass towards the British.

A chainsaw like staccato ripped through the air.

"What the-?" Wilhelm said to himself. All around him men were dropping. His men. He recognized the sound of an MG 42. Machine guns! The enemy doesn't have machine guns! The bullets caught him across the chest, tearing bloody holes diagonally from left to right. He crumpled to his knees. A terrible burning pain spread from his chest across the whole of his body. Blood began to dribble out of the corner of his mouth. As his eyes filled up with tears and his vision began to blur he thought to himself, "machine guns… German machine guns…it's not fair."

Alan's eyes opened wide with fear as he heard the loud whistle blast tear through the air. Hundreds of Germans suddenly appeared as if they had grown out of the ground and started charging towards the Fusiliers. A bugle blast pierced Alan's ears. Vincent's finger tightened on the trigger and his machine gun began to fire. More machine guns joined in. The Germans were stopped in their tracks as if they had run into a brick wall. One second there were hundreds of soldiers charging towards them and the next second there were none. The Grim Reaper had cut down the German stalks of wheat with a giant British scythe.

Another bugle blast. "Charge!" Vincent screamed, the blood lust was in his eyes, "Come on!" Alan climbed to his feet and charged after Vincent. Everywhere he looked, to his left and right; Fusiliers were scrambling out of their foxholes and charging towards the Germans. The surviving Germans quickly surrendered. The fight had been knocked out of them. Those lucky enough to escape were running towards the forest dragging their dead and dying with them.

After five minutes of fight and flight it was all over. The RRiFFS returned to their positions with more German weapons, ammunition, booty and prisoners. Sentries were set and the remaining members of the battalion fell into a deep and exhausted sleep.

Christian von Schnakenberg stared out over the battlefield numb with shock and awe as he watched the tattered remnants of his regiment straggle home. The Grenadiers stumbled and staggered into the forest in ones and twos or sometimes with a wounded comrade propped up with an arm around the waist. Many soldiers were without helmets, their uniforms torn and covered with blood, dirt and gore; most were without weapons that had been abandoned in their haste to get away. All semblances of discipline and order had disappeared. They were no longer soldiers. They were a rabble. A mob. They wandered past von Schnakenberg without a word. Defeat was written all over their faces. And something else. Shame. Shame that they had not carried the enemy position. Shame that they had been beaten so badly, by "schoolboys and old men" as their officers and N.C.O.s had described them before the attack, bragging and boasting about how they would be no match for the high and mighty Potsdam Grenadiers.

Von Schnakenberg found a disheveled looking officer. "What happened?"

"They waited until we charged. Then they opened up with machine guns at point blank range. Our machine guns. German machine guns." The words came out in a slur, dazed and halting as if he was sleep talking.

Von Schnakenberg turned to Lindau; "Freddy," he asked in a tortured voice, "how did this happen?"

"They must've captured them from the motorcycle battalion," Lindau replied. He paused, "Christian, there's something else…"

Alarm bells went off in von Schnakenberg's head. Lindau never called him by his first name unless he was either drunk or he was the bearer of bad news.

"Christian. Willy didn't make it. Alfonin, his platoon feldwebel told me…"

Von Schnakenberg's hand went up to his mouth and he bit into his knuckles. "Where is he?" He asked through clenched teeth.

"He's lying out there with the rest of his men.…" Lindau answered.

Von Schnakenberg's legs gave way as if someone had kicked them out from under him.

"I see," S.S. Brigadefuhrer Hans Schuster said. A pause. "Let me see if I get this right: the whole of our advance is being held up because the mighty Potsdam Grenadiers cannot capture trenches held by the Home Guard!" Schuster screamed the final words at the top of his voice, spittle projecting out of his mouth and his face turning bright red; "Our advance is being held up by schoolboys and old men?" he continued, his scar twitching. Hans Schuster was the commanding officer of the King's Lynn invasion force.

"I must protest, sir," Lindau interrupted; "Oberstleutnant von Schnakenberg's own brother was killed in the attack and the men fought bravely," he asserted. But they ran like cowards, he thought to himself, "Oberstleutnant…?" Lindau turned to his leader for support.

"Well, von Schnakenberg?" Schuster said, puffing out his chest.

Silence.

"I think that I've seen quite enough here. I'm bringing up the Fourth S.S. Regiment tonight and they'll take up position behind you. Tomorrow at dawn we'll attack the British and you'll see how real Germans fight. Do your best to hold your position tonight," Schuster walked forward until he stood inches from von Schnakenberg's face; "However, I do give you permission to retreat if the Home Guard launch an attack…armed with pitchforks…"

Chapter Two

Hans Schuster had fought on the Western Front during the Great War and after the war he had joined the Freikorps and he had helped to crush the Communist Sparticist Revolt. Schuster had then joined the Nazi Party and had taken part in the Munich Beer Hall Putsch. He had commanded an S.S. Death Squad during the Night of the Long Knives and had become a tried and trusted personal friend of Hitler. He had commanded the Fourth S.S. Regiment and had led his men through the campaigns in Poland, the Low Countries and France. At the end of the Blitzkrieg he had been promoted to command an S.S. Brigade-which became known as "The Triple S" -Schuster's S.S.

"Gentlemen, our guests have arrived. Let's welcome them in true Triple S fashion." His officers laughed loyally at their leader's joke.

The refugees started to clamber out of the lorries until a group of several hundred had assembled. Von Schnakenberg and Lindau walked across to where Schuster and his officers were standing.

"Brigadefuhrer Schuster," von Schnakenberg asked, "what's going on?"

"Prisoner exchange," Schuster answered, barely acknowledging him.

"Sir, with all due respect, I hardly think that this is the time or place for a prisoner exchange," Lindau said.

"I'd rather listen to my grandmother's military advice than listen to yours, Lindau. So with all due respect, keep your chicken shit opinions to yourself. "

Lindau was about to say something that would finish his career for good when von Schnakenberg grabbed his arm.

The S.S. troops ushered the refugees into a thick long line that stretched for several hundred yards. The soldiers took up position behind them.

"I don't like the look of this…" von Schnakenberg said.

"I'm getting a bad feeling…" Lindau added.

"Lindau!" Schuster shouted, "get your men into position behind mine."

"Brigadefuhrer Schuster, do the British know that we're proposing a prisoner exchange?" Lindau asked.

"No," Schuster replied with a deadpan face, returning to look at his map.

Lindau looked over the hundreds of refugees milling around aimlessly. Men, women and children, old people and babes in arms. Children holding their parent's hands, babies crying, old people sitting on the ground as they waited. Scared and bewildered, dazed and confused. S.S. soldiers hovering around the edges of the crowd like lions circling Christians in the Coliseum.

"You're not going to exchange prisoners at all, are you?" Lindau accused, "you're going to use those people as a human shield!" Lindau's eyes bulged with horror.

Schuster ignored him.

Von Schnakenberg clicked his heels to a position of attention. "Brigadefuhrer Schuster, I must protest: using civilians as a human shield directly contravenes all articles of the Geneva Convention."

"Von Schnakenberg, this may come as a terrible shock to you, but I don't give a rat shit about your precious Geneva Convention."

"If you do this you will blacken the honour of the German Army for ever," Lindau persisted.

Schuster turned to look at both of them with a look of sheer disgust and utter contempt on his face, "'Blacken the honour of the German Army?' You're not in your fancy student fencing clubs and military academies now, you're not in your fancy Prussian mansion now, you aristocratic bastards!" He was spitting as he spoke; "we should've finished off all of you Junker bastards when we dealt with the Jews!"

"I will not follow any order that contravenes the Articles of War," Lindau said as he jutted out his jaw defiantly.

"Yes, you will, Lindau, you spineless piece of shit, or I will shoot you on the spot for cowardice and for disobeying the orders of a superior officer and your men will be placed under my command." Schuster took his Luger pistol from his holster and pointed it at Lindau's face.

Von Schnakenberg stepped in front of his friend and shielded him from fire. "That will not be necessary, sir," von Schnakenberg assured him; "we will carry out your orders as instructed."

"But Christian…" Lindau protested.

"I'd like to speak with Major Lindau in private, if I may, sir." Schuster barely grunted his permission as von Schnakenber grabbed Lindau by the shoulders and steered him away from Schuster out of earshot. "Freddy, Schuster's connected straight to the top. He's a personal friend of Hitler himself! We have no choice. If we disobey him, it will not just be our heads which end up on the chopping block, but the heads of our families as well. We must do what he says. There will be time to settle the score later." He released his vice like grip.

"Christian," Lindau had not given up yet, "what about the regiment?"

"Freddy," von Schnakenberg said gently, "if we don't do as he says there will be no regiment."

Von Schnakenberg returned to Schuster and clicked his heels together standing at attention; "I apologize on behalf of myself and Major Lindau. We were both out of order. Of course, we will do our best to support you."

"You're damn right you're out of order!" Schuster exploded. He slipped on the safety catch as his face slowly returned to its normal colour; "I'm glad that you've finally seen sense," Schuster put away his Luger. "I'm willing to forget this gross insubordination, but if it happens again I guarantee that you will spend the rest of this war on garrison duty in Berlin." He banged his fist on his car bonnet and made his map jump. "Do I make myself clear?" His words were laced with poison.

"Yes sir!" von Schnakenberg and Lindau answered in unison.

"Very well, gentlemen," Schuster said, his voice returning to normal, "let's put this unfortunate incident behind us. Major Lindau, to your position. Oberstleutnant von Schnakenberg, stay here with me, if you please. Come, come Christian," von Schnakenberg winced as Schuster put his hand on his shoulder. "After all, we're on the same side."

"Come on, Al," Sam said. "Get up."

"Colonel," Captain Mason announced, "I think that you'd better come with me."

Colonel Hook finished strapping on his Sam Brown belt

and checked that his revolver was fully loaded. "What is it?" he asked following Mason.

"Hundreds of refugees are heading towards us, sir. They must've come from King's Lynn."

Hook and Mason arrived at the B Company position at the entrance to Fairfax. Refugees were spread out in a line in front of him stretching as far as the eye could see from left to right the line was at least twenty people deep and the crowd included men, women and children. There were hundreds of them. The mob carried large grubby white sheets hanging from branches.

Hook looked left and right at his men. Most of them were standing up, looking and pointing at the spectacular sight in front of them. Hardly anyone of them were in their foxholes and few of them were carrying any weapons. The refugees were still coming. They were less than three hundred yards away.

"Where are the Germans, Paul?" Hook asked, speaking to himself. "Battalion, stand to." He grabbed Mason's arm, "quickly, but quietly," he whispered. Mason sped away, spreading the word.

Hook raised his binoculars to his eyes and scanned the crowd. He couldn't spot any tell tale grey. Where could they be? They couldn't have pulled out, surely? Two hundred yards away.

"R.S.M. Order them to halt."

"Very good, sir," R.S.M. Witherspoon snapped to attention and saluted. All of the Fusiliers were now in their foxholes, weapons at the ready. "Refugees-halt!" He bellowed.

The refugees kept coming. One hundred and fifty yards away.

"Gunner," Hook tapped a machine gunner on his shoulder, "fire a burst above their heads."

The machine gun burst shattered the morning stillness. The refugees started screaming. One hundred yards away. Every one hit the ground.

That was the signal. The S.S. troops crouching behind the refugees opened fire with their own machine guns, charging forward, firing from the hip. At the same time mortar rounds began falling on the RRiFF positions, throwing up showers of earth and grass, scoring direct hits on foxholes, adding flesh and blood to the debris. Some Fusiliers took cover in their foxholes whilst others fired back. "Rapid fire! Rapid fire!" The officers and N.C.O.s screamed.

Sam and Alan worked their bolts furiously, hardly taking aim before firing. The Germans were getting nearer. Seventy-five yards. Fifty yards. S.S. troopers falling, but more taking their places. A mortar round fell short and tore a gaping hole in the German ranks, felling soldiers like trees. Shrapnel whistled through the air and thudded into the trees above the RRiFF' heads. A scream of pain. "My face! My face!" Shell splinters finding a target. The Germans charging on, bayonets fixed and glistening, shouting their war cries, throwing their grenades at the Fusilier positions. Here they come! An S.S. trooper ran towards Sam. Sam squeezed off a shot and caught him in the stomach. He fell over writhing and clutching his wounds. A second German appeared firing his Schmeisser machine gun from the hip. A RRiFF to the right of Sam crumpled and fell. Sam pointed his rifle at the S.S. man and squeezed the trigger. Click. An empty chamber. He was out of bullets. The German swung his Schmeisser towards him. Sam felt his bowels empty. "This is it," he thought to himself.

"Hande hoch!" The S.S. trooper ordered, motioning with his machine gun.

Sam remembered his schoolboy German. He raised his arms above his head. It saved his life.

Hook led Battalion H.Q. in a counter attack with fixed bayonets. "Plug the gaps!" He shouted, "hold the line!" He screamed. He emptied his Schmeisser machine gun at a group of Germans charging towards him. Hook looked to his left and right. S.S. were breaking through everywhere. Fusiliers were streaming away from their positions and abandoning their weapons. Germans were tearing after them and shooting them in the back as the British tried to escape. RRiFFs were starting to surrender on their own, in pairs and in groups. It was no use. They'd put up a good fight. "Bugler, sound the cease fire," Hook said calmly.

"Sir?" The bugler queried.

"The cease fire, son. Surrender. It's all over."

Hook raised his hands above his head. The bugle notes signaling the cease-fire sounded through the air. It was a universal symbol. The firing slackened in intensity and gradually died away as the soldiers stopped fighting.

Alan woke up with a massive headache. His ears were ringing and his temples were pounding. He was stiff and cold. He couldn't move. He was paralyzed. His heartbeat sped up and his breathing quickened. He started to hyperventilate. Calm down, calm down, he said to himself. Check yourself. . He slowly flexed and stretched his fingers. Fine so far. He rotated his wrists. No problem. Alan bent his elbows. They seemed to work. He shrugged his shoulders. Everything seemed to be in ship shape. At least his upper body was. He tried his legs. He couldn't move them. He tried to open his eyes. He couldn't open them. He slowly raised his hands to his face. His eyes were dry and glued shut. "Please God," he begged, "don't let me be blind. Anything but that." Alan blindly groped for the water bottle on his webbing belt. He found the bottle, unscrewed the top and poured some water on his hands. He splashed the water on his face, gently wiping the muck away from his eyes. He emptied the entire water bottle cleaning his face. He opened his eyes. He was not blind. He was sitting in his foxhole. A dead Fusilier was lying down head first in the foxhole trapping Alan's legs. It was his blood that had glued Alan's eyes shut. Alan pushed and pulled the RRiFF out, grunting and groaning as he did so. Alan looked at the dead man. He didn't recognize him. He cautiously peered out over the edge of the foxhole. A sudden stab of intense pain hurt his temples. It was the sun, but at least the sun was setting. What time was it? He didn't know. His watch was broken.

Alan looked across at the field. Fusiliers were digging as Germans looked on. They were collecting bodies from all over the field and were carrying the corpses to the freshly dug graves. Burying the dead. Alan looked around him, searching for his rifle. He couldn't find it. Alan looked around the RRiFF position. Plenty of dead Fusiliers, but no dead Germans. The burial party must've collected them. No weapons either. They must all have been collected. Alan suddenly remembered his captured Luger pistol, a spoil of war from the successful ambush at Wake. He patted it underneath his jacket to reassure himself.

"No rest!" a German barked. "Work! Schnell!" Sam was exhausted. They had spent the whole day burying the dead from the two battles of Fairfax. They had buried the German dead and now they were burying the civilians. Hundreds of refugees had been killed and wounded in the crossfire. The S.S. had loaded the shell-shocked survivors on to their lorries and had driven them away in the direction of King's Lynn.

After they had buried the last civilian the Fusiliers were at last allowed to rest. They collapsed in an exhausted heap on the ground.

25

"What now?" Sam asked.

"Sleep," Lance-Corporal Vincent answered.

"Alan could be alive though, couldn't he, Lance-Corporal?" Sam asked Vincent. "I mean we haven't found his body, have we?" He carried on. "That means that he could be alive." Sam looked at Vincent quickly, his eyes darting away. Reassure me. Tell me what I want to hear. Tell me that Alan's still alive.

"Sam lad," Vincent said gently, "we haven't found him, but that doesn't mean that he's alive," he said, pointing to the other digging Fusiliers. "Don't get your hopes up, Sam."

"But he can't be dead," Sam said, "he can't be..." He sank to his knees and rested his head on the spade handle. Vincent walked up behind him and placed his hands on Sam's shoulders. "Chin up, lad. Here come the Huns. Don't let them see you cry." He put a finger under Sam's chin and tilted it up.

"Yes, Lance-Corporal," Sam answered quietly.

"That's the spirit, lad," Vincent smiled. "Stiff upper lip."

"I'm bloody knackered," Sam exclaimed, leaning on his spade. "When are going to get something to eat?" He moaned.

"I'm bloody starving too, lad," Vincent said. "I don't know."

They had not eaten since the day before yesterday. The German attack had caught them at dawn before they had had time to eat breakfast and they had not had anything to eat since.

"We're dealing with people who use women and children as human shields, Sam," Vincent observed. "I don't think that feeding us is a top priority."

"I was afraid that you'd say that," Sam said.

"Hallo?" Vincent asked.

"What's going on?"

"The S.S. officer in charge is asking a question to a group of prisoners."

They saw Captain Mason step forward. The S.S. officer spoke to him. Mason turned around; "Listen in men!" He bellowed. "We are to march back to the field where we will be fed."

A spontaneous cheer. Mason smiled at his men. It was refreshing to be the bearer of good news for a change.

"Well, well, well," Vincent said with a smile on his face, "life is full of surprises." He turned towards Sam.

"About bloody time," Sam said, his stomach grumbling as if on cue, "I could eat a horse."

R.S.M Witherspoon marched the Fusiliers back to the field. "Come on lads, the birds are singing! The sun is shining!" Witherspoon marched beside the men, "stomachs in, chests out! Bags of oomph! Bags of oomph!" The RRiFFs perked up and reacted as one to Witherspoon's familiar baritone words of encouragement. They were reassuring and comforting. "Show them that you're Fusiliers!" The men marched off as if they were on the Parade Ground, determined to show the Germans that they were still soldiers.

One man started whistling "Colonel Bogey." More RRiFFs joined in. Soon they were all singing the familiar song:

"Hitler
Has only got one ball,
Goering has two
But very small,

27

Himmler
Has something similar,
But poor old Goebbels
Has no balls at all."

The Fusiliers marched into a field with Lieutenant-Colonel Hook in the lead with his swagger stick stuck under his arm. Witherspoon called a halt. As if on cue, German Army lorries arrived and parked with their rears facing the RRiFFs. The Fusiliers cheered. S.S. troops positioned themselves at the rear of the lorries to help unload the food.

"That's a lot of lorries, Lance-Corporal," Sam observed.

"Well, Sam," Vincent said, "there's a lot of us," pointing to the other RRiFFs, "there's well over a hundred of us and there'll be food in there for the Jerries as well."

"Oh yes," Sam conceded, "I hadn't thought of that."

"What's for breakfast, Jerry?" A Fusilier good naturedly asked the S.S. officer in command.

"Lead, Tommy," he replied. The S.S. officer swung the Schmessier machine gun up in an arc and sprayed a stream of bullets, catching the RRiFF in the chest and throwing him backwards like a rag doll.

The S.S. troops dropped the lorry tailgates with a loud sudden bang. The machine guns inside opened up, their crews methodically sweeping the barrels from left to right. The MG 42 machine guns spat out 1200 rounds per minute and tore great strips through the unarmed Fusiliers knocking them down like ten pins. Groaning in heaps and dying silently on their own. Head wounds, stomach wounds, leg and arm wounds. The crews traversed their machine guns from left to right until no one was left standing. Gradually the screaming and the shouting died out to be replaced by moaning and crying.

"Run, Sam! Run!" Vincent screamed. Sam ran until his chest was bursting, until his lungs were screaming for oxygen. A machine gun burst stitched a line of holes in the wall of the house to his left. He didn't know where he was going. Anywhere out of here. He was in Fairfax. I can hide in Fairfax, he thought to himself. Another burst. A yell of pain. "Keep going, Sam!" Vincent shouted his voice hoarse with pain. As Sam turned around he saw a German fifty yards behind him. Firing a burst point blank into Vincent's back as he ran past.

"Bastard!" Sam thought. No time to grieve. Keep running. Another burst. Sam tripped and fell. He lay on the ground. Where's the pain? I feel nothing. Am I paralyzed? Am I dying? Is this what it's like? His brain was still working. Not another burst. Three single shots. From ahead of him. Not behind. Sam looked over his shoulder. The German lying flat on his back. A gaping hole in the centre of his chest. Sam turned back to the front.

"What the hell's going on?" Lindau asked as he got out of the lorry.

It was painfully obvious. S.S. troops were wandering around the field which was covered in a carpet of British dead. They were firing at point blank range into the heads of the wounded to finish them off.

Von Schnakenberg spotted the S.S. officer in charge and stomped up to him.

"Hauptsturmfuhrer, what is going on here?" von Schnakenberg demanded.

The S.S. officer looked at von Schnakenberg as if he was the local village idiot. "The prisoners tried to escape, sir."

"'Tried to escape?'"

"Yes, sir."

"Over one hundred prisoners tried to escape? All at once? One hundred unarmed prisoners being guarded by thirty S.S. soldiers armed with six machine guns tried to escape?" Von Schnakenberg shook his head in disbelief.

"Yes, sir." Hauptsturmfuhrer Zorn stuck to his guns.

Von Schnakenberg had the distinct feeling that Zorn did not care one way or another whether von Schnakenberg believed him or not. "Hauptsturmfuhrer, what were your orders?"

"To take care of the prisoners, sir."

"To take care of the prisoners?" Lindau mimicked the S.S. officer. "You were doing a pretty good job of 'taking care of the prisoners' when we arrived." He spat the words out with disgust."

"Listen to you," Zorn snapped, "you make me sick. It's no wonder that we lost the War." It had been a long, hot, thirsty morning. Slaughtering prisoners was an extremely stressful business and Zorn had finally lost his temper. "Brigadefuhrer Schuster was right. We should have finished off all of you aristo pigs at the end of the War." Zorn ranted and raved.

"How dare you!" Lindau shouted. His face turned crimson and he took one step forward. He heard an ominous click as Zorn flicked off his safety catch and pointed his Luger at Lindau.

There was an answering clang as Feldwebel Alfonin, Wilhelm von Schnakenberg's old Platoon Feldwebel, cocked his Schmeisser machine gun, sending a round into the chamber. "I'd think twice if I was you, Hauptsturmfuhrer," Alfonin said menacingly as he stepped in front of Lindau.

S.S. troopers moved protectively towards Zorn and raised their weapons to waist height, flicking off their safety catches.

Von Schnakenberg's soldiers cocked their weapons and pointed them at the S.S.

No one said anything. No one did anything. A Mexican stand off. Everyone realized that one hasty move could spark off a firefight. But Zorn only had a platoon of thirty men whereas von Schnakenberg had several hundred. It was a no win situation for Zorn.

Zorn realized that he had bitten off more than he could chew. He knew that he had to quickly think of a way to get both him and his men out of a swiftly deteriorating situation. Hopefully without losing face. The honour of the S.S. was at stake. But he was rapidly running out of time. Beads of sweat ran down his forehead.

Zorn made up his mind. There was no way out. He flicked on his safety catch and lowered his Luger "Lower your weapons, men," he ordered over his shoulder.

"Drop your weapons!" von Schnakenberg barked.

The S.S. men hesitated.

Alfonin fired a Schmeisser burst above their heads. The S.S. dropped their weapons and raised their hands in the air.

"Now get on your lorries," von Schnakenberg said, his voice laced with venom, "and don't come back."

"But the British..?" Zorn protested. "Without our weapons we won't be able to defend ourselves..." His eyes bulged wide with horror.

"The British will give you the same chances that you

gave them." von Schnakenberg pointed to the sea of dead British soldiers with his Luger.

Zorn's men sheepishly boarded their lorries, crest fallen and humiliated. Zorn hung out of the lorry cab and turned to von Schnakenberg. "We won't forget this insult, Oberstleutnant." He stared at von Schnakenberg with eyes full of hate. "The S.S. has a long memory. We'll be back," he threatened.

"I look forward to it." von Schnakenberg replied.

Chapter Three

Von Schnakenberg drove into Hereward with his mixed convoy of motorcyclists and Grenadiers. He was challenged at the edge of the town by a paratrooper roadblock. The convoy was cheered by groups of grinning and cheering paras as they drove into the centre of the town. Von Schnakenberg had absolutely no trouble finding the Town Hall because he knew the layout of Hereward like the back of his hand. He had been studying a map and scale model of the town for months before the invasion.

The convoy pulled up in the Town Square and von Schnakenberg and Lindau climbed down from their lorry cabs. Von Schnakenberg gave orders to his company commanders to get their men out of their lorries and allow them to stretch their legs. However, he emphasized that he wanted them to remain alert and remain focused. Von Schnakenberg did not know if the Square and the town were secure yet and didn't want to take any chances.

Von Schnakenberg and Lindau walked up the stairs to the Town Hall past heavily sand bagged positions guarded by paratroopers. It looked as if the British defenders of the Town Hall, if there had been any, had given in without putting up much of a fight. Certainly the Town Hall and the Square showed no obvious signs of damage. The paratrooper guards seemed to have the situation well in hand and looked confident, but vigilant at the same time. Von Schnakenberg stopped at the top of the stairs and turned around to look over the Square. Hereward appeared to be safe, secure and under control. A huge Swastika flag already fluttered from the flagpole above the Town Hall.

Von Schnakenberg climbed up the stairs to the fourth floor and walked along the corridor to what he knew was the mayor's office. He stopped and knocked on the door. He was not looking forward to the meeting. The Town Hall was now the headquarters of Task Force Schuster and the mayor's office was now Schuster's personal office.

Schuster was leaning over a map on the Mayor's desk with a group of senior S.S. officers and some paratrooper officers.

"BrigadeFuhrer…" von Schnakenberg started.

Schuster raised a finger in the air and cut von Schnakenberg dead. He hadn't even lifted his eyes from the map.

Lindau looked like he was about to explode. Von Schnakenberg grabbed his arm and dragged him towards the balcony windows. He hoped that the cold September air would cool them both down. Von Schnakenberg opened the French windows that led out to the balcony. He smiled with satisfaction at the sight that greeted him. The Town Square was full of lorries as far as the eye could see. Soldiers milled about on the cobblestones like so many ants. They almost hid from view the First World War cenotaph in the centre. Surrounding the Square on three sides were handsome medieval buildings made of a mixture of brick and stone. They served as a mix of government offices, banks, shops, restaurants and cafes. Dominating the entire east side of the Square was Hereward Cathedral. Although he had seen photos of the building, von Schnakenberg was amazed by how magnificent it looked and how massive it was. The Cathedral had been built during the reign of William the Conqueror nearly nine hundred years before.

"Oberstleutnant von Schnakenberg," Schuster beckoned. He turned to one of the paratrooper officers standing beside him. "Generalmajor Wurth, may I introduce Oberstleutnant von Schnakenberg of the First Battalion the Potsdam Grenadiers and his Second-in Command, Major Lindau." Schuster introduced the two men graciously.

Von Schnakenberg and Lindau snapped to attention and gave a parade ground salute.

Wurth returned the salute. Von Schnakenberg and Lindau both noticed that it was a textbook German Army salute and not a Nazi Party salute. They wondered if this distinction was significant. Wurth stretched out his hand. "I'm delighted to meet you, Oberstleutnant von Schnakenberg and you, Major Lindau. And tell me, Oberstleutnant, how is your father these days?" Wurth asked.

"My father, sir?" Von Schnakenberg's face showed his surprise.

"Yes, Oberstleutnant. Your father, Major-General Karl von Schnakenberg," Wurth asked with a raised eyebrow. He was clearly amused by the obvious confusion that he had caused.

"The General is very well, sir." Von Schnakenberg was curious. "If you don't mind me asking, sir, how do you know my father?"

"I served as a young Oberleutnant in the Potsdam Grenadiers under your father's command during the last War."

"But you were not in the regiment when I joined, sir." Von Schnakenberg was clearly puzzled.

"That's right. I was in the Grenadiers but then I transferred across to the Luftwaffe where I flew with von Richthofen. I was an airline pilot between the wars but I rejoined the Luftwaffe when Goering got it up and running again. I was too old to fly in combat so he asked to help set up the Parachute Regiment. And here I am."

Schuster coughed. "Sorry to break up this happy reunion, Generalmajor, but perhaps we could return to the matter in hand?"

"Of course, Brigadefuhrer, please accept my apologies," Wurth said with exaggerated politeness.

"Your apologies are not necessary, Generalmajor," Schuster said icily. It was glaringly obvious that Schuster's opinion of Wurth had cooled by several degrees since he had discovered that he and von Schnakenberg were both Grenadiers. Schuster turned to the map. "As of 1200 hours G.M.T. this is the situation as it stands: we have captured Hereward and we are in complete and total control of the town. Our forces have broken out from the beachheads and are pushing north. The present front line runs roughly from the Wash here to Liverpool." Schuster used his bayonet as a pointer stick.

"What about London, sir?" von Schnakenberg asked.

"We have completely surrounded London. Our tactic is to starve them out. It is effectively one big giant prison camp," Schuster replied.

"Liverpool is still fighting, as are several other towns and cities. They haven't surrendered yet. Our troops are having to fight street by street," Wurth added.

"What about Wales, sir?" Lindau asked.

"We're pushing into Wales, but it's a slow and painful business. The roads go through the mountains and our convoys are easy targets for partisans."

"What about continued British Resistance behind our

36

front lines and along our lines of communications?" von Schnakenberg asked.

"The British are still fighting, von Schnakenberg," Schuster answered swiftly, gaining control of the conversation again. "Terrorists are cowardly attacking our men in the back and our lines of communications are not secure. However, we are taking steps to deal with the terrorist threat in order to ensure that such an unfortunate situation does not arise again."

Von Schnakenberg and Lindau both looked at each other. They knew exactly what Schuster was talking about. The execution of hostages as a reprisal action for the killing of German soldiers by partisans.

"The British Bulldog can still bite as well as bark." Wurth broke the tense silence.

Lindau breathed a sigh of relief. "Don't they realize that they're beaten?"

"Lions led by donkeys, Major Lindau," Wurth said grimly. "You were too young for the last war. They fought like lions in the last war and they're fighting like that now."

"The British are too stupid to realize that they're beaten." Schuster sneered.

"Don't underestimate the British, BrigadeFuhrer," Wurth said. "Napoleon did and so did the Kaiser and look what happened to them."

"Napoleon and the Kaiser are not fit to be mentioned in the same breath as the Fuhrer," Schuster puffed out his chest. "The Fuhrer is more than a match for the British."

"I sincerely hope you're right, Brigadefuhrer," Wurth said grimly. "For all of our sakes."

"Keep quiet," Sam whispered. He crouched down and moved towards the sound of the laughter. Alan was right behind him. They moved slowly through the forest until they could see a group of people ahead in a clearing. Sam crouched behind a tree and Alan knelt beside him.

Four people were kneeling on the ground with their hands up in the air. One man, a woman and two teenage girls. Directly opposite them were eight German soldiers. Some of them were sitting, some of them were standing and some of them were lounging about on the forest floor. A corporal sat on the ground, stabbing his bayonet into the soft moss covered forest floor, digging furrows in the grass. He pointed his bayonet at the kneeling man and spoke to another soldier who was acting as an interpreter.

The corporal asked him something. The other Germans fell about on the forest floor rolling and laughing like a pack of hyenas.

"Are your women clean?" The interpreter asked.

The man's face drained of blood as if the Grim Reaper had thrust his hand through his chest and squeezed his heart.

The Germans were doubled up on the grassy ground laughing so hard that tears were flowing freely down their cheeks.

"They're too close to our people..." Alan whispered.

"I know..." Sam started crawling forwards like a leopard.

The Germans started to recover and began to point at the woman and her daughters. They were deciding who would get whom and in which order. Some of the Germans were already putting down their weapons and starting to unloosen their belts.

The corporal suddenly barked an order. The soldiers immediately stopped talking and moving and instantly snapped to attention. He gave a series of short, sharp commands. The soldiers all stood up. One of the girls started crying. Her mother wrapped her arms around both of her children as if she could protect them from the horror that was about to come.

Alan and Sam were now a dozen yards away from the scene unfolding in front of them and quietly took cover behind a fallen tree trunk. They silently slipped off their safety catches and aimed their Schmeissers at the Germans.

The corporal moved towards the mother. Her husband intercepted him blocking the soldier's path.

"He's in the way. I can't get a clear shot," Sam whispered through gritted teeth..

The soldier stared at the man with a mild look of surprise on his face. A mild look of surprise that turned to one of grudging approval and admiration. A man trying to defend his wife and his children. What could be more natural than that? A very brave man. But an unarmed man. A very foolish man. The man fell backwards clutching his stomach, vainly trying to tug out the bayonet embedded in his intestines.

"Now!" Sam screamed.

A stream of rounds flew out towards the Germans, knocking the corporal and the two would-be-rapists standing behind him off their feet. Alan opened fire a split second later catching another pair of potential pedophiles as they scrambled for their weapons. Sam and Alan charged forwards firing their weapons from the hip. Another soldier spun around and collapsed as the bullets caught him.

"Hande hoch! Hande hoch!" Sam ordered.

The two surviving Germans automatically raised their hands.

Alan and Sam advanced on them breathing heavily.

Alan turned to Sam. "What did you do that for, Sam?"

"What are you talking about?"

"What the hell are we going to do with prisoners?"

"Christ, Al. You've changed your tune. You were like a

Good Samaritan when I shot those wounded Jerries back at Wake and now you're a regular Attila the Hun! I wish that you'd make your blasted mind up!"

Alan could tell that Sam was amused rather than annoyed. "That was then this is now," he explained slowly and patiently as if to a child. "That was before I watched the S.S. massacre the whole regiment in cold blood after they'd surrendered. I'm no longer looking at the world through rose tinted spectacles."

"For which I'm heartily grateful."

"But the question still stands: what do we do with these prisoners?" Alan gestured with his Schmeisser.

"We question them," Sam answered.

"But we don't speak German."

"Yes, but laughing boy here speaks English." Sam looked at one of the soldiers.

The interpreter had survived. Alan nodded his head in understanding. "Be my guest."

"What is the importance of Hereward?" Sam asked.

The interpreter sneered and spat onto the ground at Sam's feet.

Sam swung his Schmeisser to the left and fired a burst of bullets at the other surviving soldier. The rounds stitched a line of holes across his stomach almost sawing the German in half. He collapsed with a loud grunt in a bloody heap on the ground.

"Not laughing so much now are you, Fritzie?" Sam said. He looked at the German like a wolf leering at a lamb before it ripped its throat out. "I won't ask you again, Fritze: what is the importance of Hereward?"

Alan waved his hand in front of his face as the noxious smell that the interpreter had released when he had emptied his bowels wafted towards him.

Beads of sweat had broken out on the German's face

and his whole body was shaking uncontrollably. He knew that he could expect little mercy after they had murdered the man and were preparing to rape the women. He raised himself to his full height, managed to control his shaking for a few seconds and stood at attention. "Dieter Drucker, Private, 24860143." The German replied.

"Wrong answer, Fritzie."

The bullets thudded into the interpreter's belly and he toppled onto his back as dead as a dodo.

The family was still grieving; crying over the body of the murdered man. A husband to the woman and a father to the girls. The man lay on his back with his fingers gripping the handle of the bayonet that had been plunged into his belly so tightly that his knuckles were white. His eyes were wide open and staring. He would not be the last Briton to die defending his family from the raping and pillaging enemy.

"Is there anything that you would like to add to your report, Hauptsturmfuhrer Zorn?"

Zorn couldn't stop his hands from trembling. They seemed to have a life of their own. He was sweating like a pig. "No, sir."

Schuster sat ramrod straight in his chair and looked at Zorn like a hanging judge about to pass sentence. "Hauptsturmfuhrer Zorn, it is to your credit that your account of this incident more or less matches the reports written by your men. That is either a testimony to your honesty or to their loyalty." He paused. "I suspect that it is a mixture of both. The Fuhrer, the S.S. and I need honest men and more importantly, officers who inspire loyalty in their men. Your men were prepared to fight and die alongside you in hopeless circumstances in order to preserve the honour of the S.S. You recovered your temper and you possessed the clarity of judgment and the presence of mind to make the correct decision. Although you lost face, you saved the lives of your men. Oberstleutnant von Schnakenberg has already been to see me and he has made his report. His account of the incident also supports your story." Schuster paused.

Zorn gulped. His throat felt dry. He was desperately trying to salivate. Here it comes, he thought. The axe is about to fall.

"As you know, Hauptsturmfuhrer Zorn, the Army has no jurisdiction over the S.S., or else you would surely face a court martial on the charge of drawing a weapon on a superior office, in other words: mutiny."

Zorn's legs were shaking uncontrollably. What deal had Schuster made with von Schnakenberg in order to prevent a scandal? Had he managed to stop the rift between the S.S. and the Wermacht from widening? Or had he been sold down the river?

"I have assured Oberstleutnant von Schnakenberg that I will deal with the matter, Hauptsturmfuhrer Zorn, and he seems to be satisfied by my assurances." That was an out and out lie. Von Schnakenberg had made it blatantly clear that he had no confidence in the S.S. judicial system. Schuster knew that von Schnakenberg would have a heart attack when he discovered how Zorn had been punished. "We cannot afford to have bad blood between the S.S. and the Army in Hereward, Hauptsturmfuhrer Zorn. It is therefore necessary to make an example of you."

Zorn held his breath. This was it. The end. This was the end of his military career and possibly his life as well. He tried to stretch an extra few inches to appear taller. The hangman's noose would do a better job, he thought grimly.

"With immediate effect, you are reduced in rank from Hauptsturmfuhrer to Obersturmfuhrer and you and your men will be transferred from the Fourth S.S. Regiment to

the S.S. Military Police Company until further notice."
Schuster passed sentence. "Have you anything to say?"

"No, sir." Zorn's legs were shaking.

"Obersturmfuhrer Zorn," Schuster said. Zorn grimaced
as he heard himself being addressed by his new rank.

"Yes, sir?" Zorn remained rigidly at attention.

"You've been given a second chance to redeem yourself.
Don't let me down. Dismissed."

The boys entered Hereward in the early afternoon and
walked through the streets. There was very little evidence
of any fighting having taken place. Hereward had been
captured more or less intact. Hardly any houses or shops
had been damaged. There were no burnt out or bombed
to bits buildings. There were no windowless or door less
houses. It was if Hereward had been untouched. Suspended
in a time warp. Hereward was an island and the tide of war
had washed on by. The shops were open and the birds were
singing. Housewives wandered along the streets carrying
shopping baskets in one hand and holding onto children's
hands in the other. But there were some changes. There
were German soldiers everywhere. Manning roadblocks;
sandbagged positions; walking around in pairs on patrol,
rifles slung on shoulders; strolling around in groups, taking
photos of the sights and sounds like typical tourists. A
massive swastika flag fluttering from the flagpole above the
Town Hall. Housewives shopping, soldiers shopping. But
one thing was missing. Young men. Or more accurately,
young British men. They were fighting in the Middle East,
spiritually rotting in prisoner-of-war camps in Germany or
physically rotting on the beaches of Dunkirk or rotting on
the fields of Fairfax. The only males left in Hereward were
too young, too old, or too unsuitable for military service.

"We stand out, Sam," Alan whispered out of the corner

of his mouth as they strode self-consciously through the Town Square. People were staring at them.

"I know," Sam forced the words out through tightly clenched teeth. "We've got to get out of here."

Alan nodded. "Let's head home. I'll see you at school on Monday."

They both stopped walking.

"I'll see you when I see you," Sam said.

"Not if I see you first." They both shook hands.

Chapter Four

"I protest, sir!"

"What do you mean 'you protest?'?" Schuster demanded.

"I do not consider being reduced in rank a suitable punishment for the crime of mutiny!" Von Schnakenberg bared his teeth as if he was about to bite. He was as mad as a rabid dog.

"And I do not consider it suitable behaviour for a junior officer to question the decisions or orders of a senior officer!" Schuster was leaning on his knuckles on his desk, stretching up to his full height like a grizzly bear confronting a rival in a forest.

"I will protest through the appropriate channels."

"Would those 'appropriate channels' include running crying to your daddy, the General?" Schuster asked. Schuster's words were dripping with sarcasm.

Von Schnakenberg took an involuntary step backwards. He felt as if he had been physically punched in the stomach. He found it difficult to breathe. Schuster smiled with satisfaction that his finely chosen words had hit a raw nerve.

"Why you-" von Schnakenberg started before Lindau clamped a hand over his superior's mouth

"That's right, von Schnakenberg. It would be wise to think before you open that insubordinate mouth of yours. If you give me any more trouble I'll have you up in front of a court martial so quick that it will make your head spin. Get out of my sight and take your lap dog with you. Dismissed!"

Von Schnakenberg stood there with steam virtually coming out of his ears. It took a supreme effort of will to control his emotions. He wanted to jump across Schuster's desk and rip his throat out. Instead he clicked his heels, saluted, about turned and marched out of Schuster's office. Lindau did likewise.

Von Schnakenberg walked quickly down the stairs slapping his leather gloves in his hands, swearing to himself under his breath. Lindau hurried after him, struggling to keep up. Von Schnakenberg's face was scarlet with barely concealed rage. They left the Town Hall and entered the Square.

"We'll get him, sir." Lindau tried to reassure von Schnakenberg but he was painfully aware of how lame and inadequate his words sounded. "Don't you worry, sir."

"I've no doubt that we will, Freddy, but how?"

"Ah, Generalmajor Wurth," von Schnakenberg said suddenly, squeezing Lindau's arm as Wurth walked up behind him. "What a pleasant surprise to see you." Von Schnakenberg and Lindau both saluted.

"Good afternoon, Oberstleutnant, Major Lindau." Wurth returned the salute and shook their hands. "Just been in to see Brigadefuhrer Schuster?"

"Yes, sir." Von Schnakenberg was embarrassed to think that Wurth might know of his humiliating treatment at the hands of Schuster. Bad news traveled fast.

"I trust that you found the Brigadefuhrer as charming as ever?" Wurth smiled before his face darkened grimly. "I heard about that business with Zorn through the grapevine. Goering and Himmler are not exactly the best of friends, Oberstleutnant and the Field Marshall has eyes and ears in all sorts of places. Including the S.S."

"I see."

"Care for a spot of sight seeing, gentlemen?" Wurth walked away without waiting for an answer. He knew that von Schnakenberg and Lindau would follow. "There's a lot here that I want to show you. And tell you."

They followed Wurth down a street leading from the Square. Two of Wurth's paratroopers walked a few paces ahead and two of von Schnakenberg's Grenadiers walked a few paces behind forming a bodyguard. They were out of hearing but not out of sight, keeping potential enemies as well as potential eavesdroppers at a distance.

"I also know about the massacre at Fairfax," Wurth whispered. Von Schnakenberg and Lindau both stopped walking. They were thrown off balance by the shock of Wurth's revelation.

"How did you find out?" Von Schnakenberg asked, wide eyed with surprise.

"What is important is not 'how' I know, but 'what' I know," Wurth answered. "I have been expressly ordered by Field Marshall Goering to produce a full and comprehensive report on the massacres at Fairfax."

"Why?" Lindau asked.

"On a need to know basis, Major, you don't need to know, but since we're all Grenadiers, I will elaborate. Follow me."

The men walked for five minutes up the High Street until they came to the sandstone pillars and iron gate of St. John's Academy. The gates were open. Wurth led the way through. It was a Saturday and the school was deserted. They walked along the main path entering a beautiful cobblestone encrusted courtyard. Classrooms looked down upon the courtyard and crossed over an enclosed bridge that led over the River Ouse.

"What a lot of people don't know was that Queen Elizabeth built the school on the site of a Norman motte and bailey castle." Wurth pointed at the river. "The Ouse forms part of the motte.What do you think about the keep, Oberstleutnant?" Wurth asked.

"It's magnificent," von Schnakenberg answered.

"Go on," Wurth encouraged.

"A magnificent piece of engineering," von Schnakenberg continued. "Built on top of an artificial mound of earth constructed by slave labour made up of the local English peasantry. Superb view of the surrounding countryside and all round fields of fire. Effectively protected by the moat on three sides."

"Anything else?" Wurth prompted.

Lindau thought for a moment. "No, sir. Am I missing something?" He turned around to face Wurth.

"Look at the Coat of Arms above the main entrance. What do you notice?"

"An eagle on a shield. An eagle with outstretched wings on a shield. An Imperial eagle."

"Yes. An eagle just like the one on the flag." Wurth pointed at the swastika fluttering from the flagpole on top of the castle keep. Von Schnakenberg noticed that Wurth had said 'the flag' and not 'our flag.' Was Wurth subconsciously indicating what his attitude was towards the Nazis? Or maybe it was not a subconscious indication. Maybe it was deliberate.

Something was ticking in the back of von Schnakenberg's head. He felt as if he could hear a clock ticking, but he

48

could not tell the time. He was missing something here. Something obvious.

Wurth's words interrupted von Schnakenberg's thoughts. "Baron John St. John came over with the Duke in 1066 and fought at the battle of Hastings. He helped to capture the town of Ely from the Saxon patriot Hereward the Wake in 1069. King William gave him all of this land as far as the eye can see as a reward." Wurth spread his arms wide and slowly turned around in a circle.

The ticking was growing louder in von Schnakenberg's head.

"It seems that St. John was not without a sense of humour," Wurth continued, "he built a town on his land and he named it after his nemesis, Hereward." Wurth turned to look at von Schnakenberg. "Oberstleutnant, what is the symbol of St. John?"

"The eagle."

"And what is the symbol of the Reich?"

"The eagle," Lindau answered with a confused expression on his face. Where exactly was this conversation going?

"Why have we captured Hereward?" Wurth asked.

"Because it is of vital strategic importance," Von Schnakenberg repeated the holy mantra.

"No, my dear Oberstleutnant. Follow me." Wurth opened the heavy oak door of the keep and slowly climbed up the narrow winding staircase all the way to the roof. He opened a trapdoor at the top of the stairs and clambered through. He walked over to the eastern side and peered over the battlements. Von Schnakenberg and Lindau followed him.

Wurth put his hand on von Schnakenberg's shoulder. "Look, Christian." He pointed with an outstretched arm. A stonewall completely surrounded the keep. The keep was four stories high and the wall came up to the bottom of the fourth level. On top of the wall on the eastern side was a massive stone statue of an eagle with giant outstretched wings.

"Who do you think lived on the fourth floor?" Wurth asked.

"John St. John."

"Yes. The good Baron himself."

"What do you think he would see every morning?"

"The sun rising up and making a silhouette of the eagle."

"Yes. Casting a huge shadow onto the ground of his land as the sun rose. How do you think that he would feel seeing the eagle, his personal symbol, casting a giant shadow on his land every morning?"

Von Schnakenberg's mind traveled back through time and he imagined himself in the Baron's place, standing beside the battlements of his keep. His voice when he spoke was barely a whisper. "Powerfull, omnipotent, all conquering." The ticking was getting louder. How would anyone feel seeing their personal symbol casting a shadow on their land every morning?

Alarm bells were ringing in von Schnakenberg's head. "The Fuhrer…"

"Yes, the Fuhrer." Wurth nodded his head in confirmation.

"The Fuhrer's headquarters will be in Hereward." Lindau spoke the words with hushed tones as if merely saying the words would summon the devil himself.

Von Schnakenberg seemed stunned into silence

"Not the Fuhrer's headquarters, but his Official Residence. He will stay here when he is in England and he will wake up every morning to see his eagle cast its shadow over his land just as St. John did nearly a thousand yeas ago."

Von Schnakenberg came out of his trance. "Hereward was never of strategic importance?" A wave of nausea swept through his body

"No," Wurth confirmed, "but we had to capture it intact incase the British tried to destroy this specific tower."

Von Schnakenberg slumped against the battlements. All the strength seemed to have left his legs. The destruction of half of the King's Lynn invasion fleet. The ambush of the motorcycle battalion at Wake. The slaughter of his Grenadiers at Fairfax. Willy's death. The massacre of the civilians and prisoners-of-war at Fairfax. All for nothing. All so that Hitler could have a glorified holiday home which he might use once or twice a year if he was lucky. Bought and paid for with German blood and the blood of innocents. And Willy's blood. Was this what he had joined the Army for?

Von Schnakenberg violently vomited up his morning breakfast over the side of the battlements.

Sam and Alan both reached their respective homes in the mid afternoon. Sam arrived at the door of his family home to be greeted by his mum. Surprise, joy, relief. Michelle Roberts' tears and kisses expressed all of these emotions at her son's appearance. Sam's dad, Alex Roberts, and elder sister, Alice, soon joined them in a group hug. Where have you been? We thought you were dead! What have you been doing? Alan twisted his ankle when they marched out of Hereward. Sam stayed behind to look after him. They tried to catch up with the battalion but there were too many refugees. They had been trying to get back to Hereward ever since. Sam had to endure a barrage of questions during a late lunch, which he wolfed down like a hungry animal. After lunch he excused himself, climbed the stairs to his bedroom and collapsed onto his bed fully clothed. He was asleep before his head touched the pillow.

Alan arrived at the front door of "Cromwell" Boarding house to be met by his Headmaster, Peter Ansett. Alan repeated much the same story to Ansett who listened without interrupting until the end of Alan's story. Seven Cromwell Fourth Year students had marched out with the Fusiliers but Alan was the only one that had returned. Ansett informed Alan that as the only surviving Fourth Year student, he was the new House Captain, effective immediately. He was the only senior student left and Ansett would have to depend on his help to hold the Cromwell boys together in the dark and difficult days to come.

Both boys returned to St. John's Academy the following Monday. The school was like a ghost town. Alan and Sam were two of the few boys who were older than fourteen years old. The senior boys and senior girls' classes were amalgamated because there were so few boys left. There were also fewer staff. Many of the male teachers had volunteered for the Forces or had been conscripted at the beginning of the war. Some of the remainder had been officers in the RRiFFs and just like the Fourth Year Cromwell boys they too were missing, presumed killed. The boys were pleasantly surprised to find that they were not the only survivors of the massacre at Fairfax. Their Company Commander, Captain Peter Mason, had also miraculously survived. He seemed to have resumed his prior existence as a French and German teacher. The boys were rather put out that Mason had not enthusiastically greeted them with open arms as old comrades-in-arms. However, the boys soon discovered that Mason's reaction to their unexpected reappearance was by no means unique. In fact, it seemed to be the rule rather than the exception.

People would stop talking when the boys entered the

room and they would resume speaking when they left. When teachers spoke to them they seemed to take extra care choosing which words to use as if English was not their native language. As if they were not only foreigners from a different country but aliens from a different planet. Teachers never told them what to do and they certainly did not order them around. They took extra care to phrase their request as gentle suggestions. They treated the boys with kid gloves. Or perhaps with boxing gloves. They didn't treat the boys like kittens. Rather they treated the boys like tiger cubs. Tiger cubs that had killed and tasted blood. They had to be handled carefully because although you can take a tiger out of the wild, you can't always take the wild out of a tiger.

Sam and Alan were given the same response as Lazarus received when he was raised from the dead. They were treated like heroes one minute and they were treated like lepers the next. The boys were neither accepted nor rejected by their peers and teachers. They were frustrated by this bewildering mix of praise and persecution and they wished that people would simply make up their minds as to whether they wanted to treat them as friends or enemies. The boys endured this bizarre behaviour until the October Mid-Term holiday when they were given a welcome break from their period of purgatory.

Alan's parents lived in Hong Kong where his father was a superintendent in the Police Force. He had not heard from either of them since the invasion began. Alan usually stayed with his father's relatives during the school holidays but he had no idea if they had survived the fighting. Sam had kindly invited Alan to stay with him and his family during the holiday. Alan was happy to accept. In fact, he was overjoyed. The truth of the matter was that he had little choice. All of his friends, save Sam, were dead.

Alan was busy packing his bag in his bedroom when Ansett knocked and entered.

"How are you, Alan?" Ansett asked.

"I'm fine, sir," Alan answered. "And yourself, sir? Are you looking forward to the holidays?"

Ansett smiled good naturedly. "I certainly am, although I don't know how much of a 'holiday' I'm going to have, looking after all of the waifs and strays." Several of the boys had lost contact with their parents and relatives and had nowhere to stay during the holiday. Ansett had taken on the role of surrogate father without hesitation. He considered it an honour and a privilege to look after and care for the boys whom he regarded as members of his extended family. "You're ready to leave for Sam's?"

"Yes, sir."

"Any word from your parents?"

"No, sir. Not since the invasion." Alan leaned against his desk.

"And your relatives?"

"No, sir. Not a word. They're God knows where."

"I'm sure that they're alright." Ansett tried to reassure him.

"You're probably right, sir." But Alan couldn't look him in the eye. He didn't want Ansett to see the tears beginning to well up. Please change the subject.

Ansett spotted the warning signs. "I saw you playing rugby the other day."

"Yes, sir. I'm also coaching the Third XV team. They haven't had anyone coach them since Mr. Newry was killed." There was no point pretending any more. Everyone had finally accepted that the 'missing' Fusiliers were in fact dead. Alan would not be giving anything away by divulging that information. It no longer a secret. It was common knowledge.

"Your ankle's healed well."

"My ankle, sir?"

"Yes, Alan. The ankle that you twisted a few weeks ago."

"Oh yes, that ankle!" Alan laughed nervously. "It's fine now, sir." Alan tapped it gently. "Although it's a little bit stiff at times." He could feel a bead of sweat drip down his cheek.

"Well, I'm glad to hear it. In fact, such a rapid recovery verges on the miraculous." Ansett turned around and walked out of the room.

Chapter Five

"What's all this I hear about von Schakenberg carrying out 'defense exercises', Zorn?" Schuster was standing directly behind Zorn's right ear.

"His battalions are practicing building trenches at Fairfax, sir." Zorn stood at the position of attention facing Schuster's desk.

"At Fairfax?" Schuster was at his left ear. "Does that not strike you as rather suspicious?"

"Yes, sir, and what is more suspicious is that it is not only von Schnakenberg's Grenadiers that are carrying out the defense exercise."

"Who else?" Schuster demanded returning to his desk.

"The remnants of the motorcycle battalion and also Wurth's paras, sir."

Schuster sprang up from his chair like a Jack in the box. "Wurth as well! It's a bloody conspiracy! The Army and the Luftwaffe are in this together." Schuster slammed his hand on the desk's surface. Schuster sat down at his desk and took a few deep breaths as he calmed down. "Fatty Goering has a hand in this. You mark my words." Schuster looked up at Zorn again. "What are they doing there?"

"They're digging up the dead."

"Whores!" Alan shouted at the top of his voice. "You're a bloody disgrace! You should be ashamed of yourselves!" The German soldiers strolling in the Town Square started to turn towards the source of the abuse as their English girlfriends desperately tried to drag them away, not wanting to draw any attention to themselves and not wanting any trouble.

"Alan!" Sam grabbed Alan's arm.

"Whores!" Alan screamed, tears streaming down his cheeks.

Whistles blew. Two Military Policemen started running towards them from across the Square.

"Alan!" Sam grabbed Alan around the waist, "come on! We've got to get out of here!"

Sam seemed to startle Alan out of his trance. They took off at full pelt, running out of the Square, the Germans in hot pursuit. The boys ran up the High Street dodging in and out of pedestrians on the pavement. They turned right off the High Street and into a side street. They hid in a narrow alley and they held their breaths as the German jackboots thumped past. The whistle blasts faded into the distance.

"Phew!" Alan bent over with his hands on his knees gasping for breath. "That was a close call."

"'A close call?'" Sam said incredulously, "you stupid bastard, you nearly got us killed!"

"What are you so upset about?" Alan asked. "We got away, didn't we?"

"Listen, Alan, if I'm going to get killed, I'm going to choose the time, the place and the reason, not you," Sam explained through clenched teeth. He was trying hard to control his temper.

Alan could sense the warning signs that Sam was

about to blow. "You're right, Sam. I'm sorry. I don't know what came over me. It's just that…I feel so helpless." Alan punched his leg in frustration. "Our girls with those dirty Hun bastards and our boys not yet cold in their graves…"

"I know, Alan," Sam said. "But we're not beaten yet."

"What can we do?" Alan asked despairingly. "There are only two of us."

"Do you remember what Mr. Flinders told us in Greek?"

"No."

"It only took the Greeks four hundred years to kick out the Turks." Sam stood up and put his hands on his hips. "Tonight we'll show the Huns that the British Bulldog can bite as well as bark."

The boys put boot polish on their hands and faces and got changed into their darkest clothes. They slipped into their blackened gym shoes that they had also covered with shoe polish. The boys carefully crept out of Sam's bedroom window and climbed down the fire escape ladder. At the bottom of the ladder they tip toed up the path to the garden gate, wincing as they made crunching noises on the gravel path. Sam crossed his fingers and prayed that a German patrol did not happen to be passing. The boys reached the garden gate and gently eased it open. They kept to the shadows and cat walked to the Square, taking thirty minutes to cover a journey that would have usually taken them ten minutes. The boys approached the High Street and took cover in a darkened alley. Sam looked at his watch, shielding the face with his right hand so that no one would be able to see the luminous dials shining in the darkness. Half past ten. Thirty minutes until closing time. Ruthlessly enforced by the Military Police.

At ten to eleven a lorry pulled up outside the "Chicken

and Egg" pub, a favourite watering hole of the paratroopers in Hereward. The boys could hear the Military Policemen talking inside the lorry.

At precisely eleven o'clock the boys heard the landlord's deep voice bellow through the pub. But the landlord's polite request to finish up merely seemed to encourage them to continue drinking. Raucous singing and drunken laughter wafted out from the pub. The paras did not seem in a hurry to come out.

At five minutes past eleven the tailgate of the lorry banged open and the Military Policemen piled out. Following the command of their leader the soldiers drew their batons. The door to the pub opened and a shaft of light shot through the darkness illuminating the policemen. A drunken para staggered out and made his unsteady way around to the side alley that ran alongside the pub. Probably avoiding the queue in the inside toilet. He seemed completely oblivious to the presence of the M.P.s But Alan was not oblivious to their presence; in the split second that the policemen had been lit up he had noticed two things. The first thing that he noticed was that the policemen kept their rifles slung on their shoulders. That meant that they weren't expecting any trouble. The other thing that he noticed was that the M.P.s helmets did not bear the winged eagle of the Luftwaffe, the paratroopers' parent organization; it bore the crooked cross of the swastika and the runes of the S.S. For some unknown reason the S.S. had decided that it was their responsibility to ensure that the Luftwaffe adhered to the town's Drinking regulations. Alan smiled to himself.

The M.P.s charged into the pub like a rugby pack. The pub exploded like an anthill being kicked over and paras came pouring out in all directions and scattered to the four winds. The policemen who had entered the pub appeared to have been momentarily overwhelmed by the avalanche of escaping soldiers. However, they soon recovered from their temporary paralysis and rallied, charging out of the pub and pursuing their prey into the darkness. Some of the S.S. had caught the paras and were bringing them back to their lorry in handcuffs. Sam could tell from the tone of their voices that the captured men were protesting that they were not common criminals and it was neither necessary nor was it acceptable that they were being handcuffed.

As soon as the paras discovered that the M.P.s were S.S. and not their own Luftwaffe Police the stakes of the game changed. What had begun as a glorified game of Hide and Seek for grown ups had rapidly become an Escape and Evasion exercise. The paras were playing for real. Groups of S.S. Military Policemen and paras were wrestling and grappling on the ground.

Alan winced as he heard a sickening crunch as a baton crashed onto a skull. The fact that it was one German using a baton to attack another German did not make the sound any less disturbing.

Sam turned around as he heard two M.P.s dragging the inert form of a para between them. The soldier's feet trailed along the ground. Sam waited until the S.S. men had struggled past and then stepped out onto the street behind them

"Kamerad?" Sam said.

"Was ist das?" The nearest policeman stopped and turned around, still holding the para's arm in his right hand. Sam stepped towards him and buried a knife in the man's neck. A thick stream of blood jetted out covering Sam's face. The man's hand went up to his throat in a vain attempt to stem the bleeding.

Sam withdrew the knife from the dying man's neck. The other S.S. trooper's eyes were wide with shock as he watched his colleague collapse to the ground. He let go of the para's arm and desperately tried to unsling his Schmeisser. But it was a race that he could not hope to win. The policeman watched with impotent disbelief as Sam sawed his knife across his throat in a sideways motion. The M.P. slid to the ground and his eyes slowly closed as the life flowed out of him. Sam dropped the knife on the ground.

"Turn him over," Alan ordered, nudging the drunken para with the toe of his gym shoe. Sam used his blood soaked hands to turn the German onto his back. The soldier groaned. It was the last sound that he ever made. Sam stood up and moved out of the way. Alan picked up the dead M.P.'s Schmeisser and fired a burst of bullets at point blank range into the para's front. The man's chest exploded in an eruption of blood and bones.

Sam turned towards the mob and fired a long burst at the S.S. lorry, knocking out its headlamps. Complete darkness. Raised voices and angry questions. A long burst at the M.P.s. Another burst into the confused mass of Police and paras brawling on the road. Bodies falling. Screams of the dead and dying. Sam unclipped two grenades from the dead S.S. trooper's webbing. One into the back of the lorry where the para prisoners were handcuffed. Another into the jumbled mess of groaning and crying soldiers and M.P.s lying on the ground.

"Time to leave," Alan said.

The boys knew that they didn't have much time. German reinforcements would soon come to the rescue. Sam and Alan did not intend to be waiting at the scene of their crime when they arrived.

Chapter Six

"This is a summary of the investigations carried out by the Army Military Police team from London," Wurth said. "I'll spare you the details and cut to the total casualties:-S.S.: ten killed and three wounded. Total paratrooper casualties: eighteen killed and three wounded. 9 millimeter shell casings, shrapnel from two grenade explosions, paratrooper bayonets, Lugers and British Army Wembly revolvers were found at the scene of the incident. All S.S. weapons were accounted for. The report places the blame for the incident squarely on the shoulders of my paras and completely clears and exonerates the S.S."

Wurth screwed up the report into a tight ball and threw it into a corner of his office. "The regiment, the Luftwaffe and Goering will not stand for this. There'll be hell to pay, you mark my words."

"And as for improving Inter Service relations? Don't make me laugh," von Schnakenberg said. "This judicial joke will put back Inter Service relations by at least five years.

"Oberstleutnant, how's the digging and photography of the corpses proceeding at Fairfax?" Wurth asked, wanting to change the subject.

"It's going well," von Schnakenberg answered, "but it will take at least another month to complete."

"Well, I don't have a month," Wurth said. "I want it to be finished two weeks from now."

"Why?" Lindau asked.

"Because I have received orders to bring my brigade back to Germany and I want to personally carry the evidence of the massacre back to Germany and give it to Goering myself. This information is too dangerous to entrust to a special courier."

"When do you leave, sir?" Lindau asked.

"On Remembrance Sunday."

The two figures waited in the alley that led off Market Street. It was eleven o'clock at night and off duty S.S. soldiers were beginning to leave the "Duke of Normandy" pub. They were a rowdy bunch and the first group was singing the 'Horst Wessel', the Nazi marching song, at the top of their voices. There were too many of them. The waiting men let them stagger by. Gradually the pub emptied. Two S.S. men weaved their way across the road from side to side, leaning on each other's shoulders for support. As they approached the alley, a man in black stepped out in front of them blocking their path. The S.S. troopers shuddered to a stop. The remaining man stepped out behind the S.S. soldiers. They could neither go forward, nor could they go back. They were trapped.

"What's going on?" One of the storm troopers asked.

The S.S. soldier crumpled to the ground as a heavy object crashed into the bridge of his nose. A fountain of bright crimson blood sprayed onto the face of the other S.S. trooper. His legs were kicked out from under him before he could react. That was the signal. Both attackers piled in to their victims, punching and kicking the S.S. troopers in a frenzied and furious assault. They only stopped when the S.S. men stopped struggling.

The two men tied the hands of the S.S. soldiers behind their backs and quickly stripped them. They dragged a small bucket from the alley and prized off the lid. A noxious smell escaped from the bucket. The men turned the unconscious S.S. men onto their backs and spread eagled their legs. They dripped two large paintbrushes into the bucket and put them between the S.S. troopers' outstretched legs. The S.S. men screamed in pain as the paintbrushes touched their skin. Their tormentors continued to ladle on the liquid despite their victims' desperate pleas to stop. They only stopped when the S.S. men were completely covered from head to toe and from back to front. Each of the men slit open a pillow and emptied the contents onto the S.S. soldiers. The two men stood above their victims and allowed themselves a savage smile of satisfaction. They turned their backs on the unconscious men and disappeared into the night.

The next morning, the blood splattered body of a young paratrooper was found at the bottom of Hereward Cathedral. His wounds were consistent with those of having fallen from a great height. It appeared that following a night's drinking at "The King Arthur" pub he had decided to carry out an impromptu sight seeing tour and had climbed the many hundreds of steps to the battlements at the top of the Cathedral tower. He had been slightly the worse for wear and he appeared to have lost his footing as he peered over the parapet and had fallen to his death. Friends and eyewitnesses said that he had left the pub shortly before closing time to urinate outside (the pub's toilets were out of order) but he had not returned. His paratrooper wings had been ripped from his jacket. It was possible that they had been torn during the fall. Inside his pocket was an "Ace of spades" playing card bearing the skull and crossbones emblem of the Fourth S.S. Infantry Regiment. His friends could not recollect the young para ever having expressed an interest in playing cards and he certainly had not mentioned ever having any friends in the S.S.

"Look at them," Alan said smugly," the bastards can barely stand the sight of each other."

The boys sat on a bench in the Town Square observing a group of half a dozen paratroopers staring at a similarly sized section of S.S. soldiers. The two packs were warily circling each other like two rival gangs of schoolboys in the playground. As Alan and Sam watched an S.S. trooper suddenly lunged across the short gap separating the two groups and punched the closest para in the face sending him flying backwards through the air. A full scale fistfight erupted as the S.S. soldiers and paras piled in. Paratroopers and S.S. troopers who had been strolling across the Square minding their own business witnessed what was going on and quickly decided to make it their business and joined in to help their comrades.

"Christ!" Sam exclaimed, "We really stirred up a hornets' nest the other night!"

"We set a fox amongst the chickens!" Alan laughed at his own joke and Sam joined in.

The boys heard whistles being blown. "Uh-oh, here come the Keystone cops!" Sam said. S.S. and para Military Policemen were running across the Square, blowing their whistles and drawing their batons. Lorries were driving into the Square and were disgorging their Police reinforcements. Sam noticed that Army M.P.s were making no attempt to become involved and seemed quite content to allow their counterparts in the other two services deal with the situation. And the situation was quickly changing. A minor street scuffle involving a dozen men was rapidly escalating into a major riot involving several hundred. Attempts to break up the fight was not helped by the fact that dozens of Grenadiers and other Army soldiers were standing on the sidelines laughing and shouting, cheering on their champions like a Roman mob watching gladiators in the Colosseum.

Sam and Alan were doubled up laughing. They weren't the only civilians who found the situation funny. Several groups of people were also standing around the Square pointing and giggling at the sight of their Aryan Overlords scrambling and scrabbling about in the dust and the dirt like common criminals fighting over food scraps.

"Come on, Sam," Alan grabbed Sam's blazer as he stood up. "We'd better leave. I've got to go to tea."

"Alright," Sam wiped away tears of laughter.

Alan turned around. "Oh, hello sir," he said in surprise.

"Hallo, Alan. Hallo, Sam," Peter Ansett, Alan's Housemaster said.

How long had he been standing behind them? Alan asked himself.

"Hallo, sir," Sam said. How much had he heard?

"Enjoying the entertainment, are we?" Ansett asked.

"Yes, sir," Alan answered. "It's better than watching Laurel and Hardy!"

"Before you laugh so much that you wet your trousers, boys," which only encouraged the boys to laugh some more, "you might take time to remember that you should never laugh at another person's expense."

"Even if they're the enemy?" Sam abruptly stopped laughing.

"Even if they're the enemy, Sam. Remember, every one of those boys is a mother's son."

"Yes, sir." Who is this man?

The boys were shocked into silence. Mr. Ansett, Sam's History teacher, Alan's housemaster – a collaborator?

"Are you going to tea now, Alan?" Ansett asked.

"Yes, sir." He was too flabbergasted to give more than one syllable answers.

"Then I'll walk along with you if I may. Goodbye, Sam. See you tomorrow in History."

Alan did not even acknowledge Sam's reciprocal farewell and walked home on automatic pilot, lost in his own thoughts with his mind in turmoil. How far had this "live and let live-treat others as you would have them treat you" nonsense spread? How many more people had become infected with this defeatist disease? How many more people had Ansett managed to contaminate through his classes? Was Ansett a passive collaborator or an active traitor pushing and promoting the Nazi view that Britain should take its rightful place alongside her continental brothers in the New European Order? Did Ansett agree with puppet Prime Minister Mosley's Government of National Unity's message of peace and reconciliation? Whatever the answer was, however deep Ansett's treachery ran, he would have to be carefully watched. From now on. Alan would have to be especially careful when he sneaked out of his boarding house in the future. And if the risks became too great then Ansett would have to be cut out like a cancer before his sickness could spread any further.

"I have agreed to hold a Remembrance Day Parade at the request of the Royal British Legion in the interest of Inter-Service Unity and put the bad blood of the past few weeks behind us," Schuster explained. "A chance to bury the hatchet and smoke the peace pipe. This can be a day of reconciliation between the three services and also a day of reconciliation between the British and German peoples. People without politics remembering our War dead together, praying that THIS war will be the war to end all wars."

"Masterful, sir," Zorn said with grudging admiration. Word would get to London if Schuster allowed the parade to take place and if it was successful, word would get to Berlin. Or perhaps Schuster would tell his old comrade in arms, Hitler, himself? This parade could be the prototype for a program of reconciliation between the conquered countries and Germany. Schuster was a wily old fox. It was evident that he wished to extend his interests and influence from the military world into the world of politics. What would happen to old soldiers when the war was over? After all, the war wouldn't last forever. A man had to start carving out his niche in the post-war world now. When it was all over it would be too late. Schuster would not be content to remain Military Governor of Hereward. But Military Governor of England? Or perhaps even of Britain? Now that would be something. Perhaps Zorn should attach himself to Schuster's rising star? Zorn asked himself. His thoughts wandered. Brigadefuhreur Zorn, Military Governor of London. He smiled. Yes, that would do nicely, thank you. Or perhaps he should start carving out his own niche?

"Questions, comments, flaws in my masterful plan to take over the world?" Schuster asked.

"One question, sir: how, may I ask, have Generalmajor Wurth and Oberstleutnant von Schnakenberg reacted to your proposal?"

"London has ordered them to agree. They have each been ordered to provide a company of troops as a guard of honour and all three of us will present a wreath on behalf of our respective services."

"Very good, sir."

"Whilst we're on the subject, Zorn, what is the current state of play regarding our feud with the Luftwaffe?"

"I would say that it's rather more than a feud, sir. It's a blood vendetta in true "Romeo and Juliet" style. Ever since the "Chicken and Egg" incident there have been outbreaks of violence every night. Dozens of men have been injured on both sides and there have even been several deaths."

"My God. I had no idea that things had got so bad. How has Wurth reacted?"

"He has done absolutely nothing to stop it, sir. In fact, he has encouraged it."

"And the Army, Zorn?"

"On the surface the Army has remained neutral but under the surface Army sympathies are firmly with the paras."

"No surprises there, Zorn. Von Schnakenberg and Wurth are as thick as thieves. They're bound together by class and regimental loyalty."

"Yes, sir."

"How have the public reacted?"

"The public treat it all as a big joke," Zorn said bitterly. "Instead of wandering down to the park on a Sunday afternoon to listen to a brass band playing they walk to the Square to watch our boys scrapping with the paras. The Armed Forces as a whole have become a laughing stock. "

"All the more reason to put an end to this nonsense once and for all." Schuster stood up and slammed a clenched fist into his hand. "We must show the people of Hereward that we are not a mob of undisciplined, uncultured barbarians." He puffed out his chest like a robin. "We are members of the greatest civilization that the world has ever seen!"

"Your ankle seems to have made a full discovery," Ansett said as he walked alongside Alan.

"Sir?" Alan was confused.

"Your ankle," Ansett pointed.

"Oh yes, sir, my ankle," Alan laughed uneasily. He stopped and leant on a lamppost as he stretched and flexed it. "As good as gold, sir. Although it can be a little stiff after I've done anything physical." Such as killing Germans, you no good, low down, dirty, Hun loving traitor. Where were you when the shooting started and what were were you doing? Dusting down your welcoming mat and hanging out your swastika?

Alan started walking again.

Ansett remained where he was. "Alan."

"Yes, sir?" He stopped.

"You can give up your charade."

"Sir?" Alarm bells started to ring in his head.

"You can give up your charade about your ankle."

Alan started walking again, speeding up, "I'm afraid that I don't understand, sir." A bead of sweat ran down his cheek.

Ansett caught up with him and placed a hand on his shoulder. "I talked to Mr. Mason, or Captain Mason, your company commander. He said that both you and Sam fought bravely at Wake and Fairfax."

Alan clenched his fists as he desperately tried to fight off a rising tide of panic that threatened to engulf him. "He must've have mistaken me for someone else." He shrugged off Ansett's hand and kept walking.

"Alan, he's known you for two years in the Officer Training Corps, he taught you German last year and he teaches Sam this year. He hasn't made any mistake." Ansett said matter of factly.

Alan stopped walking. Can I trust you? His Luger pistol was pressing uncomfortably against his crotch where he had hidden it down his trousers. Both Sam and he had agreed to be armed at all times. They had been deadly serious when they had sworn that they would rather die fighting than be captured alive. "Alright, we both fought at Wake and Fairfax. So what?" Alan was rapidly losing his temper despite knowing that he had to keep his wits about him. Have you sold your soul to the Devil, Ansett? Are you a traitor? Am I going to have to start killing my own people?

"The War is not over."

"What?"

"You're not alone."

Alan's legs seemed to turn to rubber. His energy seeped out of him like air escaping from a punctured balloon. He sat down on a wall to gather his thoughts and regain his strength. Can I trust you? Is the Luger loaded? Is it made ready? Is there a round already up the spout? Can I squeeze off a round and kill you, you treacherous bastard, before you can call your Jerry friends? Too dazed and confused to think straight. I must think. I need time to think. What to say? What to do?

"What do you want from me?" Alan asked.

"Are you ready to pick up the gauntlet again?"

"What about all of that 'laughing at another's person's expense' in the square rubbish?"

"A smokescreen."

A pretty damned effective one, Alan thought.

"I know what you're thinking."

You have absolutely no idea what I'm capable of. What I've seen. What I've done. You'd run a mile and you wouldn't stop to look back. "You didn't join up. You were in the last War, you were Mentioned in Dispatches for God's sake, you were in the last War and you didn't join up for this one." The words tumbled out as soon as the thoughts entered his head.

"I had reasons for that. I can explain."

71

"How?" Alan stood with his hands on his hips.

"In fact, I can do better than that. I can show you. I can prove it to you."

Alan could almost taste and touch Ansett's desperate desire to be believed. His yearning urge to be trusted again as one of the good guys. "When?"

"Tomorrow. Come to my classroom after school."

"How close are we to finishing?" Wurth asked, surveying the field.

"The men are working flat out, sir," Lindau answered.

Wurth's paratroopers, von Schnakenberg's Grenadiers and his adopted motorcyclists were scattered across the fields are far as the eye could see, busy digging up the mass graves of the dead civilians and slaughtered British soldiers. Other soldiers were collecting documents from the murdered men, women and children and dog tags from the bodies of the executed Fusiliers. A group of desk bound soldiers were recording details from the rapidly growing mountain of mouldy and musty material. Once the documents had been catalogued they were put into empty ammunition boxes. When the ammunition box became full it was locked shut with a padlock and an armed sentry was posted to guard it. Photographers were methodically taking photos of the dead.

"How much longer?" Wurth asked.

"We should be finished by tomorrow."

"Friday?"

"Yes, sir."

"Good." Wurth nodded his head. "We have a rehearsal for the Remembrance Day Parade on Saturday, Remembrance Day takes place on Sunday and we leave for Germany that afternoon."

"You will have to intercept and destroy Wurth's Fairfax report, Zorn," Schuster said firmly.

"Me, sir? How?" Zorn was absolutely horrified.

"Wurst leaves Hereward straight after the Remembrance Day Parade and I'm sure that he will carry the report on him. We can't wait until he leaves England. You'll have to destroy it before he leaves Hereward. Afterwards will be too late."

Except that Wurth would be guarded night and day by three thousand armed to the teeth, itching for a fight paratroopers.

"Are you at all familiar with English History, Zorn?" Schuster asked, picking up a hefty looking book.

"Sir?" Where was this leading?

"Who will rid me of this troublesome priest?" Schuster quoted from the text.

"I'm afraid that I don't know what you're talking about, sir."

Schuster opened the front of the History text book and pointed to the contents page "That will tell you how to deal with Wurth."

Chapter Seven

"Where's Sam?" Ansett walked to the class room door and looked up and down the corridor.

Alan didn't answer. His silence spoke for itself. *I came alone. Incase it was a trap. Can I trust you?*

"I see." Ansett smiled grimly. He understood. "Follow me."

Ansett led the way out of the classroom, down the corridor and out of the building. Alan followed him through the school gates and down the High Street towards the Town Square.

"Where are we going?" Alan asked.

"You'll see."

Alan was aware that he was sweating profusely despite the fact that it was nearly half way through November. Adrenalin was rushing through his body in waves. He could almost hear his heart pumping his blood through his veins. His right hand strayed to his waist where he could feel the butt of the Luger pistol pressing against his belt buckle. They were walking towards German Headquarters. *If you betray me, they won't take me alive, you bastard. The first bullet will be for you, Ansett, straight in your back. I've got four* full magazines. I'll take you and some of your Nazi friends with me and I'll save the last bullet for myself. They won't take me alive.

Ansett kept walking past German Headquarters.

"Not far now." Ansett pushed open the giant oak doors of Hereward Cathedral and stepped inside. Alan followed. His hand fell away from his belt buckle. No. It could still be a trap. This is where they take you. When you think that you're safe. When you think that you've made it. When you've been lulled into a false sense of security. Ansett fought in the last war, but he didn't join up for this one. Why? The thought thudded through his mind like the persistent pulse of a headache. He could still be a traitor.

It was quiet inside. There were only a handful of worshippers scattered throughout the Cathedral sitting on the benches. Plus various groups of German tourists, both civilian and military, malingering around. But were they tourists? Was this a trap? Were they waiting for a signal from Ansett to spring the ambush?

Ansett headed towards the steps leading down to the crypt. He stopped at the bottom and drew out a large iron key. He inserted the key, turned it and opened the door. Considering its age, the door was surprisingly silent as it swung open. The hinges must be incredibly well oiled, Alan thought to himself. Ansett turned around and casually swept the Cathedral with his eyes to see if anyone had noticed him opening the door. No one seemed to have noticed anything out of the ordinary. "Come on," He whispered.

Alan followed him down the stairs. It was deathly quiet, as quiet as … a tomb. Ansett picked up a torchlight that was placed conveniently by the door. "Close the door." He ordered. Alan did as he was told and then had to pick up the pace to catch up with Ansett as the light from his torch disappeared into the darkness. Alan's heart skipped a beat in sudden panic at the thought of losing sight of Ansett and being stranded down here in the dark. The thought of spending the rest of his days wandering hopelessly amongst the dead speeded up his steps until he finally caught up with him. Alan kept close behind as they walked down the length of the crypt. Tombs stretched out in front, behind and to either side of them as far as their torchlight could see.

"This...this place gives me the creeps," Alan whispered.

"Why are you whispering? The dead can't hear you," Ansett whispered back.

"I can't help it," Alan admitted.

"They're already dead, Alan." Ansett spoke over his shoulder. "You can't kill them with that thing."

"Sorry, sir." Alan bashfully put his Luger away. How had it got there? He couldn't remember taking it out of his trousers. He wiped the sweat from the pistol grip before he placed it back inside his underpants.

They reached the end of the crypt. "Here, give me a hand. Grab the other end of this." He shined the torch on the lid of a tomb before he put the torch down on the ground.

"What? This?" Alan asked with confusion.

"Yes," Ansett answered. "On my command: lift up, alright?"

"You must be joking! It must weigh a ton!" Alan said incredulously.

"Just trust me."

Alan realized that he had no other choice. If Ansett wanted to, he could simply switch off his torch, retrace his route to the exit and leave Alan to die with the dead.

"One, two, three, lift up!"

"Wood! It's made out of wood!" Alan held the 'marble' lid in his hands.

Ansett laughed. "Yes! Now, slide it towards me about a foot."

Alan did as he was told. He watched in confusion as Ansett climbed up beside the tomb and lowered himself into it. "Come on," Ansett said. "Or are you going to stand there all day with your thumb up your arse?"

The shock of hearing Mr. Ansett uttering profanities was sufficient to jerk Alan out of his temporary paralysis. He climbed down a ladder that was built into the side of the 'tomb.' He climbed down about twelve feet and found himself standing in a room that measured about fifteen feet by fifteen feet square. Two sets of bunk beds ran alongside one wall of the room and a rack holding a collection of British and German weapons ran alongside another wall. A radio sat on top of a table that ran alongside the third wall and a small gas cooker and a woodwork bench ran alongside the fourth wall. A dining table with four chairs placed around it stood in the centre of the room. The whole scene was illuminated by a naked red light bulb. Red light so that they wouldn't lose their night vision if they were entering or leaving. Red light so that even if someone entered the crypt they wouldn't be able to see any light escaping from the hiding place. Alan noticed that there was an extra trap door where the ladder met the ceiling of the hiding place for extra security. Very clever.

"What's that?" Alan pointed at where a curtain partitioned off a corner of the room.

"Gents," Ansett answered matter of factly.

Alan laughed. Ansett was relieved. He could not remember the last time that he had heard his House Captain laugh. "Cozy." Alan wiped away the tears with the sleeve of his blazer.

"Compact and bijou," Ansett smiled. "There were four of us," Ansett explained, his tone suddenly becoming serious.

He pre-empted Alan's next question. He was giving nothing away. There were four bunks. "One of us was killed. It's not necessary for you to know who this person was."

'This person,' Alan noticed. So he/she could be male or female. "You were a Stay Behind Party."

Ansett nodded.

"Your job was to lie low and strike behind enemy lines when the Jerries passed you by."

Ansett nodded again.

"I'm sorry, sir." Alan snapped to a position of attention as if he was on a parade ground. "I thought that you were a coward."

"And worse, no doubt, Alan," Ansett said, shaking Alan's extended hand. "No apology is necessary, son. That was the general idea. And it worked. People must continue to believe that I am a coward and a defeatist at best and a collaborator and a traitor at worst. From time to time I may have to call upon you and Sam to help me to perpetuate this myth. You will have to remain silent when others condemn me even though you wish to defend me and you may even have to add your voice to theirs. You may even have to cast the first stone."

Alan nodded gravely.

"But the important thing is that you and Sam are not alone anymore." Ansett picked up a rifle from the rack, checked that the safety catch was on and cocked the weapon in one easy, practiced, fluid motion. "It's time for the Empire to strike back!"

It was ten o'clock in the morning on Remembrance Day and soldiers were busy setting up the barricades which would keep the crowds away from the route that the veterans would take to march past. The S.S, the Army and the paratroopers were each responsible for the security of a sector of the Town Square.

At 10.15 the crowds started to assemble with people picking prime positions by the barricades so that they could get the best view.

At 10.20 the Honour Guard consisting of one company each of paras, S.S. and Army soldiers marched onto the Square. All eyes were focused on the marching soldiers and no one paid any attention to four paratroopers who weaved their way through the crowd to the west side of the Square. Anyone who did notice them presumed that they were on crowd control duty. Two of the paras headed for the southwest corner of the Square and walked into the communal entrance of a block of tenement flats. They climbed the stairs to the top floor of the five floor block of flats and knocked on the door of the flat.

S.S. Hauptsturmfuhrer Andreas Schmitt was looking out of his living room window watching the parade preparations and was halfway through his breakfast when he heard a knock at the door. He swore, pulled his dressing gown chord tight, walked to the door and looked through the spy hole.

"Who is it?" Schmitt asked.

"Orders," one of the paras answered.

"Verdammt!" Schmitt swore. "Today's my day off." He swallowed his last piece of marmalade-covered toast and opened the door. "Oh well, no rest for the wicked."

"Mornin'," the para said. The rifle butt caught Schmitt square in the face before Schmitt had time to realize that the para had greeted him in English. The force of the blow sent Schmitt spinning around and the cup of Earl Grey tea that he was carrying was sent flying through the air before it smashed to pieces on the wall.

"Sorry to disturb your breakfast, Fritz," Sam said as he pointed at the dazed and confused German with his rifle. "Quick, Al. Tie him up."

At 10.30 Brigadefuhreur Schuster began his speech with an interpreter providing a simultaneous translation into English.

At 10.35 Mayor Robin Walker started his speech. He stressed the need for tolerance, a general live and let live philosophy and the necessity of accepting the present political situation.

Ansett and Mike Robinson, the second member of the Stay Behind Unit, were busy ransacking the flat of S.S.Sturmbannfuhrer Wolfgang Offenbach. The German lay flat on his back on the floor with a surprised expression on his face. Offenbach's eyes were staring wide open and a steady stream of blood trickled out of the corner of his mouth. A paratrooper bayonet was buried in his rib cage.

At 10.40 the German Army Chaplain began his service.

At 10.45 the Bishop of Hereward Cathedral, Ben Rathdowne, started his service. He talked about forgiving and forgetting, remembrance and reconciliation.

At 10.50 the Secretary of the Hereward Branch of the Royal British Legion, Richard Gill, began his speech. He spoke about pride and courage and about duty and honour. Tears started to trickle down his cheek as he talked about love and sacrifice.

Obersturmfuhrer Zorn walked up to two sentries guarding the main entrance to Hereward Cathedral.
The two sentries came to attention and Zorn returned the salute. "At ease, gentlemen. "How are things here, Gefreiter?" Zorn asked amicably.

"Fine, sir. Everything is in perfect order."

"I'm just doing a quick inspection, Gefreiter. I wonder if you would care to accompany me inside."

"We're not really supposed to abandon our post, sir," Gefreiter Wilesk explained with a pained expression on his face. He wasn't used to refusing the requests of an officer. Especially an official looking officer armed with an important looking attaché briefcase.

"You're not 'abandoning' anything." Zorn smiled good naturedly. "You're merely leaving it for a few minutes. Anyway, everything is fine out here. You said so yourself. Major Lindau asked me to come over here and check things out."

"Major Lindau said that it was alright?" Wilesek asked with raised eyebrows. "In that case, sir, it would be a pleasure and a privilege to escort you inside." He was relieved to be let off the hook. Wilesek turned to the other soldier. "Come on, Artelt."

"Do you have the keys?" Zorn asked.

"Yes, sir." Wilesek unclipped a large ring of keys from his webbing belt, selected a huge rusty iron key and unlocked the door of the Cathedral.

"After you, gentlemen."

The gefreiter stepped through the giant oak doors. Artelt followed him.

"Is there anyone else in here?" Zorn asked.

"No, sir, just Scharfuhrer Behrens at the top of the tower. He's on sniper duty." Wilesek answered.

"Is he a good shot?"

"Yes, sir." Wilesek's chest puffed up with pride. "He's the best shot in the regiment. He could shoot the skull cap off an old Jew boy's head at one hundred meters."

"I believe you," Zorn said with admiration patting

Wilesk on the shoulder. "And he has a sniper rifle?" He asked casually.

"Yes, sir. The best that money can buy."

"Thank you for being so co-operative, Gefreiter Wilesek."

"Not at all, sir." Wilesek smiled.

"You've told me everything that I need to know."

"Don't mention it. My pleasure, sir."

"That's what makes this so difficult," Zorn said gritting his teeth.

"I'm sorry sir, I don't under –." Zorn whipped out his Luger and shot Wilesek twice in the forehead. Artlet was too shocked to react. Zorn shot him twice in the chest before he could even get his rifle off his shoulder. The gunshots echoed around the vast cavern of the Cathedral, bouncing off the walls.

Zorn dragged Wilesek and Artlet behind a pile of chairs stacked in the corner by the entrance and then locked the main entrance door. He picked up the dead soldiers' rifles and thrust them through the door handles to act as an extra barrier. Now, were Wilesek and Artlet carrying any grenades?

At 10.55 the Wreath laying Ceremony started with the British contingent consisting of Mayor Walker, Bishop Rathdowne and British Legion Secretary Richard Gill laying the first flowers.

Alan and Sam took up their positions by the windows overlooking the Square. They double checked that their rifles had full magazines. Ansett and Robinson did the same in their flat.

"Feldwebel Behrens?" Zorn asked through the tower roof trap door.

"Yes?"

"Senior Obersturmfuhrer Zorn. S.S. Military Police. I've been sent up here by Major Lindau to have a final look see before the parade."

"Come on up, sir."

Zorn opened the trap door and stepped out onto the roof of the tower. He whistled as he emerged. "Mein Gott!" He exclaimed, wiping the sweat from his brow, "quite a view."

"Yes, sir," Behrens saluted. "On a clear day you can see all the way to Cambridge."

Zorn returned the salute. "How are things up here?"

"Absolutely fine, sir. The parade is proceeding like clock work. Look." Behrens pointed. "Brigadier Wurth is about to lay the wreath on behalf of the Parachute Regiment and the Luftwaffe."

"Where?" Zorn stepped closer to Behrens to get a better view.

"Over there, sir." Behrens pointed down towards the Square. Zorn stepped behind Behrens, wrenched his head back and in one fluid movement sliced his S.S. bayonet across Behrens' throat from ear to ear. Crimson bright blood spurted in an arc like a fountain as Behrens collapsed on the floor. Zorn pulled Behrens' lifeless body over to the side of the roof, picked up the discarded sniper rifle and took up the sniper's position. Zorn looked at his watch. It was 10.58.

There were six targets in total, von Schnakenberg, Wurth and Schuster and their three second-in-commands and there were four Resistance snipers. The bells would ring eleven times and the partisans would fire forty four shots at the same time as the bells tolled so that the Germans would not be able to tell where the shots were coming from.

Zorn rested his sights on the back of Wurth's head.

Business before pleasure, he smiled wickedly. Wurth first, then von Schnakenberg.

Sam looked up at the giant clock on the Cathedral tower. It was 10.59. At five seconds to eleven, he took a deep breath through his nose and slowly released it through his mouth. When the last breath of air had left his lungs he gently squeezed the trigger at exactly the same moment as the bell rung. von Schnakenberg was going down as if he had been hit by a sledge hammer. Sam felt a sudden rush of adrenalin. "Hit in the shoulder. Damn!" Sam swore. There had been no time to test fire the rifle and zero the sights of the weapon before the parade. And now they were paying for it. The last shot had been wide and off target and von Schnakenberg was down but not out.

Zorn's bullet hit Wurth square right between the eyes and drilled its way through his skull to emerge out of the back of his head which exploded in a shower of blood, bone and brain tissue. Zorn smiled. "Von Schnakenberg, you're next, you bastard."

Ansett fired at Wurth, but Wurth was already falling. He had been shot already. "Who the hell shot him? Was that you, Robbo?" Ansett asked accusingly.

"It wasn't me, Pete," Robinson replied. "It must've been one of the boys."

Alan's round hit Schuster in the arm. "Bugger! I missed Schuster!" Alan shouted disappointedly.

"Shut up and keep firing! Get him with a second shot," Sam urged.

Alan frantically worked the bolt of his rifle to get off another shot. "Calm down," Alan said to himself. "Less haste, more speed. I see you." Schuster was crouching and taking cover behind the War Memorial and Alan realized that he was too late. The German was out of sight and out of the line of fire. Alan swore in frustration. "Never mind.

Next time, Schuster. I've got a bullet with your name on it. Sam, I'm switching to secondary targets."

Robinson shot another German officer right in the centre of his chest. "Timber," Robinson said as the German toppled backwards like a tree felled by an axe.

"Von Schnakenberg, you're next," Zorn said grimly. "Where the hell are you?" Zorn took his eye away from the telescope to get a wider panoramic view. "Von Schnakenberg is already down." Zorn's brow furrowed with confusion. "What the hell is going on?" he asked himself. People were running everywhere like headless chickens. "I don't believe it. It must be a partisan attack." Zorn smiled and allowed himself a chuckle. He couldn't believe his luck. "A partisan attack will provide the perfect cover. All the deaths will be blamed on the British." It couldn't have worked out better if he had planned the whole thing himself. For the first time Zorn began to think that he might actually be able to pull this off and get away with it. "Time to get out of here, but time for one more shot." Zorn pulled the trigger and took his eye away from the telescopic sight. "Got you, Lindau, you bastard. Kiss your boyfriend goodbye, von Schnakenberg." But first things first. I need to dispose of the evidence. "Now, do you have any grenades, Behrens?" Zorn asked as he patted the pockets of the body.

The second bell rang as the wounded Lindau was leaning over von Schnakenberg, protecting him and using his own body to shield his injured friend from any further shots. Alan fired his second shot and Lindau collapsed over von Schnakenberg and lay still, not moving. Other secondary targets were also dropping. Some were S.S. and some were Army.

The third bell rang as Zorn was leaving the roof, running quickly down the stairs with his fingers crossed.

The fourth bell rang as a pack of soldiers arrived puffing

and panting at the main door to the Cathedral. They had come to stop the bells from ringing, the bells whose deafening peal was preventing the Germans from locating the enemy. "Open the doors!" A feldwebel ordered.

"I can't," a soldier replied. "They're locked shut." Some of the soldiers tried to use their rifle butts as a battering ram but the ancient oak doors were many inches thick and their energetic exertions made no impact on the doors what so ever. The doors stubbornly refused to budge.

The fifth bell rang as the soldiers fired their Schmeissers at the Cathedral doors which finally began to splinter and shatter under the combined assault of half a dozen machine guns. Two soldiers fired a machine gun burst inside the Cathedral to clear the entrance and shattered the stained glass windows which had stood inside for a thousand years. "Grenade!" A soldier shouted as two soldiers threw a pair of grenades inside in rapid succession. "Clear!" The grenadiers shouted as chunks of masonry fell from the walls.

Sixth bell. The frenzied mob of soldiers crashed through the damaged Cathedral doors. The soldiers stampeded through the foyer like a herd of wildebeest and the first man tripped the booby trapped grenade which Zorn had set earlier. The explosion ripped through the tightly packed soldiers who fell like ten pins in a jumbled heap of dead and dying men. Zorn watched the shredding of the soldiers as he ran towards the Cathedral doors stairs. I must retrieve the report from Wurst's body.

Groups of soldiers were heading for the communal entrances to the flats surrounding the Square whilst other soldiers fired indiscriminately at the windows. Soldiers continued to collapse to the ground as the assassins found new targets. Hordes of panicking civilians ran around the Square like lemmings but they were trapped by the barricades and they were trapped by the soldiers and were hopelessly caught in the crossfire.

Seventh bell. Another section of soldiers entered the Cathedral, leapfrogging over their fallen comrades. "Medic! See what you can do for the wounded." A feldwebel ordered. He spotted an S.S. officer approaching. "Sir!" The feldwebel shouted as he snapped to attention and saluted. The S.S. officer spotted the feldwebel at the same time and returned the salute.

"Over here, Feldwebel!" Zorn replied. A thin film of sweat spontaneously spread over his forehead as Zorn realized that he was at real risk of being discovered.

"Where are they, sir?" The feldwebel demanded as his forefinger itched on the trigger.

"Down that way!" Zorn pointed down the length of the Cathedral, "I'm going to get reinforcements," he said as he started heading towards the door. His heart was pounding so powerfully and so hard and fast that it threatened to burst out of his chest

Eighth bell. As the feldwebel streamed by with his section. Zorn picked up a discarded Schmeisser, cocked it, switched off the safety catch and pulled the trigger unleashing a torrent of bullets into the backs of the unsuspecting soldiers. Because you've seen me. Because I can't leave any witnesses. Because no one must know that I was here. The men fell on top of each other like dominoes. "I'm sorry," Zorn said as he finished off the wounded with a double tap to the back of the head with his Luger.

The Medic ordered to help the wounded heard the sudden burst of machinegun fire shatter the silence of the church. He slowly stood up and cautiously poked his head out from behind a column in time to see a figure disappear around a corner.

A section of S.S. troopers started to pound up the flat stairs to the top floor where Sam and Alan were firing.

"They're coming," Alan said, furiously working the bolt as he fired another shot.

"I know. We've still got time. Keep firing," Sam shouted as he squeezed off another round.

Ninth bell. Zorn realized that he couldn't leave by the main door. It was simply too conspicuous. Someone might spot him. He headed for the side exit, Luger in hand. He stepped out of the door and hurriedly jumped back to avoid being crushed by the crowd. Civilians were streaming past away from the Square, away from the shots and the shouting. Zorn cautiously started heading towards the Square, keeping an eye out for any stray German soldiers. He hoped to reach Wurst's body and either retrieve the Report or blow up the Report together with Wurst's body. Zorn found the entrance to the Square and slowly peeked around the corner. The Square was a scene of utter carnage and chaos. Isolated corpses and bodies lay all over the place and a particularly large cluster was grouped around the War Memorial. Zorn grinned wickedly at his own handiwork. However, he had always considered himself to be a fair man. Credit where credit was due. It was not all his own work. Some of it was the handiwork of his British partners in crime. He could see officers and N.C.O.s barking orders and trying to gain command and control of the situation. Dying soldiers tried to crawl out of the killing zone and wounded civilians sheltered in door ways and begged to be rescued.

Tenth bell. Germans were running up the stairs to the fourth floor.

"Time to leave," Alan said, turning around and heading for the door.

"Let's go." Sam stood up to follow him.

S.S. storm troopers pounded up the stairs to the top floor

but stopped when they saw two paratroopers emerge from a flat door. The S.S. Scharfuhrer paused. He was confused. He hesitated. "I didn't know that you boys were supposed to be in charge of security on this side of the Square."

"We're not, Adolf." Sam said as opened fire. The S.S. Scharfuhrer was going down and the next man was falling as Alan emptied a full magazine into the pack of storm troopers. Sam threw two grenades down the stairs which exploded, ripped apart the weakened banister and sent half a dozen S.S. men screaming over the side to meet their sudden deaths on the foyer flagstones at the foot of the stairs. The boys stepped over the smoking, broken and bloodied bodies and rapidly proceeded down the stairs with their weapons held at the ready with the butts pulled tight into their shoulders.

Zorn took a Red Cross armband out of his pocket and slipped it on as he ran to the War Memorial "Move out of the way. I'm a doctor!" he shouted as he reached Wurth. He felt the back of Wurth's head and his fingers came away dripping blood, bone and gore. "It's no use. He's dead." Zorn spotted the attaché brief case, which Wurth had been carrying, swapped it with the one that he had left earlier by the Cathedral door and joined a group of S.S. soldiers entering a block of flats before anyone could stop him. I must make sure that people remember that I was no where near the Cathedral. Zorn worked his way through to the front of the section and took command.

Eleventh bell. "Al, there's another group of stromtroopers coming up the stairs," Sam warned. "There's too many of them. They'll have heard the firing and the grenade blasts. The same trick won't work twice. They'll be on guard. They'll shoot first and ask questions later. We're trapped."

"No we're not, Sam," Alan replied. "Quickly! Back upstairs to the dead Germans!"

The S.S. men raced up the stairs. They had heard the shooting and the explosions and they were ready to kill anything with a pulse. The lead scout saw two shadowy figures at the third floor landing and opened fire with his Schmessier. Zorn knocked the man's barrel to the side and the bullets veered off target and drilled a neat set of holes into the wall. "You stupid bastard, they're paras!" He shouted angrily in the shooter's ear.

"Kamerad!" One of the paras shouted.

The two paras slowly limped down the stairs with one supporting the other. They were covered in blood and the crippled one was obviously badly wounded.

Zorn stepped to the side as the two paras limped by. "Are you boys alright?" He asked, tenderly placing a hand on the shoulder of the walking man.

The para tapped the side of his head with the palm of his right hand and shook his head from side to side. I can't hear you, he signaled.

Zorn squeezed the shoulder of the mime artist. "It's probably temporary," he tried to reassure them as he shouted in his ear. "Your hearing will probably return within a few days." Or a few weeks. Or never, he thought. The para shrugged his shoulders. He then braced up and saluted. Zorn was caught off guard. He returned the salute and watched the paras continue their journey down stairs.

The two paras exited the communal entrance and walked into the Square. The injured paratrooper looked to his left. Two more paras were walking towards them.

"Are you alright?" Ansett whispered as he reached them. His words were almost lost amongst the sound of the carnage and chaos around them. The Germans were still firing indiscriminately at the windows of the flats surrounding the Square. There was not a single pane of glass that had not been shattered.

"Yes, we're fine," Alan reassured him.

Ansett pointed with alarm at their blood soaked uniforms and their equally blood soaked faces.

Sam laughed at Ansett's confusion. "It's not our blood," he explained.

Ansett laughed with relief. "No, I didn't think that it was. You look like you've been at an Aztec Sacrifice! Come on. Let's get out of here."

Chapter Eight

"What's the final body count?" Schuster asked. He was sitting up in bed with his right arm in a plaster cast and in a sling. His face was pale and drawn. He had lost a lot of blood from his wound.

Zorn stood at the foot of his bed. He read the names from the casualty list which he held in his hand. "Generalmajor Wurth, commanding officer of the Seventh Parachute Brigade killed." Schuster grunted his approval. "Obersturmbannfuhrer Wrechert, your second-in-command, killed…"

"A damned shame," Schuster interrupted, "he was a good man."

"All the commanding officers and second in commands of the Fourth, Fifth and Sixth S.S. Infantry Regiment killed…"

"Christ! All of my senior officers!" Schuster interrupted angrily.

"…and Sturmbannfuhrer Offenbach the commanding officer of your Signals Company was killed. He was murdered in his flat, sir. A paratrooper bayonet was found stuck in his chest."

"Interesting." Schuster scratched his chin thoughtfully. "Go on."

"Major Lindau, Second-in-Command, First Potsdam Grenadiers killed…"

"Every cloud has a silver lining." Schuster chuckled at his own joke.

"Hauptsturmfuhrer Andreas Schmitt was murdered in his own flat as well, sir. He was executed at point blank range with two shots to the forehead. Forensics has determined that the rounds were fired from a Luger…" Zorn said grimly. "The killers had sticky fingers, sir. Schmitt's webbing and Luger are missing."

"Verdamnt! I served with his father in the last War. That's one letter that I'm not looking forward to writing. "

"The Mayor of Hereward was also killed…" Zorn continued.

"Which rules out any British Resistance involvement…"

"Unless he was shot as an example to collaborators…" Zorn interrupted.

"Three of our men survived the attack in the flats. One of them swears that the reason that the Scharfuhrer in charge hesitated before opening fire was because the attackers were paratroopers."

"Could he have been mistaken?"

"Of course it's possible, sir. However, I was in the same block of flats. Two wounded paras limped down the steps towards us and we let them go by. We found the bodies of our men and our wounded further up the stairs. A Hauptsturmfuhrer from the Fifth S.S. was in command, sir."

"Could you identify these paras if you saw them again?"

"Possibly, sir. But they were covered in blood and I

93

didn't notice which of Wurth's three para battalions they were from. Anyway, Goering would never allow the S.S. to carry out an identity parade inspecting three thousand odd paratroopers."

Schuster nodded. "Our total casualties?" Schuster braced himself for the worst.

"Twenty seven killed, sir. Eighteen wounded."

Schuster shook his head from side to side in despair and disbelief. His brigade had been decapitated. He had lost virtually all of his senior commanders. How was he to fill these dead men's shoes? He simply did not have enough good men. How could he maintain the combat effectiveness of the brigade? "Paratrooper casualties?" He asked hopefully.

Zorn gave a pregnant pause. "Only one, sir. Generalmajor Wurth."

And that was you, wasn't it, Zorn? You sneaky bastard, Schuster thought. "No more paras killed or wounded?" Schuster was grasping at straws for good news.

"No, sir."

Which would point to a paratrooper continuation of the vendetta, Schuster thought to himself. Two or more shooters in two separate flats. And you would have caused the Army casualties. "Army casualties?"

"As I said, sir, Majors Lindau and von Karajan killed. Von Schnakenberg wounded."

Schuster's eyes locked like a magnet on Zorn. He felt the rage rise inside him like a burning fire. If looks could have killed, Zorn would have fallen stone dead on the spot. Schuster automatically reached for his Luger, his eyes blind with sudden rage. But his right hand was trapped in a plaster and sling. He winced as a sharp pain lanced through his injured arm. And anyway, he was not wearing his holster. The hospital frowned upon their patients wearing their weapons in bed. He turned to look at Zorn once more. Schuster's eyes bore into him accusingly. You clumsy bastard. You missed. You only had to kill Wurth and von Schnakenberg and you missed one of them

Zorn refused to look away. He looked back at Schuster meeting him glare for glare. Staring him down. You can't say anything, Schuster, he thought. You can't complain. You can't chastise or rebuke me. Because you can't admit that you know anything. You can't acknowledge that you know that I killed Lindau and Wurth and wounded von Schnakenberg. And all in your name. All because you wanted me to. "Who will rid me of this troublesome priest?" This way, if all of this blows up, if word somehow leaks out, you can deny all responsibility. You can say that I was a rogue officer carrying out a personal vendetta against the paras and the Army. A lone wolf. A loose cannon. You can wash your hands of me and deny all knowledge of me and responsibility for my actions.

"How is he?" Schuster asked, turning away to look out of the window.

"He's still in hospital. A shoulder wound. He'll pull through."

"Any other casualties?"

"No more in the Square."

No more Army casualties. Or para casualties. Only S.S. casualties. This definitely proved that the killers were paras, Schuster thought. By God, the paras would pay in blood ten times over for what they had done, he fumed.

Zorn coughed to catch Schuster's attention. "Sir, there were Army casualties in the Cathedral."

"In the Cathedral?" Schuster was confused. "What the hell was the Army doing there?"

"The Army was responsible for the security of that part of the Square, sir. Twenty nine killed, ten wounded." Zorn answered in a monotone.

Schuster nodded his head approvingly. "I'm a bit short of company commanders," he said. "I'm looking for a good man to fill the position of company commander of A Company, Fourth S.S. your old regiment. The job's yours if you want it. Are you interested?"

Zorn smiled at Schuster's ingenuity. Schuster knew that Zorn was rather less than pleased at having been forced to play the major role in the production that had become known as the Remembrance Day Massacre. Schuster was ever the strategist and politician and understood the need to offer sugar to sweeten the bitterness of Zorn's medicine.

"I'm your man, sir." Zorn knew that he had little choice other than to swallow his pride and swallow Schuster's sugar.

"By the way. Did you manage to retrieve the report, Zorn?" Schuster asked casually.

"I'm sorry, sir," Zorn replied apologetically. "I didn't."

"Oh well," Schuster shrugged philosophically, "you win some, and you lose some." Schuster's Day of Judgment would come later. Of that Zorn had no doubt.

"Why did you shoot the mayor?" Alan asked.

"Walker was a collaborator," Ansett said matter of factly. "He was spreading dangerous ideas like 'live and let live' around. We want to keep the Jerries on their toes. We want them to be constantly looking over their shoulders, constantly worrying about whether someone is going to bury a knife between their shoulder blades. We don't want Hereward to gain the reputation as a place where the Huns come for a spot of rest and recreation. We want the Jerries to dread being posted here. We want the Huns to hate every single second of every single minute that they stay in Hereward. Anyway, the Germans will put Walker's death down to a misfire or a ricochet. Walker was simply in the wrong place at the wrong time. The Jerries won't think that we're ruthless enough to start killing our own."

"Talking of our own people. How many did we lose?" Alan asked.

"Total civilian casualties: Thirteen killed and twenty four wounded."

"Christ…"

"A mixture of men, women and children. Some killed in the crossfire. Most killed in the stampede to escape from the Square. Some gunshots wounds, but mostly crush wounds. Cuts and bruises and broken bones."

"My God. We killed nearly as many of our own people as we did Germans," Alan said bitterly. "Was it worth it, sir?" he asked with tear filled eyes.

"People always die in a war, Alan.," Ansett explained gently. "Sometimes the innocent suffer along with the guilty. What we did was necessary."

"How do I explain that to a child who's lost her mother?"

Ansett thought for a few seconds before answering. "You would tell her that her mother died in a good cause. She died for freedom."

On Christmas morning the whole household gathered around the Christmas tree. Alan was staying with the Roberts family for the holiday and he picked up a package addressed to him that he read was from Sam. The present was a wooden British Matilda tank. "Thanks, Sam. I was wondering what you had been making so secretly in woodwork class."

"It was jolly difficult trying to keep it a secret, let me tell you," Sam smiled.

"I'm glad that you like it."

Sam opened the package that Alan had given him. It was a wooden Luger pistol painted black. It was very accurate and lifelike. And well it should be, Sam smiled. They had seen, held and fired enough of the real thing. Alan had simply copied the wooden model from his metal model. Sam laughed to himself. He knew that Alan had given him a wooden Luger as a none too subtle way of rubbing in the fact that Alan had a real one and Sam did not. However, although that may well have been true when Alan had begun to carve the pistol this was no longer the case. Sam had liberated a Luger during the Remembrance Day Massacre from the recently deceased Hauptsturmfuhrer Schmitt.

The next present that Alan opened was from Alice. The contents spilled put onto the carpeted floor. The package contained badges. Alan recognized them immediately. German Armed Forces badges. S.S. paratrooper and Army. Cuff and collar badges. Rank badges, Regimental shoulder and breast pocket identification badges, Specialist insignia such as anti-tank gunner, signaler, machine gunner and even a few medals and ribbons. Alan was gob smacked. He was holding a veritable treasure trove in his hands. He looked across at Sam. He was holding a similar collection of badges in his outstretched hands. And he was in a similar state of shock. Alan knew that the same question was racing through both of their heads: How did Alice get this?

Alan could hardly trust himself to speak. But as the silence dragged into seconds he knew that he had to. "Thank… thank you, Alice," he stuttered.

"Do you like them?" Alice asked.

Alan didn't know what to say. "Yes, they're very nice," he answered lamely.

"You don't like them, do you?" Alice's brow became furrowed with creases.

"No. No, I do. You like them too, don't you, Sam?" Alan desperately searched for help.

"Yes," Sam answered with a false smile. "I think that they're… terrific. Where did you get them?"

Alice seemed to be placated by their reassurances. Her face broke out into a smile. "Trade secret. Everybody's collecting them. They're like gold dust."

"Which ones are the most valuable?" Sam asked picking up an S.S. anti-tank gunner specialist badge.

"Paratrooper, S.S. then Army."

"Why in that order?" Alan asked.

"Para badges are the most valuable because they've left Hereward. Army badges are the least valuable because they are relatively easy to get. You have to sweat blood and tears to get S.S. badges."

Alan looked across at Sam. He saw how Sam winced when Alice paraphrased the words which Churchill had used when he had become Prime Minister. It seemed disrespectful if not downright sacrilegious to use those words so flippantly.

"The S.S. make you work hard for their badges," Alice said shaking her head from side to side as if remembering how hard she had to "work" in order to get them. "They don't surrender their badges without a fight." Alice continued with a chuckle.

Alan didn't even want to think about what Alice had done to convince the S.S. to "surrender" their badges.

"What about British badges?" Sam asked through clenched teeth.

"British Badges?" Alice snorted. "They're tupence hapenny." She was completely oblivious to her brother's growing anger. "Everyone and their dogs got them. Every homeless down and out wandering the streets is an ex-soldier. Nobody wants them."

"Are you talking about the badges or our soldiers?" Sam asked with barely controlled fury.

"The badges of course, Sam," Alice stared at him as if he was the village idiot. "What's the matter with you, anyway?" she said shaking her head. "I thought that you'd like the present."

Sam stared at his sister as if he she was a stranger. He could barely conceal his contempt and loathing. He knew that a few of the older girls at the school had German boyfriends and he had wondered whether Alice had followed this growing trend.

Alan swallowed bitterly. He could feel the bile rise at the back of his throat. He knew that what Alice had said was the truth. He had seen the Police move along the jobless and homeless ex-soldiers who clustered in pathetic and pitiful groups around the Square. Unwashed and unwanted. Many of them were crippled by war wounds. They were a painful reminder of the humiliation that Britain had suffered. Out of sight out of mind. If people could not see them then it made it easier to forget about the defeat.

"Thanks for your present, Alan," Alice said, stretching up on her tiptoes to kiss him on the cheek.

"My pleasure."

"I'm going out to the garden to try it out. Are you coming?"

"We'll be along in a minute."

Alice walked out of the room. She looked down at the skipping rope that she was holding in her hand with disbelief. How old did Alan think she was? Honestly.

Chapter Nine

The sniper round had entered slightly below von Schnakenberg's collarbone narrowly missing his lung and had exited just avoiding his shoulder blade. He had nearly died from massive loss of blood. Von Schnakenberg had spent two weeks in hospital fighting for his life and it had been touch and go as to whether or not he would make it, but he had pulled through. In the meantime the Army in Hereward had been leaderless. It had drifted around like a ship without a rudder. Every single officer above the rank of major had been either killed or wounded. The Army in Hereward had coped but Army Headquarters in London had decided that one of the contributing factors that had led to the Remembrance Day Massacre had been the unequal balance of power in Hereward and so von Schnakenberg had been promoted to generalmajor and he had been given command of his own brigade. The news was a welcome morale booster to both von Schnakenberg and to his men. Although Schuster would remain officer in command of Hereward, he would no longer be able to give von Schnakenberg orders. Instead he would have to "liase" with him as an equal partner and discuss what they had to do rather than dictate and give orders.

"Gentlemen, it is a pleasure to see all of you here tonight. I must confess that for several days I was uncertain as to whether or not I would ever see any of you ever again!" Von Schakenberg looked out over the sea of familiar faces that filled the length and breadth of Hereward Cathedral Hall. "With the arrival of fresh reinforcements from the Fatherland we are now at full strength and at last we will be able to face our enemies on an equal footing!" More cheering from the troops.

He topped up and raised his champagne glass. "Gentlemen, please fill your glasses and join me in a toast." The officers filled their glasses and stood up. "The brigade, the Army and the Fatherland!" The officers repeated the toast.

"Three cheers for the Generalmajor!" Alfonin shouted, "Hip-Hip-Hooray!"

After the cheering had died down von Schnakenberg turned around to face Alfonin. "Thanks for welcoming me back, Nicky."

"My pleasure, sir." Alfonin hesitated for a second. "Sir, I wonder if I could have a word with you?"

"Certainly, Nicky. Pull up a chair," von Schnakenberg invited.

"In private, sir, if I may." Alfonin leaned in close.

Von Schnakenberg nodded. Alfonin led the way out of the hall, with von Schnakenberg following, shaking hands with well wishers, being introduced to new officers under his command and pressing flesh like a Mafia Don. Von Schnakenberg's eyes opened wide in surprise as Alfonin entered the Ladies' toilets. "Alright, Nicky, why all the cloak and dagger?"

"Because what I'm about to tell you sir, is only known

to three people. Me, one other and now your good self. And because what I'm about to tell you may well end up getting all three of us killed."

"Go on." Von Schnakenberg was intrigued. He leant back on a wash hand basin and crossed his arms.

Alfonin took a deep breath before he continued. "Sir. Not all of our men were killed in the Cathedral. One of them survived without a scratch."

"Who?"

"Private Eggers, sir. I was his platoon feldwebel. He served under your brother."

Von Schnakenberg winced at the mention of his brother. "Continue."

"Eggers was tending the wounded lying on the Cathedral floor when he heard the burst of Schmeisser fire which cut down our men. He poked his head out from behind a pillar and he caught a glimpse of the man's back as he walked away."

"Who was it?"

"An S.S. officer, sir."

"For Christ's sake," Sam's voice dripped with disgust, "I don't believe it." He pushed himself from the wall and started steaming towards the entrance to Hereward Cathedral Hall like a runaway train.

"Sam, wait!" Alan futilely tried to grab his arm, but Sam shrugged him off as if he was shrugging off a fly.

"Oh hello, Sam," Alice flashed a perfect pearly white smile and turned to the man standing next to her. "Sam, I'd like you to meet a friend of mine. Norbert, this is my brother Sam."

Sam stared at the man whom Alice had introduced. Norbert Ulrich was six foot tall and had blue eyes and blonde hair. He looked like a model from an S.S. recruitment poster or a specimen from a German Secondary School Biology textbook. A perfect example of Aryan Manhood. Sam looked at him as if he was from another planet. He simply couldn't help himself.

Norbert clicked his heels together and gave a slight bow. "I've heard a lot about you, Sam. I'm glad to finally meet you. It was very generous of Bishop Rathdowne to invite all members of the German Armed Forces to attend the annual Hereward Cathedral Christmas Dance." Norbert held out his hand. "I understand why many people disagreed with his decision, Sam."

"Sam!" Alan hissed in his ear.

Sam shook his hand in slow motion. His lips were pulled back to reveal his teeth and gums which resembled that of a corpse in the final stages of rigour mortis. If you could read my mind you would n't be smiling, you German bastard, you'd be pissing in your bright, black shiny jackboots.

"And this is Alan," Alice smiled.

"Pleased to meet you," Alan said, shaking Norbert's hand. "Excuse us," he said, placing a hand on each of Sam's shoulders and turning him around to face the dance floor. "We promised a couple of girls a dance. We'll see you later. Alice. Norbert."

"Alan." Norbert clicked his heels and bowed again.

"Save a dance for me," Alice called after him.

"Of course."

"See you later, Sam," Alice shouted after her brother.

"Yes, Sam," Norbert added. "We have a lot to talk about."

Sam did not respond.

"Roberts, you whore! What are you doing with that Nazi bastard?" The question was hurled across the length of the dance floor. The band stopped playing. Everyone stopped dancing. All eyes turned towards the door.

"Edwards…" Sam hissed out the name like a snake. "That does it…"

"Sam! Wait!" Alan urged. He hurried after Sam as he quick marched towards the door. He knew that Sam was spoiling for a fight. He was ready to fight Edwards, the Germans and the whole world if necessary.

"Edwards!" Sam barked as he halted in front of him with legs splayed and hands hanging loosely around his hips in the classic pose of a Wild West gunfighter.

"Ah, Sam Roberts, the Whore's brother, I presume." Danny Edward's cronies laughed sycophantically. They were well used to the role of playing the appreciative audience to Danny's class clown antics.

Danny Edwards was six foot two and was built like one of the brick sheds on his farm. He played tight head prop for the St. John's Academy 1st XV Rugby Team and he had the cauliflower ears, scars and abrasions and various other war wounds that accompanied that position. Edwards was a Day Pupil and he was in Fourth Year, the same year as Sam and Alan. He had also gone out with Alice earlier on in the year, but she had broken off the relationship at the end of the Christmas Term. Edwards had not accepted the break up gracefully. Although Sam also played in the Firsts as a flanker, they were not friends and at best they could be described as acquaintances.

"Edwards, take back what you just said," Sam said menacingly.

"I won't, Roberts. Your sister is a Hun whore and you know it," Edwards sneered, drilling a hole in Sam's chest with his forefinger.

"Take it back right now, Edwards," Sam snarled, flexing

and unflexing his fingers. "This is your last chance. I won't ask you again." He took one step forward.

"Who's going to make me?" Edwards stepped towards Sam.

"I am."

"Oh yeah," Edwards looked contemptuously at the lone figure of Alan standing behind Sam. "You and whose army? You and your little boyfriend here?" Edward's friends laughed like a pack of hyenas. He looked over his shoulder at his three burly friends standing behind him and then returned to look at Sam and Alan. It was painfully clear that Sam and Alan would stand little chance in a fight against Edwards and his gang. They were outnumbered two to one.

"Him and my army." Paul Mason stepped between the two quarrelling boys.

"Sir?" Sam said in surprise.

"Captain Mason?" Alan echoed.

"Keep out of this, sir," Edwards warned. "This is none of your business."

"I'm making it my business."

"Get out of the way."

"You're both students at my school and you're my responsibility."

"Responsibility? What would you know about responsibility?" Edwards asked. " My father and my two elder brothers marched out in your company under your command with you and the Fusiliers in September. You came back. They didn't. How do you explain that?"

"I don't have to explain my actions to you," Mason said defensively as his cheeks began to burn.

"And I don't have to explain my actions to a coward who abandoned his men."

Mason's uppercut landed right on the base of Edward's

chin and lifted him clean off the ground. He flew through the air in a graceful arc and landed flat on his back on the dance floor. His legs and arms were as floppy as those of a rag doll and his eyeballs rattled around in his skull. He was out cold, unconscious and completely dead to the world.

There was a stunned silence. Everyone was too shocked to react.

"Take Edwards away," Mason ordered Edward's lackeys in an ice cold voice. "Tell him when he wakes up not to come back. He's not welcome here."

Two of Edward's companions grabbed an arm each and lifted him up to a standing position. They each wrapped an arm around his waist and dragged him towards the main door. He was only just starting to come round. When they reached the exit the boy holding the door turned around and faced Mason.

"This is a warning to all whores and traitors," The boy snarled. "You haven't heard the last of this: we'll be back."

"I understand why you're so angry, Sam," Alan said as he followed Sam out of the dance hall.

"No, you don't, Al." Sam shook his head. "Edwards called Alice a whore: he insulted my sister, he insulted me and he insulted my family. He has shamed me and my family in front of the whole town."

"But Edwards is wrong, Sam. The whole town knows that."

"No, Al. Edwards is right-Alice is a Nazi whore and the whole town knows it. They're just too polite to say it. Or maybe they're just too scared. At least Edwards had the guts to say publicly what the whole town is thinking privately," Sam said bitterly.

"Now steady on, Sam. You don't know that," Alan protested. "You don't know that for sure."

"Know what for sure?" Sam asked. "That she's sleeping with the enemy?"

Alan's embarrassed silence answered Sam's question.

"Look, Al. I've had enough," Sam said. "I'm tired of sitting around on our backsides doing nothing. I'm tired of watching the Jerries swan around with our women acting as if they owned the place and I'm tired of waiting for orders from Edinburgh. As far as I'm concerned, the Christmas Truce is over."

"What about Ansett?"

"Bugger Ansett."

"What about our orders?"

"Bugger our orders," Sam swore. "I don't remember signing on the dotted line to join Ansett's chicken shit outfit."

"We swore an Oath of Allegiance, Sam," Alan said seriously.

"Yes, we swore an oath, Al, but to the King, not to Ansett. He could be a crazy vigilante for all we know. A loose cannon. Anyway, how do we know that he's following orders from the Free North? How do we know that he's got a radio? Have you seen it? Because I certainly haven't. We only have his word that he's following orders from Edinburgh. And I'm afraid that I'm not willing to put my life on the line on the basis of his word. And neither should you, Al."

Alan said nothing. He was still trying to digest what Sam had said. "What have you got in mind?" He asked finally.

Sam's eyes lit up. He had been confident that he would be able to win Alan over and he was pleased to discover that his confidence had not been misplaced. "I propose that we go freelance."

Chapter Ten

The two figures slipped through the back streets of Hereward. They were dressed completely in black and kept to the shadows. They paused at each cross roads to make sure that there were no German patrols. They glided through the streets like ghosts and made no sound.

At last they reached their destination. A two story semi-detached brick house in an up market part of town. The first of the pair lowered a tin to the ground and carefully prized open the lid with the blade of his lock knife. The figure dipped a paintbrush into the tin and started painting foot high letters on the wall. In the mean time, his companion had taken off his haversack that he had carried on his back. He took out a jerry can and two objects wrapped in paper. He unwrapped the objects that were revealed to be two beer bottles made of glass. He poured the contents of the jerry can into each of the beer bottles until they were both full to the brim. He then stuffed a soaking rag into the neck of each.

The painter kept watch to ensure that the coast was clear. He then opened the garden gate for his companion. He crept up the garden path to the front door carrying the jerry can in one hand and a hose in the other. When he reached the door he slowly lifted up the letter flap and inserted the hose. He placed the other end of the hose in the jerry can and tilted it up at an angle until it was higher than the letter flap. The contents of the jerry can flowed through the hose and gushed onto the carpet inside the house. The carpet soon became sodden and soaked through. The dark figure carefully placed the empty jerry can on the "Welcome" mat outside the door and laid the hose on the ground beside it. He then tiptoed back down the garden path. When he reached the painter at the gate they both reached into their pockets and extracted a rectangular box. The matches burned brightly in the black night as they lit the petrol soaked rags. They picked up the petrol bombs and threw them at the large bay windows at the front of the house.

The bombers exited through the gate as the windows shattered. The petrol soaked carpets went up in wall of flames as the Molotov Cocktails exploded. The arsonists couldn't resist whooping a wild war cry as they admired their handiwork. They then turned on their heels and ran off into the night disappearing as silently as they had appeared.

"How is the public reacting to the fire bomb attacks?"

"Until the first deaths there was general sympathy with the bombers' motives, but not with their actions. Since the first deaths public opinion is firmly on the side of the victims and against the attackers. The arsonists are universally hated and condemned."

"How are the British Authorities coping?"

"They're not, sir," Zorn answered. "The Fire Brigade cannot cope: they are under equipped and undermanned. The Police are not coping either. They rounded up the usual suspects, including the Edwards boy, on Monday. However, he had a watertight alibi and they had no choice but to release him after twenty four hours due to a lack of evidence."

"Lack of evidence!" Schuster guffawed contemptuously.

"Sir, a Police Constable was stabbed in the chest as he attempted to arrest a suspect last night-the suspect escaped."

"I know, Zorn. The Chief Inspector came and saw me this morning together with the Mayor and Bishop Rathdowne. They have asked for permission and authorization to increase the number of 'Special Constables' in order to deal with what the Chief Inspector called 'vigilante mobs taking the Law into their own hands.' I have granted his request. The good bishop will preach against 'anarchy and lawlessness' during his church service this Sunday and he will ask for volunteers to join the Specials. The Mayor will place an ad in the 'Hereward Herald' this week likewise asking for volunteers."

"The bishop is turning into a regular little Quisling, sir."

"Yes, the bishop has his uses," Schuster laughed. "There is one minor detail, Zorn: The Specials will be armed and the next natural step will be to transform the Specials into a paramilitary force which we can use against Jews, Communists, terrorists and other such untermensch. We are forming the nucleus of a British Fascist Militia, the beginnings of a New Order Army."

"Divide and conquer, sir."

"Precisely, Zorn." Schuster nodded. "Just as we use Frenchmen against Frenchmen in the Milice, so we will use Englishmen against Englishmen in the Specials."

"So you promise that you have absolutely nothing to do with these arson attacks?" Ansett asked. He was leaning with his back to his desk with his arms folded across his chest.

"I promise, sir," Alan replied.

"And you, Sam?"

Sam came to a position of attention. "I promise to do my best, to do my duty to God, to serve the King, help other people and to keep the Scout Guide Law." He gave the Scout salute, smirking as he recited the Scout promise.

"For God's sake, Sam!" Ansett slammed the palm of his hand on the desk making a loud bang. "This is no laughing matter!" His face was scarlet with rage. "Four people have been killed and you think that this is all one big joke!"

"Four whores and traitors," Sam retorted as quick as a flash. "Not people."

"One of the 'traitors' was a four month old baby boy," Ansett said.

"You can't make an omelet without breaking eggs."

"Are you calling a baby a traitor?" Ansett's eyes bulged in disbelief.

"No, I'm not." Sam opened and slammed a desktop. He was sick and tired of being the villain in this story. "What I am saying is that Sarah Burrows knew what she was doing. The Huns killed Fred at Fairfax and he was barely cold in his unmarked grave before she was shacked up with a Nazi. That Nazi might have killed her husband for all that she knew. Two Hun whores had already been executed and she continued to sleep with the enemy. She made a choice. She knew the risks and she took her chances. She knew what she was doing."

"Little Charlie didn't have a choice, Sam," Alan said softly.

Sam's head whipped around as if he had been slapped. He screwed up his eyes and glared at his friend. Alan refused to be stared down and slowly shook his head in disgust and disapproval. Sam realized that he wasn't going to win this time. He shrugged his shoulders with forced nonchalance.

"How can you be so callous?" Ansett asked.

"Not callous." Sam turned to face him. "Matter of fact."

"Are you telling me that you agree with what the bombers are doing?"

Sam shook his head. "I don't agree with their methods but I do agree with their motives."

Alan swore.

"Despite the fact that innocent lives have been lost?" Ansett asked.

"Depends what you mean by 'innocent.' We lost far more 'innocent lives' on Remembrance Day."

Ansett did not reply. There was nothing that he could say. Sam was right. Thirteen people had died and twenty four had been wounded that day. Some of the victims had been women and children, but all of the victims had been innocent. All of them had died as a result of the decisions that Ansett had made and the actions that he, Sam, Alan and Robinson had carried out that day.

"Guilty, innocent. Terrorists, Partisans. Words are cheap. There is absolutely no difference between the killing of the Nazi whores and the execution of the mayor." Sam continued. "They were all traitors and collaborators and they all deserved to die." Sam stuck his chin out resolutely, defying anyone to challenge him.

Ansett thought about challenging Sam, but it was rapidly becoming obvious that he was banging his head against a brick wall. He decided to change tactics. "But you promise that you have had nothing to do with these attacks?"

Sam nodded. "I may sympathize with the attackers, but I have nothing to do with them."

"Good." Ansett stood up. "I'm glad to hear it. Because

113

what's happened so far is child's play. The bombers have only had to deal with flat footed bicycle cycling Bobbies on the beat who couldn't catch a cold, never mind armed arsonists."

"So what's the problem?" Sam asked.

"Christ!" Ansett exclaimed in exasperation. "You don't get it, do you?" He started to stride purposefully around the classroom, talking and walking as he thought. "If the arsonists continue with their attacks then it will only be a matter of time before they kill a German, whether deliberately or accidentally. It doesn't matter."

"The Huns will take hostages…" Alan began.

"… And they will shoot them if they fail to find the arsonists," Sam interrupted, "thus turning the people against them and scoring a spectacular own goal." He shrugged. "So what's the problem?"

Ansett bit his tongue. He refused to let Sam's question provoke him. "Most of us," Ansett emphasized, "can see what is going to happen if the attacks do not stop."

"What are you suggesting?" Sam suddenly stood up. He could see where Ansett's train of thought was leading.

"That we stop them ourselves." Alan beat Ansett to the punch.

"What?" Sam exclaimed as if he had been burnt with a red hot poker. He turned around to stare at Alan in disbelief. "'We stop them ourselves?' We help the Nazis to catch our own people?" Sam asked rhetorically.

"They're not 'our own people', Sam," Ansett answered. "These arsonists are killing British men, women and children. It doesn't matter whether they, or anyone else, consider them to be innocent or guilty."

"You're going to do the Germans' dirty work," Sam accused. "You might as well join up with Mosley and his mob."

"No, Sam," Ansett said patiently. "We're going to stop the arsonists before the Jerries can start their work."

"How?" Sam asked.

Ansett did not answer.

"How?" Sam repeated.

"I don't know yet," Ansett admitted. He stopped stomping around the classroom and resumed his position perched on the desk. "But if we work together then we can come up with a plan."

"The problem with you, sir, is that you ask all of the right questions, but you don't have the right answers. Well, the fire bombers do have the answers. They've cleaned the Hun whores and their Boche boyfriends off the streets and that is absolutely fine with me." Sam stormed out of the classroom and slammed the door before either Alan or Ansett could reply.

"Ah, good morning, Paul." Harold Ashworth stood up from behind his desk and walked around to the front as Paul Mason walked in. Ashworth was grinning like a Cheshire Cat.

"Good morning, Rector." Mason shook Ashworth's hand.

"I believe that you know the Mayor; Mr. Brunswick; Chief Inspector Brown and Bishop Rathdowne?"

The men all stood up and Mason shook their hands in turn before sitting down.

"Paul, you are no doubt curious as to why we have asked you to join us here."

"You could say that."

"Well, perhaps it would be better if Chief Inspector Brown explained."

"Thank you, Harold," Brown said, leaning forward

in his chair. "Captain Mason, as you know we are in the process of expanding the existing Special Constabulary Unit in order to help the Police deal with the criminal activities of various hooligan elements in Hereward."

"Yes, Chief Inspector. I am aware of the plan." Mason noticed that Brown considered the arsonists' actions to be criminally and not politically motivated. The attackers were cowardly criminals. Plain and simple.

"What are your views on the subject, Captain?" Brown asked.

"I think that it's a good idea." Mason could sense Mayor Brunswick and Bishop Rathdowne nodding their heads with approval. "You can't allow people to take the law into their own hands."

"We cannot allow mob rule in Hereward nor will we allow anarchy to take hold," Ashworth continued.

"Have you thought about joining up, Paul?" Rathdowne asked.

"To be honest, Ben, I hadn't actually paid it much thought," Mason admitted.

"The Special Constabulary needs a commander, Captain Mason," Brown used Mason's RRiFF rank, "someone with proven natural leadership abilities, a man whom the men can look up to and we think that you're the man for the job."

"But my work at school. I wouldn't have time," Mason protested.

"You would have more time for work outside school in the Specials if you spent less time teaching. I need a new deputy rector." Ashworth dangled the carrot in front of Mason's nose. "Less teaching time, but more responsibility points, a pay rise and a rent free house within the grounds of the school would accompany that position."

"And my rank?" Mason asked Brown.

116

"Inspector. It's a fully paid position."

Mason's eyes lit up at the thought of what was being offered. Promotion, privelage, prestige. Power. "Is there anything else that I should know?"

Brown coughed before he answered. "Brigadefuhreur Schuster is supplying the Police and the Specials with captured British revolvers."

"You're going to work for the Germans?" Mason asked with horror as he nearly leaped off the chair.

Brown's face turned red with fury. The hackles of his moustache rose as he opened his mouth to reply.

But Rathdowne preempted him and cut Brown off at the pass. "Not for the Germans, Paul," he explained gently. "We will not work for the Germans," he emphasized. "It just so happens that at this moment in time we share the same enemy-the arsonists."

"The Jerries are only supplying weapons, correct?" Mason asked.

"Correct," Brown answered who had recovered his self-control.

"They're not supplying us with 'advisers' or anything like that? We're not having joint patrols?"

"No."

"The Specials will only deal with civil matters, not political?"

"Yes. I guarantee it."

Mason looked into the expectant faces of the four most powerful and influential men in Hereward. He felt a wave of adrenalin surge through his body. The success or failure of this entire venture depended on the decision that he was about to make. "I've made up my mind."

The men sat forward on the edge of their seats with expectation.

"I accept."

117

Chapter Eleven

"Do you love me, Hans?" Margaret Paterson asked as she lay in bed.

"Yes, of course I love you, Maggie," Hans answered earnestly. "You know I do."

Hans Wagner had taught German for three years at Ellis Academy, a prestigious independent school for boys in Cambridge. He had reluctantly returned to Germany during the Munich Crisis in 1938 and he had planned to return to England but he had been conscripted into the Army. Wagner was a passionate Anglophile and he considered it a great tragedy that Germany and Britain were at war.

Margaret Patterson taught French and German at St. Mary's School for Girls in Cambridge and she had met and fallen in love with Hans during her summer holidays in Germany in 1935. Unfortunately, when Hans was conscripted their wedding plans were put on hold and when the war began both Hans and Maggie buckled under the weight of intense parental pressure from both sides and broke off their engagement.

However, Han's unexpected arrival in Hereward as a leutnant in the Potsdam Grenadiers had changed everything.

Both Margaret and Hans felt that fortune was smiling on them and the Gods had given them a second chance.

"So, it's all set then, Hans?" Margaret asked.

"Yes, my love. Everything is set. I've saved up most of my pay for the last four months and we should have enough money to get a train to Wales and a ferry across to Ireland."

"You're sure that you won't be missed until Monday?"

"I'm certain that I won't." Hans nodded. "I've got Weekend Leave and as far as my commanding officer is concerned I'm living it up in London as we speak. I won't be missed until morning parade on Monday."

"Tomorrow's Saturday so that will give us two whole days to get away before we're missed."

"Yes."

Margaret thought for a moment. "Are you sure that we're doing the right thing?"

"What choice do we have? Your parents disapprove. My parents disapprove…?" Hans shrugged his shoulders.

"And there are all of these firebomb attacks."

"Exactly." Hans hugged Margaret tightly. "We have absolutely no choice. It is far too dangerous here. We can't be seen in public."

"Even people who knew that we were engaged before the War won't speak to us." Margaret sighed.

"Don't be too hard on them, Maggie." Hans gently placed his hand on her arm. "It's not them, it's not us. It's the War."

"Will we be safe in Ireland?"

"We'll be safe as long as it stays neutral."

"What if your mob invades?"

"Stop saying 'my mob,' Maggie!" Hans' face turned crimson with anger and he jumped off the bed as if someone had rammed a red-hot poker up his behind. "They're not my mob! I voted Communist in'33; I broke my hand fighting the Nazis in the streets! I was conscripted into the Army, I didn't volunteer! I've deserted! I'll be shot if I'm captured!"

"I'm sorry, my love," Maggie laughed. "Come back to bed." She patted the pillow. "I know how much you hate the Nazis. I'm only teasing you."

"Well, don't." Hans sulked. "I hate the Nazis as much as you do. They took me away from England and away from you and I won't let it happen again."

"If the Nazis attack Ireland we'll escape to America." Maggie threw her pillow into the air.

"And if they attack America then we'll escape to the moon!" Hans copied her.

"They'll never catch us!" Margaret hooked Hans across the chin with her pillow and sent him tumbling out of the bed. Hans grabbed a pillow and brought it crashing down on top of Margaret's head. The pillow exploded and Margaret became covered in a thin layer of feathers. She launched herself at Hans and sent him sprawling across the width of the bed. Margaret leaped onto Hans' chest and raised her own pillow above her head to deliver the coup de grace. "What was that?" She suddenly sat bolt upright.

"A squeaking door?"

"Not a door." Margaret swung her legs onto the floor. "A letterbox!"

There was a loud crash of shattering glass followed a split second later by the sound of two explosions in quick succession.

"Firebomb attack!" Margaret shouted. "Quick! Down the stairs!"

Hans jumped out of bed and grabbed his Sam Browne belt holding his holster and Luger pistol.

Margaret grabbed her dressing gown and opened the bedroom door. She rushed along the corridor to the stairs leading down to the ground floor with Hans hot on her heels.

"Too late," Margaret said. A wall of flames blocked off their escape route to the front door. Smoke was billowing throughout the ground floor and the flames were starting to creep up the stairs.

"Is there another way out of here?" Hans shouted above the sound of the fire.

"Yes. Through the skylight in the attic. Here. Help me grab the pole to pull down the trapdoor." They knelt down on the floor and felt their way along the skirting board at the bottom of the wall until they found a pole with a hook at one end. Smoke was rapidly filling up the first floor corridor making it difficult to see. They both stood up and raised the hook pole to a vertical position. Margaret guided the pole as they searched for the ring in the ceiling that would release the trap door.

"Hurry, Maggie!" Hans urged. The flames were half way up the stairs and it was becoming increasingly difficult to see and breathe.

"Nearly there." Maggie spotted the ring in the roof through the smoke and lunged with the pole. Missed.

"Maggie, the flames are nearly at the top of the …"

"I know! I know!" Maggie shouted. She saw the ring again and thrust the pole out like a lance. Missed again.

Hans looked over his shoulder. The flames were now at the top of the stairs and they were advancing over the threshold. Hans said nothing. There was nothing to say. If Maggie missed this time then they would not get out.

"Third time lucky," Maggie muttered to herself under her breath. She reached out and hooked the ring. "Thank God! Pull, Hans!" They both pulled on the pole with all of their strength. The trap door immediately swung open.

Flames were now licking their way along the corridor towards them.

"How do we get up?" Hans asked.

"Step ladder in the spare bedroom." But the spare bedroom was now cut off. There was no time left and no way out.

"Quick, Maggie. Climb onto my shoulders." Hans knelt down on the floor and Maggie climbed onto his shoulders. Hans gingerly stood up, coughing and spluttering, the smoke was making it extremely difficult to breathe. "Grab the edge and pull yourself up," he ordered.

Maggie grabbed the edge of the trap door entrance as Hans tottered backwards and forwards beneath her trying to keep his balance. She summoned up all of her strength and pulled herself through the hole, standing on Hans' shoulders.

"Hans!" Maggie shouted through the smoke. "How will you get up?"

Hans rushed through to Maggie's bedroom and grabbed hold of a chest of drawers. He quickly emptied the drawers out onto the floor and dragged it down the smoke filled corridor. He positioned it beneath the trap door and climbed on top. He stood up and stretched out his arms. His fingertips just managed to curl around the edge of the entrance. The flames were spiraling up the legs of the chest of drawers.

One pull up, Hans thought to himself, then Wales, Ireland and we're home Scot-free.

He hesitated for a split second as the welcome thought raced through his head. The first floor collapsed and the chest of drawers disappeared. The shock made Hans lose his grip. The last sound that he heard was Maggie's scream as he fell into the flames below.

The couple walked along the street arm-in-arm without a care in the world, meandering aimlessly from one side of the deserted street to the other and back again as if they were a ship that had lost control of its rudder. They finally stopped outside a gate. The woman leaned back against the wall and the man leaned against her.

Two black figures increased their pace and rapidly closed the gap between them and their prey. The kissing couple remained blissfully unaware of the approaching danger. Their pursuers stopped walking and stood on the opposite side of the road to their quarry. They were taking their time. There was no need to rush things. This was the best bit. The moment of realization. The moment when their victims realized that they were about to die.

The man whispered a sweet nothing in the woman's ear. She laughed and opened her eyes. She gasped. The man's head whipped around and his right hand raced for his revolver.

"Not so fast, Fritz." One of the black clad figures warned. The man's hand stopped in mid air.

"Hands in the air, Adolf," the other black clad figure ordered. "You too, you Nazi whore," he snarled. The woman flinched at the insult. She knew who these people were now. A thin, hot stream of urine dribbled down her legs and formed a rapidly expanding pool of fear on the ground.

"What...what do you want?" The man stammered, his hands trembling.

"Your life." The two rounds shattered the German's collarbone and punched into his heart. He fell to the ground with an astonished look on his face and died quickly as the blood pumped out of him.

"And yours, you treacherous whore." The gunman fired two bullets into the woman's chest. She died before she had time to beg for mercy.

"I've got nothing to say to either of you," Sam said belligerently. He stood up from behind his class room desk and started heading for the door. Ansett quickly moved to the door and blocked the exit.

"I think that you'll want to listen to this," Ansett said. "Just hear me out and then you can go."

"Alright." Sam nodded his head. "But make it quick. I've got people to do and things to see." He turned around and walked back to his desk. He leaned with his back against it and folded his arms.

Ansett did not pay attention to Sam's deliberately rude response. Instead he paid attention to Sam himself. Sam had recovered his pride and self confidence since the firebomb attacks had started. He was more sure of himself and he had rediscovered a sense of purpose.

Alan was also watching Sam as he settled down. He also thought that Sam had changed. For one thing he and Sam had barely exchanged half a dozen civil words since their argument in Ansett's classroom last week. Sam had found a new group of friends at school. The new group of friends bizarrely included Danny Edwards and his cronies. It appeared that all had been forgiven since the incident at the New Year's Eve Party. Both boys had blamed each other for their public humiliation and here they were now, bosom buddies. Alan couldn't figure it out. He also knew that Sam had hardly spoken a word to Alice since the New Year Eve Party five weeks ago. Alan was certain that Sam was an arsonist. He knew that Ansett thought that he was one too. Well, What Ansett was about to say would prove it one way or another.

"Did you know that Mary Butler was murdered last night?" Ansett asked.

"Another Hun whore bites the dust," Sam sneered. "So what?"

Ansett ignored Sam's deliberately provocative remark. "Did you know that an S.S. Hauptsturmfuhrer was also killed?"

"Yes."

"How did you find out?" Alan asked.

"What is this? The Spanish inquisition?"

"Just answer the question," Ansett demanded.

"I heard it on the grapevine," Sam answered smugly. He gave Alan a withering look of contempt.

"Whatever you may have heard and wherever you may have heard it is neither here nor there," Ansett said. "Tonight the S.S. will arrest and take into custody twenty hostages and unless the attackers surrender or are captured by 1p.m. on Wednesday, the hostages will be hung in public in the town Square…"

"And then public opinion will turn against the Nazis and swing back towards us," Sam broke in again. "You can't make an omelet without breaking eggs."

"Your father is on the list."

Sam Roberts raced downstairs at the first knock. He had lain awake the whole night. He hadn't slept a wink worrying about what would happen that morning. After finding Captain (now Inspector) Mason that Monday afternoon and joining the Specials he had hurried home and waited for his father to return after work. He had bitten his lip half a dozen times that evening in order to stop himself from warning his father. Sam reached the main entrance and opened the door on its chain. A flashlight blinded him.

"Turn that damn light off!" A voice ordered in German from outside the door.

Sam turned on the downstairs light. "What the hell's going on?" Sam asked, pretending to rub sleeping dust out of his eyes. "It's three o'clock in the morning."

"Good morning, Sam." The German voice switched to English. "It's Norbert Ulrich. Alice introduced us last year."

"My God, Norbert. I know that you like my sister, but this is a bit early for a social call. Can't you wait until tomorrow to see her?"

"I'm afraid that I can't, Sam." Ulrich shook his head. "This isn't a social call: this is official business."

"Now, sir?" A voice enthusiastically interrupted in German, the soldier's white teeth shining in the black night, testing the weight of the sledgehammer in his arms.

"Not now, Mueller!" Ulrich said sharply.

"Sam! What's going on?" Alice entered the hall, wrapped in a dressing gown. "It's three o'clock in the morning."

"It's your boyfriend," Sam replied dryly. "He's late for your midnight rendezvous. He must still be on German time."

"Hallo, Alice." Ulrich ignored Sam's sarcasm. Sam stepped out of the way so that Alice could speak to him.

"Norbert," Alice whispered, "what on Earth is going on?"

"'What's going on?'" Ulrich repeated in disbelief. "'What's going on?'" He swiftly looked over both of his shoulders to make sure that none of his men were eavesdropping. He breathed a sigh of relief when he realized that his fears were groundless: none of his men could speak English. "I told you that this was going to happen. I told you to get your father away."

Ulrich was deafened by Alice's silent reply.

"You did tell him, didn't you? You did get him away. Please tell me that he's not still here…"

"Alice, what in heaven's name is going on?" Alex Roberts' dulcet tones echoed down the corridor.

"I told you that I couldn't!" Alice lowered her voice. "If my father went missing then Zorn would put two and two together and figure out that you had warned me…"

"I was willing to take the risk…"

"…And I wasn't…"

"You were willing to risk your father's life to protect me?"

"You were willing to risk your life to protect my father."

"Alice, I didn't…"

"Alice, who are you speaking to?" Roberts interrupted the conversation. Sam and Alice's mother, Michelle, stood behind him.

"It's Norbert, papa."

"Good morning, Mr. Roberts." Ulrich gave a small bow.

"Good morning, Norbert." Roberts returned the bow.

"I had hoped that we would be introduced under more pleasant circumstances, Mr. Roberts, but I regret that it was not to be."

"So had I," Roberts agreed. "What's this all about, Norbert?"

Ulrich straightened to attention. "I have been instructed to take you into protective custody, sir."

"'Protective custody?'" Roberts asked incredulously. "Protection from whom, may I ask?"

"From terrorists. We have reason to believe that your life is in danger."

"The only terrorists we have in Hereward have swastikas on their helmets!" Sam interjected.

"You would be wise to hold your tongue, Sam. My

comrades in the S.S. are not as tolerant as I am," Ulrich warned.

"My life is no more in danger from so called 'terrorists' than any father whose daughter is sleeping with the enemy."

Ulrich winced. He knew fine well that his actions and Alice's actions placed not only their own lives, but also the lives of their friends and families in danger. He ignored Robert's remark. "Your threat assessment does not change my orders. I am to take you to Gestapo Headquarters."

"'Gestapo headquarters?' You Nazi bastards!" Sam swore.

"I'm warning you, Mr. Roberts, control your son, or I'll deliver two Roberts to the Gestapo instead of one!" Ulrich threatened.

"Sam! Please!" Roberts said. "Am I under arrest?"

"No, you are not. You will be released when the terrorists have been captured or have surrendered."

"Now, sir?" Mueller asked.

"Not now, Mueller!" Ulrich barked.

"I'm touched by your concern for my safety, Norbert, but I'm perfectly safe and I'm capable of looking after myself and my family," Roberts kept up the charade.

"Look, Mr. Roberts, I have neither the time nor the inclination to argue with you. My orders are to take you into protective custody and deliver you to Gestapo Headquarters, with or without your cooperation. What will it be?"

"Without!" Sam slammed the door shut trapping Ulrich's fingers which were resting on the door chain.

"Now, Mueller! Now!" Ulrich screamed in agony.

Mueller swung the sledgehammer over his head in a huge arc and the door splintered as if it was made of plywood. Two soldiers armed with Schmeissers burst through the shattered remnants of the door, flicking off their safety catches and resting their forefingers alongside their trigger guards as they did so.

"Take him alive." Ulrich ordered through clenched teeth. He was kneeling on the floor supporting his wounded hand with his other arm.

One of the S.S. troopers stepped up to Sam and thrust the barrel of his Schmeisser into Sam's stomach. Sam groaned as he doubled over. As he bent over, the same soldier kneed Sam viciously in the face. Sam straightened up again. The other German swung his Schmeisser in a wide horizontal arc and the butt caught Sam square on the chin. Sam spun around and collapsed in a crumpled heap on the floor. Michelle Roberts rushed over to her son. The first S.S. trooper came over and kicked Sam's mother in the stomach.

Alice screamed.

Ulrich's hand whipped up and he pointed his Luger pistol in the soldier's face. "That's enough, Brandt! Get Roberts and let's go!"

But Alex Roberts remained rooted to the spot. He was shell shocked by the ferocity of the punishment meted out to his son and wife.

"Gott in Himmel!" Brandt cursed, reversed his Schmeisser and hit Roberts right between the eyes with the butt of his machine gun

Roberts fell to the ground.

Ulrich groaned. "Alive, Brandt!"

"Don't worry, Obersturmfuhrer," Brandt answered. "He'll wake up tomorrow with nothing worse than a nasty hangover."

Ulrich looked at his watch. 3.15 a.m. Time to leave. "Alright, men. Let's go."

"What about him, sir?" Brandt pointed at Sam lying unconscious on the ground.

"Leave him. We'll come back for him if we need to."

"But, sir…!"

"Brandt!" Ulrich grunted through pain gritted teeth. "Do as you're bloody well told!"

Brandt grinded his teeth with frustration. "Pick him up," he ordered.

Three soldiers picked up Alex Roberts and dragged him out through the splintered door with his feet carving a path through the shattered pieces of wood.

Another soldier tried to help Ulrich to stand up, but Ulrich reacted as if he had been touched by a leper. "I'm not a cripple!" He barked sharply. Ulrich recovered his composure and said more gently, "it's alright, Mueller. I can get up by myself. Thank you." Ulrich bowed his head slightly in gratitude as he apologized for his harsh words.

Mueller stood back to give Ulrich space to stand up. Ulrich faced Alice who was kneeling on the floor beside her unconscious brother and her distraught mother. "If Sam had let us in none of this would've happened."

"You've obviously forgotten that an Englishman's home is his castle," Alice replied defiantly.

Ulrich clicked his heels and bowed in the traditional Prussian gesture of respect. "I'll see what I can do for your father, Alice." Ulrich turned around and walked out of the house. His soldiers followed him.

The last storm trooper covered Alice with his Schmeisser and backed out slowly. At the door he paused and said "The Obersturmfuhrer may be willing to forgive and forget," gesturing at Sam, "but I'm not. The S.S. has a long memory."

Alice was rooted to the spot with shock. The soldier had spoken clear, fluent English.

Chapter Twelve

Alan studied his reflection in the shop window as he walked along the High Street. He was dressed completely in black from his peaked cap bearing a silver badge showing a crown above the letters "S.C." through his tightly fitted wool tunic to his jodhpurs and his laced up knee high riding boots. On his right arm he wore a bright blue armband with a white circle. In the centre of the circle were the capital letters "S.C." Special Constabulary, written in scarlet. He wore a highly polished black Sam Browne belt that held his holstered Wembly Revolver, ammunition, handcuffs and foot long truncheon. The uniform made Alan feel like a Greek God. The uniform was black and silver and sexy. It made a man look and feel like a medieval knight dressed in a suit of armour. Black armour. Dark and foreboding. Invincible and invulnerable.

Alan walked along the High Street with a regular Police Officer, Sergeant Hitch.

"Where are we going, Sergeant Hitch?" Alan asked as they walked down High Street.

"Call me 'Hitchy,' Alan." Hitch smiled good-naturedly. "Everyone does."

"Alright, Hitchy," Alan said self consciously. It felt strange calling an adult by his nickname.

"Each patrol has a certain designated beat to cover. We have to organize the beat areas very carefully or else some patrols will overlap and cover the same area, whilst some areas would not get covered at all."

"Oh, I see. And what happens if a patrol gets into trouble?"

"We use this."

"I am hardly brimming with confidence, Hitchy," Alan said sarcastically as he looked at the whistle which Hitch was holding.

Hitch chuckled. "I know exactly how you feel, lad. But with the increased number of patrols around it shouldn't take longer than ten minutes for another patrol to arrive."

"But ten minutes is a long time in politics. It's even longer in a gunfight," Alan said grimly.

"I know." Hitch nodded his head. "But we have to make do with what we have."

"The old 'Dunkirk spirit,' eh?'"

"Yes. Fat lot of good it did us," Hitch muttered to himself. His words dripped with bitterness. He looked at Alan to see if he had heard him. He had. Hitch had not mumbled quietly enough. Hitch looked away as if he had been caught eavesdropping. He lowered his eyes and looked at his shoes. He couldn't look Alan in the face. He couldn't bear to be thought of as a defeatist. He listened to the B.B.C. broadcasts from the Free North. He heard Churchill and the King telling them not to give up hope, promising them that the Occupied South would soon be liberated. Hitch tried to be a good patriot. He wanted to believe in final victory. But it was hard. Damn hard. With jackboots goose-stepping across the Town Square and a giant swastika flying from the flag pole above the Town Hall.

Alan walked over to Hitch. "Our time will come." He put his hand on Hitch's shoulder and squeezed.

Hitch nodded his head. Wanting to believe that Alan's prophecy would bear fruit.

They continued walking down High Street.

"What was that?" Alan asked, cocking his head like a Spaniel.

"What was what?" Hitch asked. "I didn't hear anything."

"Well, I did. I'm going to check it out. I'll be back in a tick." Alan took off like a bat out of hell up a side street.

"Alan! Where the hell are you going? Come back here!" Hitch's shouting shattered the silence of the curfew.

"I'll come back!" Alan's voice echoed down the street.

"Mitchell, you disobedient bastard! Come back here! That's an order! I'll have you court-martialed!"

But by this time Alan had long since disappeared into the darkness. Hitch cursed his name to high heaven, shrugged his shoulders and started quick marching up the street.

Alan ran up Brighton Street until he was sure that he had left Hitch behind. He stopped running and started to walk quickly allowing himself time to recover and catch his breath. After quick marching for a few minutes he slowed down until he was barely walking. He reached into his back pocket and took out a pair of tights. Silk tights were like gold dust in the Occupied South, but Alan had managed to trade them with a primary school boy for a small treasure chest worth of German Army and S.S. badges. The boy had stolen the tights from his mum's lingerie drawer. At least Alice's Christmas presents had been put to good use, Alan smiled to himself.

Alan pulled the tights over his head to conceal his face. He opened his holster and withdrew his revolver which he cocked. He flicked off the safety catch and waited in the shadows provided by a giant oak tree. This was a tree that he always used to wait beside. He waited a few minutes until he heard footsteps approaching. But from which direction were they coming? Alan edged further back into the shadows. The footsteps stopped on the other side of the tree, thank God. The footsteps had come from Fitzroy Street.

"Sam?" The voice whispered. "Is that you?"

"Yes," Alan replied.

"I've got my stuff. Have you got yours?" The figure stepped out from behind the tree. Dressed completely in black from head to toe. Black woolen hat, black shoe polished face, black overalls and black gym shoes. Black S.S. officer's webbing belt with holster and revolver. No doubt taken from a dead Nazi. The holster still buttoned up. Big mistake, Alan thought to himself. The figure carried a jerry can in one hand and a length of hose in the other.

"Yes." Alan applied first pressure to the revolver trigger. "Where's everyone else tonight?" Alan stayed on his side of the tree and used one hand to muffle his voice.

"Everyone else?" The figure repeated. "I don't know what Danny's up to. What's the matter with your voice?" He asked with furrowed brow.

Alan's heart missed a beat. "I've got a cold." He tried to keep conversation to a minimum.

"Danny's probably with Pete."

Peter Miller, Alan thought to himself. One of Danny Edward's friends.

"You were the one who said that it would be better if we didn't know what the other two were doing and visa versa. Better for security, you said. Why the sudden interest?" The boy in black asked suspiciously.

'The other two,' Alan thought. Sam and this bloke,

Danny and Pete. Four in total that meant that the other arsonists were copy cats.

Alan stepped out of the shadows.

The figure spotted the Specials uniform. "What the-?"

The two bullets hit the boy in the chest. "I'm sorry," Alan said. "I truly am." You are a sacrificial lamb. Your corpse, your body, your life. Your death will free the hostages. You will free Alex Roberts, the father of my best friend. You will not have died in vain.

Alan knelt beside the corpse and unbuttoned the dead boy's holster. He withdrew the revolver and flicked off the safety catch. He stood up and pointed the weapon at the all too familiar oak tree. He took careful aim and fired two rounds at the tree in quick succession. The bullets embedded themselves in the thick bark.

"Mitchell! What the hell do you think you're doing?"

The voice coming out of the darkness made Alan jump out of his skin.

"Hitchy?" Alan pointed his revolver down the street.

"Of course it's me! Who else could it be at this time of night? And stop waving that thing about. You might shoot someone!" Hitch stepped out of the shadows.

"Thank God it's you." Alan breathed a genuine sigh of relief. "I thought that you were one of his friends." He pointed at the corpse with his weapon.

"Who is it?" Hitch asked as he walked over.

"I don't know." Alan holstered his own revolver and quickly placed the dead boy's weapon in the corpse's hand. He pulled off the woolen mask and turned on his flashlight. Short dark hair. Alan used the hat to wipe some of the shoe polish from the dead boy's face. He sighed and stood up. "Davie Jones."

"Do you know him?"

"Yes, he's in my class at school."

"I knew his father well. We fought together in the Fusiliers in the last war and we both joined the Force at the same time after the War."

"Christ. What a waste." Alan shook his head.

"Yes. Nick will be turning in his unmarked grave. I guess that Davie just wanted revenge. His dad died of lung cancer shortly after Davie was born. He contracted the disease as a result of suffering a gas attack during the last war."

They both stood in silence.

"Did he say anything before he died?" Hitch asked.

"No." Alan lied. "He must've realized that he'd made a noise. He heard me coming and opened fire as I reached him. Fortunately, his aim was as poor as his judgment and he missed. Look." Alan walked over to the oak tree and pointed at the bullet entry points.

"I see." Hitch examined the entry points. "You can still see the bullets stuck in the tree." He shined his torch on the tree. "And then you fired back?"

"Yes. Two shots."

"And both shots hit him in the chest?" Hitch looked at the still warm corpse of his friend's son. "Good shooting, Alan."

"Beginners' luck." Alan shrugged modestly.

"Luck has got nothing to do with it. You fought at Wake and Fairfax. Jones is not the first person that you've killed."

"Davie Jones was British. He was a person. The others were just Huns. This is different," Alan said with a heavy heart through gritted teeth.

"Jones and his friends are responsible for the deaths of British men, women and children. He acted as judge, jury and executioner. He's exactly the same as a Jerry pilot who drops bombs on defenseless refugees," Hitch said resolutely. "Jones didn't say anything before he died, you said."

"No. Not a word." Stick to the story, Alan thought to himself.

"Except that we're standing here on the corner of Brighton and Fitzroy Street."

"So what?" Alan asked. He was beginning to feel uneasy.

"Whose house is that over there?" Hitch pointed at the house on the corner. Hitch knew fine well that Alan knew.

"The Roberts House."

"And who lives there?"

"The Roberts Family," Alan answered impatiently. "For Christ's sake, Hitchy, where is all of this leading?"

"You tell me, Alan. You tell me," Hitch said slowly.

"Look, Hitchy. The Roberts Family has nothing to do with any of this. Alice is going out with an S.S. officer, for crying out loud."

"And their house is one of the few that hasn't been firebombed."

"It doesn't mean anything," Alan said stubbornly.

"It means everything!" Hitch snarled. "These killers are not lone vigilantes. They work in pairs. They are organized. Danny Edwards, Peter Miller, Davie Jones and..." Hitch paused, "Sam Roberts."

"How-?"

"I've been a Policeman for twenty years, Alan," Hitch interrupted. "I know all of the shortcuts, back streets and alleyways. I heard the entire conversation. I heard everything. The game's up."

Alan was too shocked to reply. All of his scheming had come to naught. "I know that you murdered Davie Jones in cold blood." Alan's heart missed a beat. "But I'm willing to forget that minor detail. What ever my personal feelings might be about him being Nick Jones's son, Davie Jones knew what he was getting himself mixed up in and he got what he deserved."

"What do you want me to do?" Alan's shoulders slumped in abject defeat and misery.

"We'll return to the Station, gather reinforcements and arrest everyone tonight. No exceptions. No warnings. No tip offs. Do you understand?" Hitch looked at Alan right between the eyes.

"Yes," Alan replied weakly.

"Say it!" Hitch demanded.

"I understand."

"You'd better, Alan. Or I'll send you down the river with the rest of them!" Hitch threatened.

Alan nodded.

"You'll back up my story and help to convince Chief Inspector Brown to take action," Hitch ordered.

"What will the Jerries do?"

Hitch looked at Alan as if he was the village idiot. "The Jerries? This has got nothing to do with the Jerries. This is British business. This is Police business. It's a civil matter; not political. The prisoners will be brought to trial and convicted," Hitch pressed on.

"And executed?"

"That's for the Courts to decide. They'll be hung if they're found guilty of murder."

Alan slumped to his knees beside the corpse. He heard whistles being blown in the darkness and saw torch lights flashing in the distance. The sound of running footsteps echoed down the streets.

"Other patrols will be here soon, son," Hitch said. "Just agree with everything that I say. If you play your cards right we can both come out of this with a promotion and medals."

"You're asking me to betray my friend."

"I'm asking you to do the right thing, Alan. Your 'friend' has murdered several people: men, women and children. He may even have been planning to murder his own sister."

That hit a nerve. Because Alan knew it was true.

"By putting Sam Roberts and his friends behind bars you'll be helping to save the lives of countless people."

"Is there no other way?"

"I'm sorry, Alan."

"So am I." The two rounds sped straight through Hitch's flimsy woolen tunic into his heart and burst through his back leaving two bloody exit wounds. The bullets buried themselves into a wall on the other side of the road. Hitch collapsed on his back. Alan walked over and calmly checked his pulse with trembling fingers. He walked back to Jones and placed the smoking revolver back in his lifeless fingers. Alan blew sharply on his whistle three times and walked back to Hitch. He knelt down beside him and cradled Hitch's head in his arms. Tears were still rolling down Alan's cheeks when the first Policemen found him.

Chapter Thirteen

"It must have been difficult to arrest Alex Roberts," Zorn said casually.

"What do you mean, sir?" Ulrich's back tensed.

"Ulrich. Everyone knows that you and Alice are an item," Zorn smiled amicably.

"I did my duty, sir." Ulrich came to a position of attention.

"I'm not suggesting otherwise, Ulrich. And no one is suggesting that you didn't." Zorn cast the first fishing line. "Were you aware that a terrorist was shot dead last night?"

"No, sir. I had not heard."

"Yes. A lone terrorist was shot dead last night. The terrorist used a revolver which formerly belonged to S.S. Hauptsturmfuhrer Josef Heiner to murder a Policeman."

Ulrich breathed a sigh of relief. Thank God, he thought. Alex Roberts and the rest of the hostages would be released.

"Does anything strike you as strange?"

"The terrorist was acting on his own?"

"Exactly!" Zorn slapped a pair of leather gloves in his hand. "We had always assumed that the terrorists worked in small groups or at least in pairs. He was carrying a jerry can full of petrol and a hose."

"Let me guess: but no bottles with which to make Molotov cocktails?" Ulrich was grateful that he had managed to change the subject away from his relationship with Alice Roberts. "So he was waiting for someone?"

"Yes. But that someone didn't turn up. Or perhaps another person turned up instead. " Zorn cast the second fishing line.

"Where was he waiting?"

"The corner of Brighton and Fitzroy Street." Zorn watched as the blood drained from Ulrich's face.

The corner of Brighton and Fitzroy Street. He had walked with Alice up that street to her house more times than he could remember. Ulrich knew whom the terrorist had been waiting for: Sam Roberts. But Sam Roberts had not been able to rendezvous with the terrorist because Ulrich's men had beaten him unconscious.

"The dead terrorist has been identified as one David Jones, a Fourth Year student at St. John's Academy." Zorn cast the third fishing line. The same school as Sam Roberts. The same year as Sam Roberts. Zorn could almost read Ulrich's mind. "And do you know who shot David Jones? A young Special who also joined up yesterday, Alan Mitchell."

Zorn cast the fourth fishing line.

"Incidentally, Mitchell joined up with Roberts."

"What… what will happen now?" Ulrich struggled to keep his voice steady.

"Roberts will be arrested and handed over to the Gestapo for interrogation." There was no need to spell out what would happen there. "And then he will be shot." That was if he actually survived being tortured.

"And… and his family?" Alice. What about Alice?

"They will be handed over to the Gestapo as well…"

Ulrich screamed silently.

"...If they are found guilty of terrorist activites," which they will be, "then they will be shot." Zorn paused. "And if they are not found guilty then they will be sent to a concentration camp in Cornwell as punishment for harbouring a terrorist." Zorn cast the hook to reel Ulrich in.

Ulrich was speechless. What could he say? He tried not to think of Alice in the hands of those animals. "Is there anything. Is there anything that can be done...?" Ulrich asked pathetically.

"There is nothing that anyone can do, Ulrich," Zorn said slowly. "The death of one teenage terrorist is not enough. Both the Army and the S.S. are baying for blood. We want our revenge. Not even a schoolboy would believe that one child terrorist caused all of these deaths and all of this destruction. It will not satisfy Schuster or von Schnakenberg and it will certainly not satisfy Headquarters in London. They all want their pound of flesh." He glanced at Ulrich. He looked completely drained of energy. Of hope. "We can't hope to catch all of the terrorists. Many of them are copycat killings anyway. But... but, if we can capture or kill a few more terrorists as an example, maybe this will scare off the copycats."

Ulrich appeared deep in thought. Zorn could almost hear the cogwheels turning in his head. "Let me get this right: if we capture or kill some more terrorists then Schuster will free the hostages?"

"Yes." Zorn nodded. "The Brigadefuhreur does not want to shoot the hostages. At the moment the townspeople are on our side. He doesn't want to alienate them. If he shoots the hostages then London will think that he can't control the situation here and replace him. He is searching for a reason to release the hostages without losing face. We can provide him with a reason."

"By murdering innocent people?"

"If we have to. Yes." Zorn shrugged his shoulders dismissively.

"I... I don't know if I can do it again, sir," Ulrich mumbled.

Zorn slammed the palm of his hand onto the desk. "I'm sick of playing games with you, Ulrich!" He screamed, his face turning red with rage. "I'm not asking you! I'm ordering you!"

Ulrich was stunned by Zorn's outburst. He'd never heard him raise his voice before.

"You don't get it, do you, Ulrich?" Zorn snarled, his lips curling in an ugly grimace. "I know. I know that you warned Alice that we were going to arrest her father!"

The colour drained from Ulrich's face. How? The word formed on his lips, but he had been struck dumb.

"It doesn't matter 'how' and why: I just do."

Ulrich was speechless. Spies. In his own platoon. His own men. Men he would kill for. Men he would die for. He swayed from side to side like a tall tree caught in a strong wind.

Zorn walked up to Ulrich and stood so close that their noses were almost touching. "Senior Obersturmfuhrer Norbert Ulrich, I charge you with passing secret information to the enemy. You have tried to aid and abet the enemy to evade lawful arrest and by your treacherous actions you have endangered the lives of German soldiers."

Ulrich was nearly lifted bodily off the ground by the enormity of Zorn's accusation. His bottom lip began to quiver. Zorn's spittle covered his face. "Yes, Ulrich! Treachery! You passed secret information to Alice Roberts, the sister of Sam Roberts who murdered German soldiers! You are a traitor and you should be shot!" Zorn stabbed his forefinger in the air, inches from Ulrich's face. "However…" Zorn lowered his voice to a conversational level and circled behind Ulrich like a tiger circling its prey. "However…I'm willing to take a chance on you, Ulrich, I believe that you're not beyond redemption. I think that you can be saved." Zorn paused dramatically. "I am willing to forgive your…how can I put it? Error of judgment and forget the involvement of the Roberts Family in terrorist activities in return for your full co-operation."

"What do you want me to do?" Ulrich sobbed.

"Exactly as I say."

"Achtung!" The harsh guttural voice shouted. "Raus! Raus!"

The dozen men reluctantly rose to their feet and wiped the sleeping dust from their red eyes with dirt-encrusted hands. The men watched as an S.S. officer entered the room. "You are to be freed," the German announced in French. "You will be transported to London immediately. Tomorrow you will be taken to Dover and then you will be repatriated across the Channel. By this time tomorrow you will be in France."

The prisoners were too shocked to react. It took a few seconds for the news to sink in. Realization gradually dawned. Pandemonium broke out as the men broke out in a barrage of mutual backslapping and hugs. Tears washed away the grime as they trickled down dirty faces. Someone started singing "The Marseillaise." More men joined in until a dozen voices drowned out the sounds of the guards in joyful celebration of their imminent liberation. When they had finished singing the prisoners continued their orgy of backslapping, Gallic kisses and hugs.

The S.S. officer's lips curled downwards in Teutonic

distaste at this unaryan display of emotion. He looked at his watch. Timing was of the essence. He had fifteen minutes to reach the disembarkation point. "You've got one minute to grab your things," he announced. "If you're not ready then we'll leave without you."

There was an avalanche of activity as the prisoners hurriedly gathered up their blankets and other meager possessions. They quickly exited the small and cramped room that had served as their cell. They shivered as they walked out of a side entrance and stamped their feet and hugged themselves in a futile attempt to keep out the biting cold of the January night. They waited by the back of the lorry. Two S.S. troopers undid the tailgate and they both motioned the prisoners to get on by waving their Schmeisser machine guns. The prisoners climbed on board, chattering excitedly despite the chill. They sat down on the benches that ran along each side of the lorry. One of the soldiers climbed on board and sat on the bench at the back of the lorry.

The S.S. officer appeared against the tailgate. The S.S. trooper beside him lifted a large box onto the lorry. "A present from Germany as a gesture of goodwill," he announced, "in the hope that peace will once again be restored between our two great countries."

The prisoner nearest the box reached in his hand. He pulled out a bottle. "Vin!" He exclaimed. He looked at the German in shocked disbelief. "Merci beaucoup, monsieur," he said.

"Avec plaisir," the officer replied. He nodded his head to the soldier standing beside him. The German threw a handful of small cartons into the lorry. The prisoners scrambled around and picked them up.

"Tabac!" They shouted. The prisoners ripped the packets open in frenzy and frantically lit up, cramming one, two, three cigarettes into their mouths at the same time in their desperation. Other prisoners were passing around the bottles.

"We'll be stopping in about ten minutes to allow you to stretch your legs," the S.S. Officer announced. "It's a long lorry ride to London."

The prisoners were too busy boozing and stuffing their faces to reply.

"Alright." the German said to the driver. "Let's get this over with."

Sam's head was thumping as he walked along the street and it was not just because of the cold. Ulrich's men had given him a good going over the night before and had left him with a nasty headache. Although it had largely gone away, he was still not feeling 100%. However, he had insisted on coming out on patrol.

Chief Inspector Brown had ordered the patrols to be beefed up in response to the German threat to execute the hostages. Brown had decided that the only way to prevent the Germans from murdering the men and women was to capture any terrorists still at large. Instead of a patrol consisting of one Policeman and one Special, each patrol was now made up of one Policeman and three Specials.

Sam looked to his left and felt Alan's reassuring presence. A few yards in front of the pair walked Bill Linsdell, another sixteen year old Special and a fellow student at St. John's. The patrol commander, P.C. Alf "Jock" MacDonald, a regular Police officer, walked to Bill's right. All four men walked along the street with revolvers drawn. They were not going to be caught unawares like poor Hitchy was last night. They were determined to deal with the criminals and take them dead or alive.

The S.S. Officer and driver sat in silence as the lorry traveled through the dark streets of Hereward. The prisoners sitting in the back of the lorry were singing songs at the top of their voices and were becoming drunk and disorderly at a rapid rate of knots.

The prisoners were the flotsam and jetsam of the defeated French Army that had washed up on the southern shores of England following the "miracle" of Dunkirk and they were united by one overwhelming desire: the desire to return to France. Although prior to the Invasion their accommodation had been far from luxurious, their living quarters had at least been above ground level and they had been allowed to go to the toilet and wash themselves without having to ask for permission and without being accompanied by an armed escort. Unfortunately, Hereward had experienced a rather dramatic change of management. Their new German hosts were not quite as hospitable as the original owners.

Not all of the French soldiers intended to return to France to demob and resume the life of a civilian.

Captain Vincent Berraud and Sergeant Davide Renaud of the French Foreign Legion had not touched a drop of wine. They had originally escaped to England with the intention of joining the Free French Forces of General De Gaulle. Unfortunately, the successful Boche invasion and occupation of England had put their plans on hold somewhat. Following their capture in Hereward, they had thought of escaping to Scotland, but now they decided that the best way to liberate France was to return to the Patrie and join the Resistance.

Berraud took a puff from his cigarette and spoke quietly to Renaud. "I don't like it, Davide. It's not like the Boche to be so generous."

"But what about the news? It is possible that Petain

has made a deal to obtain the release and repatriation of all prisoners of war," Renaud reasoned.

"It's possible. I wouldn't put it past that dirty traitor to make a deal." He spat on the floor in disgust. "Whatever happens, Davide: stick closely to me and follow my lead," Berraud ordered grimly.

Renaud nodded his head in the darkness.

The lorry gradually slowed to a halt. The French soldiers who had been standing up were thrown off their feet and landed on their comrades who had been sitting on the benches. There was much good natured swearing and banter.

The S.S. Obersturmfuhrer appeared again at the tailgate. "We're stopping here for five minutes to allow you to stretch your legs. Everybody out!"

The French soldiers piled out of the lorry laughing and joking around in obvious high spirits at the thought of finally returning home.

The driver remained in the cab. One storm trooper stood at the back of the lorry.

The officer walked up to him and whispered in his ear. Berraud watched as the S.S. officer turned around and headed back towards the driving compartment. The S.S. trooper followed him. The Frenchman saw the officer slap the driver's door twice.

Realization suddenly dawned. "Take cover!" Berraud warned.

The loud blare of the lorry's horn shattered the night's silence. Machine gun bullets tore through the air cutting down half of the unarmed prisoners in the first burst. The surviving Frenchmen did not know where to run and were caught in the glare of the lorry's lights like frightened rabbits. The alcohol had served its purpose by dulling their senses and reaction times. Most of the defenseless men died before they realized that their lives were in danger.

Berraud grabbed Renaud by the lapels of his greatcoat. "Run!" He screamed in Renaud's ear.

"Where?"

"Anywhere away from here!" Berraud turned around and saw the S.S. officer. He was holding his right arm awkwardly. "That way!" Berraud charged towards the German like an angry bull and lowered his shoulder. He caught the Nazi in his solar plexus and brought his knee up into the man's stomach for good measure driving the air from the S.S. man's lungs. The German fell backwards, striking his skull on the pavement with a loud crack.

Renaud didn't break his stride and scooped up the S.S. officer's Luger pistol from his limp fingers.

"Come on!" Berraud shouted over his shoulder. They ran towards the front of the lorry and raced past it. Renaud twisted around and fired two shots at the lorry shattering one headlamp, missing the other, but forcing the driver to duck.

The driver swore loudly as he watched the two escaping prisoners disappearing around the corner. He grabbed his Schmeisser machine gun from under his seat and jumped out of the cab. He ignored the inert form of his platoon commander lying on the ground and took off in hot pursuit of the Frenchmen.

"Come on!" Sam shouted as he heard the first shots.

"Which way do we go?" Alan asked.

"Towards the sound of the guns!" Sam answered excitedly. "Come on!" He repeated. Sam raced off towards the gunfire, with Alan and the other Special, Bill Linsdell, following hot on his heels.

"For God's sake, slow down!" P.C. MacDonald shouted after them as he struggled to keep up.

The driver saw the prisoners in the distance. "Halt!" He ordered as he fired a short burst over their heads.

Renaud stopped and fired two shots towards the sound of the firing.

The bullets whistled over the S.S. trooper's head like angry hornets.

"My God! They're armed!" The Nazi was shocked. He stopped and fired two controlled bursts at the prisoners.

Renaud grunted and fell onto his front. "Vincent…" he croaked through pain clenched teeth. Berraud ran on for a few more steps before he realized that Renaud was not running alongside him. He turned around. Renaud was lying face down in a rapidly expanding pool of blood. "Davide!" He shouted as he ran towards him. "Where are you hit?" he asked urgently.

"In my… in my back…" Renaud gasped.

"Get up," Berraud urged.

"I'm not going to make it." A burst of machine gun fire tore through the night.

"Sergeant Renaud, get up! That's an order!"

"Vincent…" Renaud wrapped a bloody hand around Berraud's wrist. "Listen to me…," he whispered. "I'm not going to make it…" Another burst of bullets.

"Come on. I'll help you." Berraud tried to loop his arms under his friend's armpits. He caught a glimpse of Renaud's back. It looked as if someone had scrapped a giant cheese grater down its entire length. It was torn, shredded and bleeding. Renaud must have taken the full force of bullets in the back at a distance of less than one hundred yards. He gently lowered his friend to the ground. Renaud was not going anywhere.

"Vincent…I'm finished… he's right behind us…" Renaud's fingers tightened into a vice like grip. "Save yourself…" He placed the Luger into Berraud's sweaty palm. The pistol grip was warm and sticky with his blood.

Berraud looked down the road from where he had come. He could hear the German running towards him. He wrapped Renaud's hand in his own. It was rapidly growing cold. "Farewell my friend." He squeezed Renaud's blood soaked fingers. "I'll see you in the next life."

"In…the…next…life…" Renaud's teeth shone white in the darkness.

By the time the German reached him he was dead.

"There! Look!" Sam pointed at a figure flashing a torchlight and kicking something on the ground. The figure turned at the sound of Sam's voice and fired off a burst of bullets. Bill Linsdell fell to the ground. His hands clutched his throat in a futile attempt to stem the flow of blood pumping from his neck.

"Alan! Help him!" Sam ordered. He fired two rounds towards the figure. Alan turned around and crawled towards Linsdell. He was making strangled gurgling noises as his blood and his life seeped out of him.

Jock MacDonald reached Linsdell before Alan. "I'll help Bill," he shouted above the sound of the gunfire, "you sort that bastard out." He pointed down the street.

But the figure was already down. "Cover me!" Sam shouted. He ran a few yards towards the fallen figure and then dropped to one knee pointing his revolver down the street. Alan ran down the street as Sam provided cover. The boys leapfrogged each other until they reached the figure. Correction. Two figures. One lying on his back with a bullet hole in his chest where his heart was. German and very dead. The other figure lay on his front. Nationality unknown. But shabbily dressed. Wearing some type of uniform. British? Possibly.

"What the hell's going on?" Alan asked, picking up the dead German's helmet.

"I don't know," Sam answered, picking up the Schmeisser. "We'll soon find out. I have a cunning plan." His eyes twinkled mischievously in the moonlight.

"Cease fire! Cease fire!" Hauptsturmfuhrer Zorn shouted at the top of his voice. The gunfire gradually died out. "Scharfuhrer Schmitt. Check the dead," he ordered. Schmitt and a couple of men wandered amongst the dead and dying Frenchmen, administering a coup de grace, a bullet to the nape of the neck, to those still breathing. "Rottenfuhrer Zimmermann, grab the gear from the lorry." Zimmermann walked to the back of the lorry that had carried the Killing Group to the ambush site. Two S.S. troopers inside the lorry started to pass out a selection of jerry cans, hosepipes, empty bottles and weapons.

"Spread them around." Zorn ordered. The soldiers began to randomly place the equipment around the still warm bodies of the dead Frenchmen. "A job well done, boys," Zorn congratulated his men, rubbing his hands together in glee. "There'll be medals and promotions all around, I promise you." Zorn could sense that his men were smiling. "Where's Obersturmfuhrer Ulrich?" He asked another S.S. trooper.

"I don't know, sir," Brandt replied. "I haven't seen him since the shooting started."

Zorn's eyebrows narrowed in puzzlement.

"Sir," Zimmermann said, "what do you want me to do with the left over weapons?" He held up a rifle in each of his hands.

"What do you mean?"

"There are twelve weapons, sir, but only ten bodies." Zimmermann pointed at the dead Frenchmen.

"Are you sure?"

"Quite sure, sir. I've counted them twice."

Zorn scratched his head. "Twelve weapons and only ten bodies. Plus one of my Obersturmfuhrers is missing." He swore under his breath. "This is not a good sign."

"He's probably with Mueller, sir," Brandt suggested.

"Who the hell is Mueller?"

"The lorry driver. Ah, here comes Obersturmfuhrer Ulrich now, sir." He pointed up the street towards two figures walking towards them. The one in front had his hands placed on top of his head in the universal gesture of surrender. The one behind was holding a Schmeisser machine gun and was prodding the man in front of him repeatedly. He appeared to be trying to drill a hole in his back.

"Obersturmfuhrer Ulrich," Brandt asked. "Where's the other prisoner, sir? And where's Mueller?"

Brandt was answered by a burst of machine gun fire that cut a neat line of holes across his chest. He fell backwards with a grunt trapping Zorn, who had been standing immediately behind him, onto the road. The next burst cut down Zimmermann and the two soldiers standing next to him. A potato masher grenade sailed through the air from where it had been hiding behind the head of the 'prisoner' and landed in the middle of the massacred and murdered Frenchmen. The explosion sent shrapnel flying into the face of Scharfuhrer Schmitt who had just completed finishing off the wounded prisoners. The grenade blast punctured several jerry cans that had been lying nearby. They caught fire and exploded and covered another two Germans in fiery fuel. The 'prisoner' fired shots from his revolver at the Nazis as

153

they collapsed screaming, smoking and burning onto the road. The 'machine gunner' fired another couple of bursts into the back of the Killing Group's lorry catching the two S.S. troopers who had passed Zimmermann the equipment in the chest. The 'prisoner' threw in another grenade for good measure. The Nazis were dead before they had time to unsling their weapons.

Sam quickly changed his empty magazine for a full one as he surveyed the scene of complete and utter death and destruction that he had helped to create. He moved amongst the dead and dying Germans and fired a short burst into the chests of any that showed signs of life. Alan picked up a Schmeisser and joined in with Sam liberally spraying the bodies with bullets.

"Christ…" Alan was disgusted, "What a bloody mess."

"Bloody hell, boys! What have you done?"

"Damn!" Sam swore. "Here comes the cavalry. Late as usual."

"More like the Keystone Cops. P.C. MacDonald, how good of you to join us!"

"What the hell happened here?" MacDonald's eyes bulged wide with disbelief. He had not seen so many corpses and so much carnage since the Somme.

"One heck of a gunfight, Jock, one heck of a gunfight…" Alan answered. " They were like this when we got here."

"But I don't know who came off worse-the Jerries or the other mob," Sam added.

"The other mob?" MacDonald said. "Who are they?"

"I don't know," Sam shook his head. "They don't appear to be British. They're not wearing British uniform."

"Well, it doesn't matter who the hell they are," MacDonald said. "We've got to get out of here." They could hear the sound of whistles being blown in the distance.

"The Police will be here soon and the Huns will be here

soon after," Alan said. He suddenly remembered. "How's Bill?" He was horrified that in the heat and excitement he had forgotten all about him.

"Dead," MacDonald stated simply. "He bled to death in my arms. There was nothing that I could do."

"Forget about the dead," Sam said abruptly. "Let's remember the living: what are we going to do?"

"We've got a live one here!" Alan suddenly said, but before he could react, MacDonald had whipped his revolver around and had shot a wriggling and wounded German twice between the eyes.

"I guess that you didn't win your Military Cross for nothing," Alan observed, pointing at his M. C. ribbons sewn onto his tunic.

"You won the Military Cross?" Sam asked.

"This may come as a surprise to you, young Roberts, but despite the fact that I may not be as light on my feet as I used to be, not everyone surrendered without a fight when the Jerry paras landed. He's not the first Hun that I've killed and he certainly won't be the last."

Sam and Alan both looked at MacDonald with newfound respect in their eyes. They both understood what he was saying. MacDonald was one of the few who had fought against the paras with pitchforks, petrol bombs and shotguns when they had entered Hereward.

They could hear the sound of lorries rumbling along the road towards them.

"Come on, lads," MacDonald drew his revolver and reloaded. "Let's get out of here."

Zoon lay trapped underneath Brandt and watched helplessly as the two men in black murdered his men. He tried to undo his holster with his right hand and withdraw his Luger, but he couldn't reach it. Tears began to roll down his cheeks and he ground his teeth in frustration at his own impotence. He had no hope of helping as his soldiers lay dying. Finally, the figures stopped firing. They had completely wiped out his section of eight troopers in as many seconds. They were all lying on the road or in the lorry burning and bleeding to death.

His heart missed a beat as he saw the two killers move amongst his soldiers, laughing and joking as they finished off the wounded. He was reminded of the cold and callous way in which his own men had killed the British wounded at Fairfax. It seemed that fate was not without a sense of humour. Zorn's heart rate started to race as the men in black walked towards him.

Another figure appeared revolver in hand. Christ, Zorn thought to himself. Was there no end to them? They were springing from the ground like the Hydra's teeth. The newcomer spoke to the machine gunners. They stopped shooting. He seemed to be the leader. They were having a discussion of some kind. They appeared to be moving away. Preparing to go. Thank God. Sweet Jesus, if you let me live, I promise that I'll go to church every Sunday for the rest of my life. Zorn's heart began to slow down and beat more regularly as he started to hope that he might escape with his life. And then Brandt groaned. Jesus Christ. He wasn't dead. Maybe the killers hadn't heard. Then Brandt moved. One of the shooters shouted in alarm. A jet of hot urine rushed down Zorn's leg. My God. This is it. Two shots. Darkness.

Chapter Fourteen

The Town Hall tower read 12.45 p.m. as a large crowd filled the Town Square. They were held back from the gallows by a double line of S.S. and Army soldiers. The sunlight glinted on the steel of their fixed bayonets as the Germans warily watched the crowd. The crowd was sullen and silent and was separated from the soldiers by a metal barricade.

The Hereward men and women talked quietly amongst themselves. It was 12.50 p.m. At 1 p.m. twenty men were going to be executed. Twenty local men who were friends and colleagues of other local men and women. Twenty Hereward men who had families: wives; brothers and sisters; fathers and mothers; sons and daughters. Twenty husbands; twenty brothers; twenty fathers; twenty sons whose deaths would rip the heart out of the small, close knit town and rip the heart out of those who loved them

At 12.55 p.m. An S.S.sturmbannfuhrer and an Army major walked out of the Town Hall and climbed the stairs to the gallows platform. Eight S.S. troopers and eight Army soldiers followed the officers in double file. The sturmbannfuhrer and major stopped in the centre and turned to face the crowd. The S.S. men stood on the right hand side of their officer and the Army men stood on the left hand side of their officer. The soldiers pointed their Schmessier machine guns at the crowd. A sudden hush descended over the Square.

Then the hostages emerged. They walked out one by one, flanked by a soldier on either side. First the ten hostages held by the S.S. and then the ten hostages held by the Army. When the hostages appeared friends and family members shouted their names. People broke down in tears. As more and more hostages climbed the stairs to the gallows more and more people began crying until the whole Square seemed to be sobbing with sorrow. The wind whipped up the sound of peoples' tears until it sounded like the wailing of ten thousand grief stricken banshees. The sense of sadness and dark despair spread from person to person like a virus causing people who did not know any of the prisoners to burst out crying.

The soldiers placed the first four hostages underneath the gallows. The Army engineers had not had enough time to construct more than four gallows. The hostages were to be executed in five groups of four. The people interpreted the fact that there were twenty hostages, but only four gallows as a cruel and calculated Nazi plot to prolong the agony of the prisoners and the people.

The two officers turned and faced each other. They consulted their wristwatches. The second hand of the Town Hall clock tick tocked around to one o'clock. The crowd stood in silence as the bells chimed thirteen times.

The S.S.sturmbannfuhrer nodded at his Army counterpart. It's time. The S.S.sturmbannfuhrer about turned and gave the order to the gallows guard. The soldiers standing to either side of the first four hostages grabbed them by the arms and moved then towards the trapdoors.

One of the condemned men started to struggle. "No! No!" He screamed. "I don't want to die!" His pitiful cries drifted out over the crowd. His legs seemed to turn to jelly as he fell to the floor.

"Pick him up!" The S.S.sturmbannfuhrer ordered. The guards tried to haul him up to his feet, but he was too heavy. "Help them!" An S.S. soldier left his position by the sturmbannfuhrer to aid his comrades.

"Please God!" The hostage wailed. "Don't let me die!"

The hair on the back of the necks of the bayonet fixed soldiers stood on end. They did not have to understand English to recognize the cries of a man begging for his life. Several of the soldiers facing the crowd turned around and took a step backwards to look at the condemned man.

"Eyes front!" An officer shouted.

"Turn around!" Another echoed.

Too late. Too many soldiers had stepped backwards. The double line that had previously been straight now resembled a sidewinder snake. Non-Commissioned – Officers stepped out of the line to shout and shove and push and punch their curiously morbid men back into their ranks. But the officers and N.C.O.s in their quest to restore order had themselves created gaps in the line.

The crowd sensed the sudden vulnerability of the Germans and surged forwards until they were barging and banging against the barrier. The soldiers and civilians were almost eyeball to eyeball. The soldiers' eyes were wide open and bulging with fear. The civilians' eyes were wide open and blood shot with hatred.

The struggling man lost control of his bowels. The stench of faeces wafted over the waiting crowd as the condemned man soiled himself and fainted. Another soldier left his position beside the S.S.sturmbannfuhrer to haul the unconscious man to his feet. But what to do? The sturmbannfuhrer asked himself. They couldn't hang an unconscious man, could they? Wouldn't that be breaking the rules? He bit his lip in indecision. Whilst he was mauling this over in his mind an S.S. motorcycle dispatch rider mounted the stairs, walked across the gallows platform, saluted and gave the sturmbannfuhrer an envelope.

"What now, for God's sake?" The sturmbannfuhrer was exasperated. "I'm rather busy here."

The dispatch rider ignored the sturmbannfuhrer's hostility and kept an expressionless poker face. "From Brigadefuhreur Schuster. You are to read the letter immediately."

"Christ. My hands are tied up at the moment. I'll deal with this later." He thrust the envelope inside the breast pocket of his tunic.

"But sir!" The dispatch rider protested. "My instructions were to make sure that you read…"

"Drag him to the rear." The sturmbannfuhrer interrupted, pointing at the unconscious prisoner. "Bring another hostage forward to take his place. And while we're at it, drag this idiot to the rear as well." He pointed at the dispatch rider. "One more word out of you, son, and I'll string you up with the rest of them!" He threatened. "Get him out of my sight!"

The two S.S. troopers who had originally been guarding the unconscious man and the two S.S. soldiers who had left their position to help each picked up a limb and dragged the helpless hostage from the platform. Another two storm troopers left their positions to pull another prisoner forward. Yet another S.S. man left the sturmbannfuhrer to escort the dispatch rider to the rear.

But the struggling hostage had set a precedent. The man who was being brought forward to replace him began to scream and shout and kick out his legs. A lucky kick

160

caught the knee of an S.S. guard who collapsed with howls of pain as he clutched his damaged kneecap. The prisoner's hands were tied behind his back. He was off balance and unsteady on his feet. He refused to cooperate and slumped to the ground. The sturmbannfuhrer detailed another two of his men to help. The hostage continued to struggle. The soldiers couldn't pull him to his feet. A storm trooper lost his patience and snapped. There was a sickening crunch as the hard wood and steel of the soldier's rifle butt smacked into the soft flesh and bone of the hostage's head. The man's screams were cut off abruptly like a gramophone record whose needle had been broken.

The crowd sighed like a huge wounded primeval beast. The crowd was no longer a collection of isolated independent individuals. The crowd had become a living breathing organism with a heart and a soul. A single entity. A creature made of flesh and blood. And that blood now surged through its body. Pumping up towards its brain. A brain which now thought. A brain with a will. A brain that wanted revenge. The crowd ebbed and surged against the barrier like a wave breaking on the beach. Each successive surge wore away at the confidence of the soldiers facing them like a wave wearing away at a cliff face. The wave would find the weakest point in the cliff face and would create a hole and cause the cliff face to crumble. The soldiers would erode-it was simply a matter of time.

The crowd found the weakest point. The S.S. sturmbannfuhrer now only had one man standing beside him. He seemed oblivious to his complete lack of protection. The crowd pushed against the barrier and forced it to bend just beyond the right hand limit of the sturmbannfuhrer's peripheral vision. The sturmbannfuhrer did not notice. His attention was focused solely on the struggling hostages and getting the prisoners to the gallows. The front rank of S.S.

troops involuntarily took a step back. They caught the rear rank unawares and some soldiers were pushed of balance and stumbled and fell. The crowd pushed again. A young storm trooper raised his rifle and tried to jab his bayonet at a face in the crowd but the lunge was off balance and over reached itself. The man evaded the clumsy thrust, grabbed the rifle barrel and wrenched the weapon straight out the hands of the bewildered soldier. The S.S. trooper standing next to the recruit was absolutely horrified and reacted instinctively. He emptied the entire contents of his Schmessier machine gun into the man's stomach. The soldiers near the machine gunner opened fire into the crowd at point blank range. Men, women and children were knocked down like stalks of wheat cut down by a giant scythe. The dead and the dying lay in a tangled, torn and bloody mound as the people standing behind them panicked, turned around and began to run.

The first shots acted as a signal. Shots rippled along the double line of S.S. and Army soldiers like a Mexican wave as they fired into the helpless civilians, hurrying to escape from the Square. The soldiers were swearing and hurling abuse at the stampeding people as they released all of their pent up rage and anger.

"Cease fire! Cease fire!" The S.S. sturmbannfuhrer shouted. But the men ignored him. They were pumped up and full of blood lust. They calmly replaced their empty magazines with full ones as if they were at the shooting range. As soon as they had loaded their new magazines they continued to pour their fire into the retreating crowd.

Only when there were no more people to kill did the soldiers stop firing. Their breathing began to slow and their heart beats gradually returned to normal as the blood lust seeped out of them like air escaping from a balloon.

"My God...what have we done?" The S.S. sturmbannfuhrer mumbled to himself under his breath. He gazed out over the scene of total death and destruction that he and his men had created. He walked down the stairs from the gallows platform to the ground. He did not notice the Army major following him. When he reached the bottom of the stairs he gazed up at the hangman's nooses dangling at the end of the ropes. The empty hangman's nooses. They had failed to hang a single hostage. He shook his head.

"Major."

The S.S. sturmbannfuhrer was jolted out of his daydreaming. "Yes. What is it? "

"The orders, sir." The dispatch rider seemed to materialize at his elbow like a genie. "I must confirm to the Brigadefuhreur that you read and carried out his orders." The dispatch rider insisted.

The sturmbannfuhrer found the envelope in his breast pocket and took out the envelope. It was addressed to him. "Urgent!" He read. He recognized the Brigadefuhreur's handwriting. His eyes glided over the writing.

"Sir," the dispatch rider said. "My instructions were that the Army major was also to read the orders."

The S.S. sturmbannfuhrer let the letter fall from his fingers. The paper fluttered gently to the ground and landed before the dispatch rider could catch it. The messenger swore. He picked up the paper and handed it to the Army major.

The shot made the Army major drop the paper. He was covered in a shower of skull fragments, brain tissue and globules of blood. He followed the sound of the gunfire. The S.S. sturmbannfuhrer was lying on the ground. The top of his skull was missing. His Luger lay in the lifeless fingers of his right hand. He had stuck his pistol in his mouth and blown his head off.

The man was debriefed at Glencourse Barracks in

Edinburgh the day after he had arrived in Scotland. He described the battles that he had fought with pride. He described his capture with shame and he described the massacre of his men with anger. He talked of his escape. Of how the men with whom he had traveling had been killed. The weeks that he spent hiding during the day, walking during the night, trekking across the countryside, scavenging for scraps of food from rubbish bins. Avoiding villages, towns and cities. Not seeing anyone for days. Not speaking to anyone for weeks. Trusting no one. Endangering no one. Packs of wild dogs loose in the countryside. Deserted and derelict villages. The bombed and burnt out towns and cities. The English people defeated and depressed. The Germans victorious and triumphant.

But he would not give up. He had walked steadily northwards up the length of England. He had swum across the River Tweed and had nearly drowned in the process. He had reached Berwick-Upon-Tweed, the city that had been built to guard the border. But now the border not only separated Scotland from England, it also separated the Free North from the Occupied South.

Edinburgh was security conscious to the point of paranoia. Everyone who claimed to have 'escaped' from the Occupied South to the Free North was vetted and verified. If their identity could be proven then all was well and good and suitable employment would be found for them. However, the escapees were placed on probation. The Germans and their British puppets could still have a hold on them and they could be working under duress. For example, they could be holding their family as hostages. Edinburgh wanted to be sure that they were loyal and true. If they were not then it was a short hop, skip and jump to the gallows and the hangman's noose, or, if they were lucky, internment in a Detention Camp in the Highlands for the duration.

The man sat on a stiff backed chair drumming his fingers on the table in front of him. He was nervous and he was apprehensive. He had given the Debriefing Officer a list of names of people who could vouch for him and prove his identity. But what were the chances that any of them were in Scotland? He tensed in his chair as he heard the echo of two sets of footsteps marching down the long corridor. There was a knock at the door and an armed guard marched into the room, halted and saluted. "Identifying witness to see you, sir," he said.

The 'identifying witness' entered the room. His face broke out into a smile as he strode towards the escapee with an outstretched hand. "Dickey, old boy," he said with concern, "you're as thin as a rake. What on earth have they been feeding you?"

"Sauerkraut and black bread," the escapee replied. He grabbed the outstretched hand and gave the witness a giant bear hug. The gates opened and rivers of tears of relief ran down his cheeks. He shook as he cried his heart out. The tension and stress of the past year drained out of his body like water draining out of a bath. At last. After weeks on the run. After months of captivity. He was safe. Lieutenant-Colonel Richard Hook, Commanding Officer, Third Battalion, The Royal Regiment of Fens Fusiliers had arrived home.

Ansett shook his head. "You should have checked the dead better…"

"Oh no…" Sam's hand covered his mouth.

"Oh yes…two of the Germans survived."

The colour drained from Alan's face. Sam turned as white as a sheet.

"My God," Sam croaked, "What are we going to do?"

"Can the Jerries identify us?" Alan asked.

"You signed your names on Jock's report, didn't you?" Ansett asked.

"The Germans know who we are..." Sam groaned. "That's it. We're buggered. Game's up. Show's over. We might as well pack our bags right now. Put a bullet through our heads and save the Jerries the trouble."

"Not necessarily," Ansett said. "Panic ye not."

Please, Mr. Ansett. Give us a glimmer of hope. Alan looked down in his hands. His fingers were interlaced in the position of prayer.

"You told me that you found a massacre when you arrived. Correct?" Ansett asked.

The boys nodded. "That's right. The Jerries had already massacred the other mob. They were all lying together in a heap. That's when we killed the Huns. The Police arrived soon after." Sam stood up straighter. Maybe there was a chance of getting away with this.

"But in your report you stated that there was full scale fight going on when you arrived?"

Alan and Sam nodded.

"If the Germans want to cover up the massacre of the prisoners then they might decide that it's in their best interests not to dispute their story," Ansett said.

"Why would they do that?" Sam asked.

"The Jerries have just set up the Specials. How would it sound if it came out that a joint Specials/ Police patrol wiped out an S.S. section? After all, they're all supposed to be on the same side," Ansett answered.

"It would be a major embarrassment for Schuster," Alan said. "He set it up."

"He would be forced to disband it and he would probably be demoted, if not sent back to Germany in disgrace," Sam added.

"My money is that Schuster will cover up this disaster," Ansett said.

"He might decide to support our statement rather than dispute it," Alan said.

"Exactly," Ansett said. "After all, you and Jock are the only 'reliable' witnesses. The Jerry survivors are wounded. The Huns can't afford another scandal like the slaughter in the Square yesterday."

"Any idea about casualties yet, sir?" Alan asked.

"The Germans are saying that less than one hundred civilians were killed and wounded. But we reckon that it's nearer to a thousand," Ansett answered. "We were lucky to escape with our lives."

"My father's alive," Sam announced. "The S.S. dropped him off at our house this morning."

"Thank God." Alan walked over and squeezed Sam's shoulder.

"The Nazis said that shots were fired from the crowd at the soldiers," Ansett said.

"What a crock of shit!" Sam exclaimed.

"We know that and they know that, Sam," Ansett said. "This is purely a face saving gesture. They're playing the blame game."

"The cynical bastards." Alan swore.

"Talking of bastards," Ansett said "Although the rational course of action for the S.S. who survived your private Guy Fawkes party would be to support your statement," the boys chuckled, "I think that it would be wise for you two boys to be prepared to flee at a moment's notice. Do you agree?"

"Absolutely," Alan answered for both of them.

"Do you have a place where you can hide?" Ansett asked.

"We have places to hide and places to go," Sam answered.

"What about Jock?" Alan asked.

"You take care of yourselves. I'll take care of Jock." One way or another, Ansett said to himself.

Chapter Fifteen

Colonel Hook spent the rest of the day catching up on news and gossip with his 'identity witness,' Brigadier John Daylesford. Before the invasion, Daylesford had been the Commanding Officer of the First Battalion The Royal Regiment of Fens Fusiliers. He had managed to escape from Dunkirk to Dover and he had been promoted from Lieutenant-Colonel to his present rank. Daylesford and Hook had served together in the First World War and had remained firm friends ever since.

"I take it that you haven't heard about what happened in Hereward yesterday?"

"No. I've been stuck in here all day. What's happened?" The hair on the back of Hook's neck stood on end. "My wife is still in Hereward. I haven't seen Jackie since I marched out on the day of the invasion."

"The Germans had threatened to execute twenty hostages unless certain 'terrorists' surrendered by one o'clock yesterday." Daylesford paused. "A crowd gathered in the Town Square, the hostages were brought forward to be executed and then the Jerries opened fire on the crowd..."

"My God!" Hook's hand went to his mouth in horror.

"We don't know why the Huns opened fire yet," Daylesford continued.

"Casualties?"

"We don't know. Hundreds. Possibly thousands."

"Sweet Jesus…" What about Jackie? Was she safe?

"We don't have a list of casualties, Dickey."

Hook nodded slowly as if in a daze.

"I'll let you know when we do." Daylesford squeezed Hook's shoulder. "I'm sure that Jackie's alright."

Hook smiled weakly. 'Alright,' but not safe. Not with Nazis roaming the streets at random.

"The Jerries then freed the hostages."

"Any idea why?"

"None what so ever."

"How bizarre." Hook thought for a minute. "A change of heart, perhaps?"

"Rather like shutting the barn door after the horse has bolted."

"Who ordered the execution of the hostages?" Hook asked.

"I'll give you three guesses."

"Schuster?"

"Yes. The Prince of Darkness himself."

"The bastard." Hook ground his teeth. "I knew it would be him. He was the swine who ordered the massacre of my men at Fairfax."

"I know, Dickey. The question is: what are we going to do about it?"

"What do you mean?" Hook sat up straighter in his chair.

"There will be spontaneous uprisings all over the country."

"Where?"

"London, Coventry, Leeds, Manchester, Liverpool…"

"All over?"

"Yes."

"But how will the people find out?"

"About 'Bloody Wednesday?' Because we'll bloody well tell them, Dickey. 'We' being S.O.E. Special Operations Executive, the organization that I work for."

"And you're sure that these 'spontaneous uprisings' will take place?"

Daylesford nodded. "We already have people in place."

"Johnny, I asked you this question once before: do you have any jobs for me?"

"I was wondering when you would ask." Daylesford smiled and stretched out his hand. "Welcome aboard. Welcome to S.O.E."

"Hauptsturmfuhrer Zorn? Hauptsturmfuhrer Zorn? Can you hear me?"

Zorn heard his name being called. He tried to open his eyes, but it was like trying to see through thick fog. He couldn't hear very well either. All sounds were muffled. It was as if cotton wool was stuffed into both of his ears. He tried to sit up, but a sharp pain stabbed across the back of his eyes from one temple to the other.

"It's the concussion," the voice said. "Lie back down on your pillow."

Zorn groaned and did as he was told.

"You have a visitor. It's Schuster," the voice whispered.

Zorn recognized the voice. Ulrich.

"Listen Hauptsturmfuhrer," Ulrich said. "He'll want to know what happened on Tuesday night…"

"What day is it?" Zorn interrupted.

"It's Friday," Ulrich answered impatiently. "Listen Hauptsturmfuhrer. You must back up my story or we'll be court martialled and …"

"Obersturmfuhrer Ulrich! Hauptsturmfuhrer Zorn! The two luckiest men in the Brigade!" The voice thundered through the room.

"Too late…" Ulrich whispered. He stood awkwardly at attention and clicked his heels together. He couldn't salute because his right arm was still in a sling.

"At ease, Ulrich. Take a seat, my wounded soldier." Schuster pulled up a chair for his subordinate and sat down on another one himself. Ulrich sat down. "How are you, Zorn?" Schuster asked.

"Not very well, sir. My head feels as if someone has been using it as a punch bag and my mouth feels like a badger's bottom."

"I'm not surprised!" Schuster laughed. "The doctors say that you're lucky to be alive."

"How's that, sir?" Zorn asked.

"Look at this." Schuster clicked his fingers. A member of his bodyguard standing behind him handed Schuster a helmet. Schuster placed the helmet on his knee. "Recognize the helmet, Zorn?"

Zorn shook his head.

"You should do-it's yours."

Zorn looked at the front of the helmet. There was a hole. "What happened?" He asked.

"The doctors say that a bullet entered the front of your helmet, rattled and ricocheted around the inside and then must have fallen out. The bullet first hit one of your men in the face, passed through his skull and then penetrated your helmet. Luckily for you, the bullet had lost most of its force by then."

Yes, Zorn thought morbidly; flesh, blood and bone had a tendency to slow bullets down. "Obviously, that bullet didn't have my name on it."

"No, it didn't. But it did have Brandt's," Ulrich said somberly.

"There but for the grace of God go I," Zorn said. "About what happened, sir..." Zorn decided to preempt Schuster's question.

"Yes, Zorn. I was just about to come to that. Before I hear your version of events, perhaps you'd like to hear Obersturmfuhrer Ulrich's?" Schuster asked rhetorically.

Ulrich began: "On Tuesday night, I accompanied Hauptsturmfuhrer Zorn on patrol in a last ditch effort to capture the terrorists responsible for the arson attacks..." He looked at Schuster.

"Go on..." Schuster prompted.

"At approximately 3 a.m. we came across a group of men acting suspiciously and we ordered them to halt. They opened fire on us and then...my world went black. I don't remember anything."

"The Police found you unconscious, Ulrich," Schuster explained. "You and Hauptsturmfuhrer Zorn here were the only survivors of your patrol."

"How many men did we lose, sir?" Ulrich asked.

"Ten," Schuster answered. "The Police found eleven dead terrorists. One of the Policemen was also killed."

Eleven terrorists? Ulrich thought. But there were twelve prisoners. So one of them was on the run. One of them had escaped. Did Schuster know that one of the prisoners had escaped?

Schuster turned around in his chair to face Zorn. "Before we hear your story, Hauptsturmfuhrer, I want to give you the Police report." He began to read from a folder that rested on his lap. "The first Police patrol on the scene stated that when they arrived they found a full scale fire fight in progress. One of their men was killed in the crossfire. Forensics found out that he'd been killed by 9mm rounds fired by a Schmessier machine gun. The firing rapidly died out. Another Police patrol then arrived at the scene and the second patrol found you and Ulrich here. The first Police patrol had already left the scene to take their comrade to hospital. S.S. and Army patrols arrived soon afterwards." Schuster looked up from the folder. "No doubt you were aware that twenty hostages were to be executed on Wednesday." Zorn and Ulrich nodded their heads. "Unfortunately, I was summoned to London on Tuesday at short notice. I found out about the gun battle and the deaths of the terrorists on Wednesday morning. I tried to get a message to Sturmbannfuhrer Munchausen to free the hostages, but terrorists had cut the telephone lines between London and Hereward and for some reason we couldn't raise Hereward on the radio," Schuster explained. "So I sent a dispatch rider. He didn't get there in time. By this time the crowd had got ugly. Our men opened fire on the crowd. We still don't know why yet. The Gestapo is still investigating. Publicly, we're saying that shots were fired from the crowd at our troops."

"Any idea of casualties, sir?" Zorn asked.

"We found nearly one thousand dead and dying civilians in the Square."

"My God…" Ulrich whispered in shock, "a massacre…"

"Not a 'massacre,' Ulrich!" Schuster slapped his gloves on his thigh, "our men were fired on first, and we reacted in self defense. Get that through your thick skull, Ulrich and you too, Zorn. If you can't then you'll found yourself fighting partisans in Poland for the rest of the war faster than you can say bratwurst and sauerkraut!" Schuster threatened.

"Yes, sir," Ulrich and Zorn replied in unison.

Schuster's fury subsided as quickly as a spent geyser. "Now gentlemen, as I was saying, the only good thing that has happened in the last few days has been your encounter with the terrorists. The fact that ten of our men were killed is an unexpected bonus…"

Try telling that to their wives and families, Ulrich thought.

"It is the icing on the cake," Schuster continued. "I can see the headlines in the papers back home right now," Schuster sketched the words in the air with his hands, "'Foreign Jewish-Bolshevik terrorist threat to Hereward destroyed: Ten German soldiers killed whilst fighting alongside their British Police comrades. The good citizens of Hereward can sleep safely in their beds once more' Brothers-in-arms. Racial unity. That sort of thing. You get the idea." Schuster was smiling like a Cheshire cat who'd got the cream. "You'll both be mentioned by name of course, as the two officers who destroyed the terrorists. Heroically wounded in the attempt. You'll be famous both here and at home. I've recommended you both for the Iron Cross First Class." Schuster went on. "There'll be a medal presentation ceremony in the Square as soon as you're released from hospital. The whole Brigade will be there and there'll be top brass up from London as well. Newspaper reporters, photographers, the lot. Also…" Schuster wanted to keep on the roll; "Sturmbannfuhrer Munchausen blew his head off when he read the dispatch rider's order to free the hostages so I have a vacancy on my staff." Schuster looked directly at Zorn. "Now, what is your version of events, Hauptsturmfuhrer?"

"Exactly the same as Obersturmfuhrer Ulrich's, sir," Zorn confirmed confidently.

"Hallo, Dickey," Daylesford said, extending his right hand. "How are tricks?"

"Can't complain, Johnny," Hook said as he shook his friend's hand.

"How are they treating you?" Daylesford asked.

"To be honest, Johnny, I don't know who's worse: the Huns or my trainers here," Hook answered.

"They mean well, Dickey," Daylesford assured him.

"They mean to kill me, Johnny. That's what they mean to do," Hook said only half joking.

Daylesford steered Hook back towards the Alligin Hotel on the northern shore of Loch Torridon which served as the Training Centre for the Special Operation Executive. He only started to speak when he was certain that he was well out of earshot of any potential eavesdroppers. "Listen, old boy, something's come up. Ideally, we'd like to train you here for six weeks, but I'm afraid that that's not going to be possible. Your trainers have said that it will take at least another two weeks to give you the minimum amount of training." Daylesford paused to let the gravity of what he was saying sink in. " I've given them a week to get you ready." Daylesford turned to face Hook. "Dickey. Understand that with only two weeks intensive training you will only have a 50-50 chance of surviving at best.

Hook nodded.

"But the truth is that we need you down south."

Hook put his hand on Daylesford's arm. "I understand, Johnny. I've never had as good odds in my life. What was our life expectancy as young officers in the trenches? Six weeks?"

"Two weeks," Daylesford corrected him.

"Exactly." Hook squeezed Daylesford's shoulder. "Anyway, I like a challenge."

During the week following 'Bloody Wednesday' there were general strikes in Liverpool, Manchester and Leeds. There were riots in Coventry, Cambridge and York. German Navy warships were sabotaged and sunk in Plymouth,

King's Lynn and Bristol. Luftwaffe aeroplanes were firebombed in Ripon, Ely and Southampton. There were mass demonstrations against Sir Oswald Mosley's puppet government in Cheltenham. Italian Occupation troops refused to open fire on protestors in Canterbury. There was a mass break out from a Prisoner-of-War camp for French soldiers in Dover.

Traitors and collaborators were a main target for the Resistance forces. In response to these attacks, Brigadefuhreur Schuster intensified his 'Specials' program. Special Constabulary units were established in all major towns and cities. Both the Police and the Specials were to be equipped with weapons supplied by the S.S. Sir Oswald Mosley, Prime Minister of the Government of National Unity, asked for permission to raise his own paramilitary forces to be used for internal defense and security against people he described as "warmongering Jewish-Bolshevik gangsters." The German occupation authorities in London eagerly grasped the opportunity to kill two birds with one stone: they would be able to solve their manpower shortage crisis on the one hand and on the other hand they would be able to achieve their long term aim of setting Englishmen against Englishmen. Divide and conquer. It had worked in Occupied Europe; the Germans were confidant that it would work in Occupied Britain.

On February First, Mosley announced the creation of "The Legion of Saint George." Major-General J.F.C. Fuller, Mosley's pre-War Military Advisor, was named Commanding Officer of the Legion.

Sam and Alan continued with their studies during the day at St. John's Academy and with their duties once per week with the Specials. Sergeant Hitch and Special P.C. Linsdell were buried in Hereward Cemetery in a joint ceremony. Family, friends, students and every single Special and Policeman who was not on duty attended the funerals. Bishop Rathdowne led the service and stressed the virtues of love, devotion, duty and sacrifice.

The following day Mayor Brunswick publicly presented Alan with a Police Medal for Gallantry in the Town Hall. Chief Inspector Brown and Inspector Mason were also there. All flashing white teeth and beaming smiles over Golden Boy. More accurately, Superintendent Brown and Chief Inspector Mason. Schuster had made a recommendation to S.S. headquarters in London that Scotland Yard should be 'persuaded' to promote Brown and Mason as a result of their sterling contribution to the fight against terrorism. Their promotions would also show that collaboration, if not crime, paid.

Ansett and Sam also attended the ceremony. Alan had been awarded the medal because he had shot the fire bomber, David Jones, who had shot Sergeant Hitch. Or so the World thought. Alan had never admitted that it was he who had killed Hitch and not Jones who had killed him. Alan had never admitted that he had killed both of them to anyone, but Ansett had put two and two together. Alan had shot Hitch because he had gathered proof that Sam was also an arsonist. Alan had killed Hitch to protect Sam. Sam seemed oblivious to all of Alan's Machiavellian machinations. Or perhaps Sam was reluctant to give thanks where thanks were due.

Chapter Sixteen

The R.A.F. Special Duties Squadron Lysander flew over the Scottish border into England. The pilot flew low and hugged the ground, ducking and diving between houses, hedges and stonewalls in order to evade enemy radar.

The S.O.E. secret agent had been tasked with re-establishing contact with any Auxiliary Units of the British Resistance which had become activated when the Germans had invaded. The units had been divided into three separate groups:-fighting groups, intelligence groups and communication groups. Each group acted independently without physical contact with other groups and without the knowledge of the whereabouts or makeup of the other groups.

Edinburgh had given specific coded instructions to each group to carry out various tasks during the 'Bloody Wednesday' uprisings in order to discover which groups had survived the invasion and were still active or could be activated. For example, one fighting unit in Southampton had been ordered to attack an airfield. An attack on an airfield had taken place in Southampton so Edinburgh concluded that the unit was still active. Another fighting unit in Southampton had been ordered to attack harbour and dock facilities. This attack had not taken place so Edinburgh concluded that the unit had either been destroyed or, for whatever reason, was inactive.

The agent's primary mission was fourfold:-to secure lines of communication between Edinburgh and active Auxiliary Units; to 'persuade' inactive units to reactivate; to recruit new members for existing units and to establish brand new units. All of the agent's activities were confined to South-East England. The agent's secondary mission was to bring a message of hope from the Free North to the Occupied South. To let his fellow countrymen and countrywomen know that all was not lost, that Britain may have lost the battle, but they had not lost the War, Britain was down, but not out and Resistance and the struggle would continue until liberation and final victory.

The Lysander landed in the middle of the night on a farmer's field to the south of the Cathedral city of Ely that was situated ten minutes by train north of Hereward. The family who had owned the land had fled and the farmhouse lay deserted. The agent code named Ivanhoe jumped out of the aeroplane and was met by three members of an Ely Auxiliary Fighting Unit. The group walked through the countryside to another farmhouse where Ivanhoe and the Resistance fighters ate a delicious meal of rabbit stew.

During the meal the unit leader gave Ivanhoe a full situation report. When 'Bloody Wednesday' took place in neighbouring Hereward, it was if dam burst. Months and months of pent up anger and hatred poured out into the open. A peaceful candlelit procession through the town rapidly escalated into a full scale riot when the marchers refused to disperse when ordered do so, first by the Police and then by the German Army. Squadrons of German

cavalrymen on giant warhorses charged the crowd knee-to –
knee and cut and slashed at the defensenseless men, women
and children. The casualties ran into the hundreds. The next
day there was a general strike in Ely. Troops tried to force
shops to open and a butcher was bludgeoned and battered
to death with rifle butts when he refused to comply. On the
following day, isolated groups of Germans were attacked
in the streets. The next day, a German soldier was chased
and captured by a mob. They lynched him from the nearest
lamppost. The Germans had reacted ruthlessly. They had
picked up twenty random men and women from the streets
and had hung them that evening in the Market Square.

Ivanhoe said goodbye to the Ely Resistance group on the
outskirts of the city. From here on in, he was on his own.
Ivanhoe traveled on the train and walked through the streets
of Hereward without a care in the world as if he was walking
home from work. Although it was only five o'clock, people
were hurrying home. The curfew began at 7 p.m. and the
deadline was rigorously enforced.

Ivanhoe crossed the street and walked towards his
contacts who were waiting, as arranged, beneath a lamppost.
They heard him coming and turned his way. He whistled
the tune that accompanied Gilbert and Sullivan's 'Pirates of
Penzance' Policeman song, "When Constabulary duties to
be done, to be done…" the two Specials finished the second
part of the password: one of them whistled "A Policeman's
lot is not a happy one, happy one."

"That's my favourite Gilbert and Sullivan." Ivanhoe
said.

"I prefer the 'Mikado,'" one of the Specials returned.

Ivanhoe breathed out a sigh of relief. "Ivanhoe," he
said.

"Batman," the Special said. "And this is Robin." He

pointed to his companion. His companion gave him a 'I can't believe you just said that' look.

"Take me to the gates of St. John's Academy," He ordered. Ivanhoe knew fine well where the gates were. After all, he had been teaching there since he finished his teacher training in the twenties. But he had to pretend that he had never visited Hereward before.

"Ivanhoe," Batman said. "Written by Sir Walter Scott."

"Have you read it?" Ivanhoe asked.

Batman nodded. "The most boring book that I've ever read."

"What's it about?" Robin asked.

"The Normans invade…Ivanhoe's a Saxon hero…blah, blah, blah," Batman began, "boy meets girl, a Templar knight falls in love with Rebecca who's Jewish…blah, blah, blah…Templars put Rebecca on trial…"

"What for?" Robin interrupted.

"Basically for being Jewish."

"What?" Robin was confused.

"The Templars were slightly to the right of Genghis Khan and slightly to the left of Adolf Hitler," Ivanhoe interjected.

"Ah. I see," Robin said.

"Anyway," Batman continued, "Rebecca's due to be burnt at the stake…Templars force Templar lover boy to fight on behalf of the Order…Ivanhoe fights on behalf of Rebecca…if lover boy loses then Rebecca will be released… if lover boy wins then she'll roast…"

"Ouch!"

"Lover boy allows Ivanhoe to kill him."

"What?" Robin exclaimed incredulously. "The Templar lets Ivanhoe kill him?"

"Yes," Batman confirmed.

"He sacrifices his own life?" Robin continued. "For a girl?"

"Yes," Batman said patiently.

"I don't believe it." Robin shook his head.

"What don't you believe?" Batman asked. "He sacrificed himself for love. It's like giving up your life to save your best friend. Greater love hath no man," he quoted.

"That's different."

"How is it?"

"That's dying to save a mate," Robin replied. "Not dying to save a girl," he maintained stubbornly.

"You may do the same yourself one day," Ivanhoe said.

"And the Templar turned traitor," Robin said. "That's unforgivable. I'd never do that."

"We'll see…" Ivanhoe said.

"Here we are," Batman said. "St. John's Academy." He pointed at the giant gates that guarded the driveway leading up to the school. As if you didn't know how to get here, you sly old fox, Batman thought to himself. "When shall we meet you?"

"Give me an hour," Ivanhoe answered. "Say a quarter past six?" he said as he looked at his watch. "Will that give us enough time to get to the safe house?"

"Plenty of time," Robin assured him.

"6.15 it is then," Ivanhoe confirmed.

"Ivanhoe," Robin hesitated momentarily as he spoke. "There's one last thing."

Batman and Ivanhoe both tensed. Was Robin about to blow their cover?

"Yes?" Ivanhoe asked.

"She's alright," Robin said.

"Who?"

"Mrs. Ivanhoe," Robin reassured him. "She's alive and well and she's teaching English at school."

Jackie. Hook said to himself. He squeezed Sam's shoulder in gratitude. "Thanks, Sam." He felt a wave of relief flood through his body. "I mean Robin."

They all laughed.

"We have to keep up appearances." Hook chuckled. "Your news means a lot to me." he smiled at the two boys. "But I want you to promise me one thing, boys."

"Yes, sir?" They said in unison. Old habits died hard.

"She must not know that you've met me and she must not know that I'm still alive."

"Hallo, Paul," Hook said.

Paul Mason's mouth hung open. He was completely speechless. Gob smacked.

"You look as if you've seen a ghost." Hook smiled. He was clearly enjoying the experience.

"I have." Mason looked Hook up and down. "You're supposed to be dead." He cautiously stretched out his hand and gingerly touched Hook's greatcoat sleeve. No. Hook was not an apparition. He was not the ghost of a soldier past. He was real.

"Well, I'm glad to disappoint you, Paul. I'm very much alive."

"So I see. Welcome back to the land of the living." Mason shook Hook's hand. "Like Lazarus arisen from the dead." Mason shook his head in awe and wonder. "Come in, come in."

Hook followed Mason down the hallway into the living room "You've done very well for yourself, Paul." Hook looked around and admired the décor.

"Perks of the job. Comes with the territory," Mason said over his shoulder as they walked down the corridor. "I'm deputy rector now."

"And you're an Inspector in the Specials as well, I hear."

"Chief Inspector actually," Mason corrected him. "I've recently been promoted. By the way, Richard. Did anyone see you come in here?" He asked as they entered the living room.

"No."

"Good. Safer that way," Mason said. "You're remarkably well informed for a man who's supposed to be dead." He poured a whiskey for both of them.

Single malt, Hook noticed. In heavy crystal tumblers, no less. Yes, Hook thought to himself, Mason was doing very well for himself.

"But enough about me," Mason interrupted Hook's thoughts. "What happened to you?"

Hook described how when the S.S. had opened fire, the R.S.M. had jumped in front and shielded him with his body. However, in the fall he had broken his ankle. A tear dripped down Hook's cheek as he spoke. He had served with Jim Witherspoon on the Western Front during the war and in Ireland afterwards. They had gone through a lot together. It was a tragedy that he had ended his days being slaughtered in cold blood like a farmyard animal in an abattoir. German Army troops had then appeared and had prevented the S.S. troops from finishing off the wounded. He had spent a week in a German Army hospital in King's Lynn and then he been transferred to a Prisoner-of-War Camp where he had spent another six weeks hobbling around on a pair of crutches. On Christmas day he had escaped from the camp with five other survivors of the massacre. They had split up into pairs, but his companion had become seriously ill and had died. It had taken Hook about a month to reach Scotland.

Mason described how he had managed to run away when the S.S. men began firing. He had hidden that night in a forest and had stripped off any insignia identifying him as a soldier and an officer. He had joined a column of refugees fleeing towards Hereward. In Hereward he had picked up the threads of his pre-Invasion life.

"How did you explain your survival?" Hook asked.

Mason shrugged. "I said that I had twisted my ankle during the advance to contact and was forced to drop out of the march."

"What about when people asked what had happened to the rest of the battalion?"

"I pleaded ignorance."

"That couldn't have been easy."

"It wasn't," Mason agreed. "It was hard when mothers asked what had happened to their sons." Mason's voice became more subdued as he remembered. "Or when wives asked you if you knew what had happened to their husbands." He looked directly at Hook.

"Paul," Hook began, "has…?"

"Yes, Richard." Mason put his hand on Hook's shoulder. "She has. Jackie asked if I knew what had happened to you. She used to ask every day. I had to lie. I had to tell her that I didn't know. She's stopped asking."

"I…I understand, Paul," Hook said somberly. Jackie thought that he was dead. However, Hook recognized that he had the power to change that. The question was: should he? And for what purpose? Who would suffer and who would benefit from such a revelation? Jackie may have moved on by now. The thought stuck in Hook's throat. After all, September was five long months ago. How long was a person expected to mourn in wartime when people were killing and being killed all of the time? And what if he did tell Jackie? She would be in danger. Would she be able to keep the information to herself? She would be a security risk to his life as well as to her own. And he would have made her a risk. And what if he was killed further down the road? Jackie would have to mourn him all over again. Could he put her through that again?

"People aren't stupid, Richard." Mason's words scythed through Hook's thoughts. "There are rumours and stories. Farmers' tales of ghosts roaming the countryside in the dead of night. Stories to frighten the children before bedtime. Spirits searching and calling out for their loved ones. For friends. For revenge. Fairfax has been blown up and bull dozed to the ground. It no longer exists. It's forbidden to go there and it's part of a restricted zone that also includes Wake. The Army and the Luftwaffe dug up all of the dead civilians at Wake. God knows what they've done with the bodies. But people know that something terrible happened there as well. The Jerries can't have killed everybody. Some people will have survived at Wake just as some people survived at Fairfax."

"Do you know of anyone else who survived the massacre at Fairfax?"

"Yes." Mason nodded. "Sam Roberts and Alan Mitchell. Both Fourth Year boys."

"Yes. I remember them. How did they explain their miraculous escape?"

"They used the same excuse as me." Mason laughed "A twisted ankle."

"You three must've been born with two left feet."

"I prefer to think of it more in terms of great minds think alike."

"What are Sam and Alan up to now?" Hook was not going to let on that he had already met the boys.

"They're in the Specials under my command." Hook could almost swear that he saw Mason's chest puff up with pride. "Alan was decorated for Gallantry. Do you remember Sam's sister, Alice?" Mason asked.

"Good looking girl in the Sixth Form?"

"The same," Mason said. "She's going out with an S.S. officer."

"Christ! Alice Roberts a Hun whore!" Hook was genuinely shocked. "That didn't take long, did it?"

"We've all had to adapt, Richard," Mason said defensively. He was surprised to find himself leaping to Alice's defense. "You don't know what it's been like for us down south."

"Evidently not." Hook snorted derisively.

An uncomfortable silence fell.

Hook broke it. "And how about you, Paul?" He asked. "How have you 'adapted?'"

"Look out!" Someone shouted.

The Armoured Personnel Carrier missed the ramp leading up to a hump backed bridge and ploughed straight through a fence as if it was made out of paper. Senior Leutnant Alfonin watched in horror as the half-track plunged down the riverbank and into the Ouse. He managed to take one breath of air before the A.P.C. disappeared beneath the surface.

"What was that?" Alan asked.

"I don't know," Sam answered. "But it came from over there." He pointed towards the river. "Come on!" Sam took off running down the street.

"What about Ivanhoe?" Alan shouted after him.

"It's only 5.30," Sam shouted over his shoulder. "We've got plenty of time. Come on!"

"Sam! Wait!" Alan shouted.

But Sam had already disappeared.

Mason poured Hook another whiskey.

"I've adapted as best as I could," Mason said. "I've had to make the best of a bad situation."

"Well, I think that you've done very well for yourself, Paul," Hook said sincerely. "Your father would've been very proud of you. Here's to you, Paul. Cheers!" Hook raised his glass and clinked it against Mason's.

"You knew my father?" Mason asked.

"I did." Hook nodded his head. "Roger Mason was well respected and regarded through out the Regiment. It was a terrible tragedy when he was killed. A stray Jerry shell hit the hospital where your father was operating. He was killed out right."

"I was only thirteen years old when the Great War started." Mason said somberly. "You probably knew him better than I did."

"I'm sorry, Paul." Hook reached across and patted Mason's shoulder in sympathy for his loss. He tried to raise his friend's spirits by changing the subject. "Your mother was from South Africa, wasn't she?"

"Yes, she was. They met there during the Boer War."

"Really?" Hook's eyebrows raised in surprise. "I didn't know that."

"There are a lot of things that you don't know about me, Richard."

The driver of the second A.P.C. jammed on the breaks. The wheels and tracks crunched and screeched as the half-track came to a halt. "Everybody out!" The platoon feldwebel shouted as the first A.P.C.'s antennae disappeared beneath the waves.

The ten men infantry section piled out over the side and through the rear exit of the half-track onto the road.

The platoon sergeant barked out orders as his men swarmed around the A.P.C. like ants scrambling around an ant mound which had just been kicked over. They grabbed ropes, blankets, spare jumpers, jackets and everything else that they could get their hands on.

The platoon sergeant counted heads as the first half-track crew bobbed to the surface. One…two…three…commander…yes, there was Mr.Alfonin…four…five…Schellenberg, the driver…my God, would Schellenberg be for the high jump when they got back to barracks!

Sam arrived on the scene as the S.S. troopers from the second A.P.C. gathered by the riverbank. He could see that the soldiers' sense of anxiety was rapidly transforming into a sense of amusement as they realized that all of their swimming comrades had been accounted for.

Alan caught up with Sam at the street corner where they were now sheltering in the shadows. Sam turned around and bared his teeth in a wolf like grin.

"What say we put the Huns out of our misery, Alan?" Sam asked rhetorically. He didn't expect an answer. And if Alan gave him a negative one, he was going to do it anyway.

"Sam, wait!" Alan said. But it was too late. Sam had sprinted towards the rear door of the half-track. "Oh well. So much for staying out of trouble." Alan sighed in resignation. "Here we go again." He checked the safety catch on his weapon and ran after Sam.

"How did your parents meet?" Hook asked. He was genuinely interested in Mason's personal history.

"They met in a concentration camp," Mason answered.

"In a concentration camp?" Hook asked with raised eyebrows.

Mason nodded as he took a drink of whiskey.

"Your mother was a nurse?"

Mason shook his head as the amber nectar flowed down his throat. "She was a prisoner."

Sam slowly pulled open the rear door of the A.P.C. and climbed up the rungs of the ladder. He looked over his shoulder and saw Alan at the street corner covering him with his revolver. Sam crawled along the bottom of the open air passenger compartment until he reached the belt fed M.G. 42 machine gun at the front. He looked behind him and he saw Alan gingerly climb into the half-track. He took up position at the rear M.G. 42 machine gun. Both of the boys crouched down out of sight below the weapons. Sam turned sideways to look at Alan. "On the count of three," he whispered. Alan nodded.

Hook was speechless. "I'm...I'm sorry, Paul. I didn't know."

"There's no need to be sorry, Richard," Mason said. "The War was a long time ago. These things happen during wars." He took another sip of whiskey. It felt as if a small fire was burning in his stomach. It was warm and reassuring. "If my step father had not met my mother then we may have all died."

Stepfather, Hook said to himself. So Mason's father as well as his mother were Boers. He had always assumed that Roger Mason was Paul Mason's natural father. He had never had any reason to assume otherwise. "I guess so...terrible things happen in wars..." Hook said lamely. He knew that it was an inadequate response, but what could he say? It was perfectly true: terrible things did happen in wars.

"So, why did you come to see me?"

"Well, in light of what you've just told me, I don't know

if I should tell you," Hook joked. At least, he hoped that it sounded like a joke.

Mason laughed good-naturedly. "I'm still the same person, Richard. I'm still my father's son."

Yes, Hook thought to himself. But that's part of the problem-which father was he the son of?

"Trust me," Mason said.

Oh well, Hook said to himself. In for a penny, in for a pound. "I've been sent to recruit members for a Resistance cell…

"Go on…"

"A small, select four person team. You were to be the leader and you were to choose three other members. Edinburgh thought that your position as an Inspector in the Specials would be the perfect cover."

"I see." Mason swirled the contents of his glass as he thought. "Are there any other cells in Hereward?"

"I'm not at liberty to say."

Of course there are, Mason said to himself. How else would you have been able to get here? You certainly didn't walk all of the way from Scotland. "You're right, Richard. It would be the perfect cover. Especially now that I've been promoted to chief inspector. I do have a position of responsibility and power here and I agree that it would be the perfect cover for a leader of the Resistance…does anyone know that you're here?"

"No," Hook replied. Which was only partly accurate. Sam and Alan had seen him enter the grounds of the school, but they had not known where he was going.

Sam jumped up, cocked the machine gun and switched off the safety catch in one fluid and practiced movement. He traversed the M.G. 42 until it centered on the middle of the soldier giving the orders. He heard the reassuring clang

192

and click of Alan cocking his machine gun and changing the safety catch to fire.

The platoon feldwebel's ears pricked up at the familiar sound of an M.G. 42 being made ready to fire. The hair on the nape of his neck stood on end. "What the-?"

The machine gun bullets ripped through the soldiers standing on the river bank at the rate of one thousand two hundred rounds per minute, twenty rounds per second. The men collapsed at the edge of the bank, half in and half out of the water, their blood pumped into the river rapidly turning it red. More machine gun bullets raced into the river biting into bobbing heads and bodies. Sam and Alan methodically swept their M.G. 42s from side to side searching for survivors. Sam finished his belt of bullets and dived into the ammunition box to attach another belt.

"Sam!" Alan shouted.

"What?" Sam asked as he attached the new belt to the machine gun.

"They're dead."

"How can you be so sure?" Sam asked as he cocked the weapon to resume firing.

"Look at them." Alan pointed at the river. The scene resembled what the Red Sea might have looked like when God brought it crashing down on top of the Egyptians. Dead bodies and debris floated everywhere.

"Alright, already!" Sam said with frustration. As far as he was concerned, the only good German was a dead German. He just wanted to make sure that they had all gone to meet their maker. "It's twenty five to six," he said. "We've got plenty of time yet."

"To do what exactly?" Alan didn't like the sound of that.

"To pour fuel on the fire," Sam answered. "Come on. Let's get these bodies into the river."

"Would you care for another whiskey, Richard?" Mason asked.

"I don't mind if I do," Hook replied. Mason poured him another glass. "Thank you."

Mason picked up the now empty whiskey bottle and disappeared into the kitchen.

"Do you have any suggestions whom I should approach to recruit?" Mason asked from the kitchen.

"I've got a few people in mind, but to be honest, I'd rather leave the choice to you."

"Why?" Mason walked back through to the living room.

"For reasons of security," Hook answered. "I don't want to know the names of who you've recruited and neither does Edinburgh. In fact, Headquarters doesn't want to know anything about you either."

"I see. So you don't know the names of the people who brought you here and they don't know my name either. That makes it easier then."

Hook looked at the box that Mason was carrying. "King Edward V Cigars" the box said. He approved. "I agree that the recruitment of another cell in Hereward is a cause for celebration."

'Another cell?' Mason observed. So his was not going to be the first. There already were Resistance people in Hereward. Probably the very people who had escorted Hook to his house. The whiskey was beginning to loosen tongues and work its magic.

Hook was relieved to see Mason reach into the cigar box. He laughed. It was good to see his old friend relax and lighten up a little.

The bullet thudded into Hook's chest. The glass of whiskey slipped from Hook's fingers and shattered onto the floor spilling its contents onto the carpet. The pool of whiskey mingled with the blood that dripped from Hook's fingertips. The cigar fell smoking onto the carpet and lay smoldering for a nanosecond before Mason casually ground it out with the heel of his jackboot. Hook lay slumped back on his chair with a look of utter surprise and shock on his face. His eyes were staring to glaze over as his life gradually ebbed out of him. His lips asked the silent question.

"Why?" Mason returned to his chair and sat down. "I'll tell you why. Because the Uitlanders killed my father in the Boer War. Because you Uitlander scum let my elder brother and younger sister starve to death in one of their concentration camps. Because my mother became an Englishman's whore in order to save my life. Because even though I grew up in England, living amongst the English, speaking English, in my heart I have always been a Boer."

"Rebecca...Rebecca Templar." Hook croaked.

"What?" Mason sat up in his chair. "What did you say?" He leapt up from his chair and grabbed Hook roughly by the shoulder. "What did you say, damn you?" He tried to shake the words out of Hook's mouth, but it was no use. Hook was already dead.

Chapter Seventeen

"An accident, you say?" Sturmbannfuhrer Zorn asked.

"Looks like it, sir," Hauptsturmfuhrer Ulrich answered. "The driver of the first A.P.C. probably fell asleep and came off the road here." Ulrich pointed with his arm. "The driver of the second half-track probably wasn't paying any attention and blindly followed the first A.P.C…"

"…And the first half-track ploughed straight through the fence and into the river and the second A.P.C. followed," Zorn interrupted. "What a bloody disaster."

Ulrich was sorely tempted to say 'I told you so.' The men were absolutely exhausted by the relentless round of round the clock anti-Resistance patrols.

"How many men did the Army lose?"

"We estimate twenty plus, sir."

"Every cloud has a silver lining."

So much for Inter Service camaraderie, Ulrich wryly thought. "Do you want the river dredged for bodies, sir?" He asked.

Zorn shrugged his shoulders dismissively. "No. We don't need to find the bodies. We know what they died of.

They drowned. Write that in the report. If the Army wants the bodies then they'll have to dredge the river."

"What about the A.P.C.s, sir?" Ulrich asked.

"What?"

"What about the A.P.C.s? I think that they can be salvaged."

Zorn's eyes lit up like Fagin's. The penny dropped. Half-tracks were like gold dust. "Where's the nearest S.S. engineer unit?"

"Cambridge, sir," Ulrich answered.

"Ask them if they're interested in laying their hands on a slightly waterlogged. A.P.C. with one previous owner."

"And if they are interested, sir?"

"Tell them to get over here at the double with heavy lifting equipment. They get one half-track. We get the other. Finder's fee." Zorn smiled.

"What about the Army, sir?" Ulrich asked.

"What about them?" Zorn asked as he struck a match and lit up.

"What should we tell them if they ask about their missing A.P.C.s?" Ulrich let Zorn light his cigar.

"I don't know and I don't care. Use your imagination, Ulrich," Zorn replied nonchalantly.

"How long did you wait?" Ansett asked the boys. The three of them were sitting on chairs in the underground bunker in the Cathedral Crypt.

"We waited for half an hour until a quarter to seven." Alan replied. "We then left because an S.S. patrol drove by and we didn't want them to see us in the area."

"For all we knew, they could've been looking for us. The Huns might already have captured Ivanhoe and they could've squeezed our descriptions out of him," Sam added.

Ansett winced at Sam's choice of words. It was a very

real possibility that the Germans had captured Ivanhoe and had squeezed the information out of him. Quite Literally. "You did the right thing, boys. Do you have any idea who he was going to meet?"

"No idea, sir." Alan shook his head. "Only that we met him and escorted him to the gates of St. Johns as he requested. He told us to meet him back there at 6.15 p.m."

"He could've been going to visit anyone," Sam said. "There are half a dozen entrances and exits to the school. He could've been using the school grounds as a shortcut to go somewhere else."

Ansett nodded in confirmation. "Alright. So, worse case scenario. Ivanhoe's been picked up by the Police or Specials. What would they do?"

"If he's not on the 'Wanted' list of known or suspected criminals or terrorists and his identification documents stand up to inspection then they'll throw him in a cell overnight and release him in the morning with a stern warning not to break curfew," Alan answered. He was very familiar with Specials' standard procedure.

"I agree. If Edinburgh's worth its salt, then the false I.D. should stand up to a casual examination," Ansett said.

"Alan and I could go back to the Police station and casually ask if anyone interesting has been arrested," Sam suggested.

"Good idea, Sam," Ansett agreed. "But who's Duty Sergeant at the station at the moment?"

"P.C., now Sergeant MacDonald. He was promoted to replace Sergeant Hitch," Alan answered. "He can be trusted. He wrote the report regarding the deaths of the S.S. troops the night before 'Bloody Wednesday.'"

"But will he be suspicious?" Ansett pressed.

"He may be suspicious, but he can be trusted not to ask

scary questions and poke his nose where it doesn't belong," Alan said.

"I hope so. For both of your sakes," Ansett said grimly.

"So that's the Police taken care of," Sam said. "What about the Army and the S.S? If they've captured him then it's a completely different ball game."

"If the Huns have captured him and they don't suspect anything, then they'll hand him over to the Police," Ansett answered.

"And if they do suspect anything?" Alan asked rhetorically. He already knew the answer to that question.

"Then they'll torture him until he tells them something."

"But what can he tell them?" Alan asked.

"He can tell them about the Free North and the people who delivered him to you. But he can only provide them with descriptions and code names, but not real names. He can tell them that he met two Specials or Police in Hereward. How many are there now?"

"Hundreds…" Sam answered.

"Exactly. Hundreds of Specials and Police. The important thing is that he can't put any names to the faces."

Sam and Alan exchanged meaningful glances.

"Sir…" Alan began.

"Yes, what is it?"

"Ivanhoe is Mr. Hook."

"What?" Ansett jumped out of his chair.

"Ivanhoe is Richard Hook, our Chemistry teacher, Lieutenant-Colonel Hook of the Fusiliers."

"He can't be! You must've made a mistake. Hook is dead. You told me yourself. He was killed at Fairfax!"

"He's alive, sir." Sam backed Alan up. "At least he was until late this afternoon. We both recognized him. We told him that Mrs. Hook was still alive."

"My God!" Ansett put a hand to his head. "What madness is this? To send a man back to his home town where anyone could recognize him walking down the street…" He slumped back into his chair in shock.

"I guess that Edinburgh thought that a local man would know the area and know who to contact," Alan suggested.

"But not whom to trust." A thunderbolt of thought hit Ansett right between the shoulder blades as he grabbed Sam's arm. "And Ivanhoe…did he recognize you?" He asked desperately.

The boys nodded their heads.

"Then we must assume the worst," Ansett announced as he stood up. "They could be searching for the both of you at this very moment. You boys will have to stay here until I find out what happened to Ivanhoe."

"But what about you, sir?" Alan asked.

"They won't find out about me until they capture you, Alan. They've got nothing to link me to Ivanhoe at the moment. Sam, I'll tell your parents that you're staying with Alan at the boarding house.

"Thank you, sir," Sam said.

Ansett nodded. "Now listen carefully, boys: If I'm not back by this time tomorrow then you must assume that the Jerries know about us. If I'm not back by 7p.m. tomorrow night then I want you boys to stock up with a week's worth of weapons, ammo, food and equipment and break out of Hereward."

"Where should we go?" Alan asked.

"To the Free North: to Scotland."

"How will we know if it's you coming back to the Crypt and not the Germans?" Sam asked.

"Or if the Huns aren't forcing you to guide them?" Alan added.

Ansett thought for a moment. "I'll whistle the tune to 'I'll take the high road and you'll take the low road…

"'…And I'll be in Scotland before you," Sam finished.

"How appropriate," Alan commented dryly.

"But if I'm not whistling that tune then I want you to burst out of that bunker with all guns blazing."

"Yes, sir," both boys answered in unison.

"And boys. One more thing."

"Yes, sir?" Alan said.

"Don't let them take you alive. Save the last bullet for yourselves."

"Alan. Wake up." Sam shook him by the shoulder. "Footsteps," he whispered.

"Make ready." Sam checked that he'd loaded his magazine correctly and attached it to his Schmeisser. He cocked the weapon and lined his forefinger alongside the trigger guard. "Ready?"

"I was born ready," Alan answered with a wolfish grin as he cocked his weapon.

"Let's go," Sam whispered. He quickly moved to the base of the ladder and began to climb.

"How close is he?"

"Close." Sam said as he switched off his safety catch. "Any second now he should start whistling…"

"Because if he doesn't, he'll start dying…"

And then it came. Not whistling, not humming, but singing. Echoing eerily and bouncing from wall to wall of the Crypt "I'll take the high road and you'll take the low road and I'll be in Scotland before you…"

The boys breathed out a collective sigh of relief, switched on their safety catches, looked at each other and grinned. Ansett.

"MacDonald mentioned an interesting thing," Ansett said slowly. "He said that two Army A.P.C.s crashed into the river at the Fairfax Road Bridge."

"Oh, which bridge is that?" Sam asked innocently.

Alan would've kicked him if he'd been able to reach him. Sam knew fine well where the bridge was. He had lived in Hereward for the last eleven years and Ansett was all too aware of that.

"You know the one, Sam. The humped back bridge," Ansett answered. He was playing with Sam like a cat plays with a mouse.

"Oh yes," Sam said. "Now I remember."

"So you should," Ansett said testily. "It's only five minutes walk from the school gates. Ivanhoe may have turned up early in need of help and you two weren't there. You weren't there when he needed you," Ansett said gravely. His voice sounded like rumbling thunder. "You two were too busy carrying out your own private little war." He sneered as he said the words. "Your lack of discipline may have led to Ivanhoe's capture, torture and death. Your recklessness may well result in us suffering the same fate and the destruction of all Resistance in Hereward." Ansett's voice had been gradually building in terms of both volume and intensity and the final words exploded from his lips like a volcano erupting.

"Now, wait a minute," Sam protested. "That's not fair!" He was not prepared to take this amount of flak from anyone and especially not from Ansett. "We were there twenty minutes early and he never showed up!"

"Then why didn't you tell me about the half-tracks?" Ansett asked. Sam's face turned the colour of a beetroot as his cheeks blushed with embarrassment at the discovery of their deception.

"Because on a need to know basis you didn't need to know," Sam threw Ansett's oft repeated mantra back in his face. Ansett reacted as if a bowl of cold water had just been thrown at him.

"I see," Ansett said slowly. Through a supreme effort of will and self control he managed to begin his temper back under control. He noticed for the first time that Alan had remained silent through out the whole exchange. That was not a good sign. "What about you, Alan?" Ansett asked his house captain.

"I agree with everything that Sam has said, sir. What about the Army and the S.S.? They could still have him." Alan tried to defuse the situation by changing the subject. He also knew that if the argument continued he might be tempted to say something rash. He realized that he must continue to play the role of peacemaker and mediator.

"The S.S. doesn't have him," Ansett said bluntly.

Sam was about to ask 'how do you know?' but thought better of it. This was perhaps not the most appropriate time to ask how Ansett got his information.

"And what about the Army?" Alan asked.

"The Army doesn't have him either," Ansett answered.

"But the question remains: if the Police, the S.S. and the Army don't have him…?" Ansett started.

"…Then who does?" Sam finished.

Sam and Alan left the Police station after they had had a look at the corpse which the German Navy had fished out of the River Ouse. They talked to each other as they walked.

"That was definitely Hook," Sam said to Alan in hushed tones.

"Yes, it was." Alan nodded his head. "And you know what that means?"

"Hook was not killed by a Policeman or a Special or a German."

"Hook was killed by someone he knew. Did you get a look at the bullet wound?"

"Yes. Dr. Caruthers said that he was shot at point blank range. Probably at a distance of less than three yards…"

"Hook was executed. But why?" Alan asked.

"Not so much 'why?' but by whom?"

Chapter Eighteen

Senior Leutnant Alfonin, Schellenberg the driver and another soldier had survived the machine gun attack on their A.P.C.s. They had dived underwater when the bullets had started flying and they had allowed the current to carry them out of the killing zone. They had not been able to climb out of the fast flowing river and they had been swept down river until they had bumped against boats moored against the pier at Ely. Alfonin and his men had spent two days so far in hospital because they were suffering from severe hypothermia. Unfortunately, Schellenberg never recovered and died.

Generalmajor von Schnakenberg came to visit his men on their third day in hospital. "How are you feeling, Nicky?"

"I feel like a drowned rat, sir," Alfonin answered. "But I feel far better than Schellenberg," he said bitterly.

"I know, Nicky." Von Schnakenberg put his hand on Alfonin's shoulder and squeezed sympathetically. "Damned bad luck."

"It wasn't his fault, sir." Alfonin tried to raise himself to a better sitting position in bed. "Schellenberg was exhausted. The men were exhausted and I was exhausted."

"I know." If Alfonin was inferring that von Schnakenberg was at fault for issuing the orders in the first place, then he was prepared to accept the criticism with good grace. After all, Alfonin was right. Von Schnakenberg's punishing work schedule had sent those men to their deaths and he was painfully aware of it. He was also prepared to take full responsibility for their deaths.

"Have they found any of the others, sir?"

"No, Nicky." Von Schnakenberg shook his head sadly. "The three of you were the only ones that the Navy found. The remaining twenty men of your platoon are still missing, presumed drowned. They'll be in the middle of the North Sea by now."

"I see, sir." Alfonin shrugged with resignation. Then his eyebrows furrowed. "Wait a minute, sir. I must have misheard you: you said that 'twenty men' were missing and that they were 'presumed drowned?'"

"Yes, that's correct." Von Schnakenberg was confused. "The crew of your half-track plus the crew of Feldwebel Kaiser's A.P.C."

"What do you mean Kaiser and his crew?" Alfonin was sitting bolt upright in his bed.

"The S.S. reported that when they arrived two half-tracks were in the river and there was absolutely no sight or sound of either your crew or Kaiser's."

"I don't understand, sir." Alfonin had thrown his legs off the bed. "We drove into the Ouse, but Kaiser didn't. He stopped his half-track and he and his men jumped out to give us a hand."

"So how did his A.P.C. end up in the river and what happened to Kaiser and his men?"

"The Partisans must've killed them."

"What Partisans?" Von Schnakenberg asked in confusion.

"The Partisans who massacred me and my men in the water!"

"'Massacred?'" Von Schnakenberg repeated incredulously. "I thought that your men had drowned."

"No, sir." Alfonin slumped back into his bed. He suddenly felt sick. Nausea was attacking his head and stomach in waves. "I thought that you knew that partisans had attacked us. I thought that you were going to tell me that you had caught or killed them. In fact, I expected to see Kaiser here today to report to me in person."

"Neither you nor your men had any gunshot wounds..."

"And those of my men who did die from gunshot wounds will be at the bottom of the sea by now," Alfonin said. He suddenly sat upright like a jack-in-the-box. "What about the A.P.C.s, sir? They'll have empty shell cases in them and they might have clues which would lead us to our attackers!"

"The S.S. has them," Von Schnakenberg said bitterly.

"What!"

"When Army patrols turned up at the scene of the crime the following morning the half-tracks had gone."

"I don't believe it," Alfonin was completely gob smacked.

"Well, you'd better believe it." Von Schnakenberg shook his head in sympathy. He could remember exactly how he felt when he was told. "Disappeared. Neither sign nor trace of them. The S.S. maintain that our two A.P.C.s were still there when they left the scene at midnight." Von Schnakenberg punched his thigh in frustration. "We know that they have them and they know that we know that they have them. The infuriating thing is that we don't have any proof that they have them. And the bastards know it! They will have repainted them by now and removed all Army identification that would link them to the Potsdam Grenadiers."

"Does Schuster know?"

"What do you think, Nicky?" Von Schnakenberg said. "It was probably his idea! Or his lapdog, Zorn's. It doesn't really matter. The question is: What are we going to do about it?"

"I've told Edinburgh about the death of Ivanhoe and I've told them that there's a very strong possibility that he was betrayed and killed by someone that he contacted," Ansett said to the boys. They were all sitting and standing in their customary positions in his classroom.

"More than a very strong possibility." Sam emphasized. "More like a definite, one hundred percent, water tight, possibility."

"Anyway," Ansett continued, ignoring Sam's attempt to correct him. "Edinburgh has ordered us to keep a low profile and that means you boys," he pointed his pipe at Alan and Sam. "No more personal vendettas, alright? That's an order. Understood?"

"Yes, sir," the boys answered in unison.

"Edinburgh has also confirmed what we had already suspected," Ansett carried on, "something big is brewing. What day is April 23rd?"

"Shakespeare's birthday," Alan answered.

"Correct, Alan." Ansett was genuinely impressed. "We'll make a scholar of you yet. What else?" Ansett pressed.

"St. George's Day," Alan said.

"Correct again!" Ansett laughed. "Give the man a coconut! And guess who's coming to dinner?"

Ansett's question was met with blank faces and shrugged shoulders.

"Reichsstatthalter Scheimann, head of the German Occupation Authority and Prime Minister Sir Oswald Mosley, leader of the Government of National Unity." Ansett announced the news like a butler announcing their arrival at a ball.

"Blimey! The Leader himself!" Sam was thunderstruck.

"Il Duce," Alan added in a daze.

"They will be visiting Hereward on April 23rd, St.George's Day."

"And what are our orders?" Alan asked.

"We are to stand by and await further instructions," Ansett answered. "So we'll do just that," he said with pursed lips. Ansett looked as if he had been sucking a lemon. "No hell raising of your own, boys, alright?"

"Yes, sir," Sam saluted. "Message received and understood."

"I hope so, lads." And Ansett really did hope so. Sam was a loose cannon. He didn't trust Sam as far as he could throw him. There was no way of knowing if Sam's promise was sincere. No way of knowing, that is, until his next wanton act of death and destruction. "Dismissed."

Ansett watched the two boys leave. He had work to do. Ivanhoe had come to Hereward specifically to set up another fighting group for the express purpose of helping to deal with the proposed visit on April 23rd. Ansett now had to step into dead man's shoes and complete Ivanhoe's mission of recruiting and setting up another cell.

Sam and Alan carried on with their studies at school five days per week and with their duties with the Specials one night per week. They followed Ansett's orders to keep a low profile. Sam carried out his instructions under duress with much mumbling and grumbling. Alan noticed how Sam always put his hand on the butt of his revolver whenever Germans approached. He knew that Sam had an itchy trigger finger and it was only through an immense effort of will and self control that he was able to suppress the urge to whip out his six shooter and blaze away like Wyatt Earp at the OK Corral. Alan, on the other side, was positively relieved to receive the order to stand down. He welcomed the chance to have a breather and relax. He was glad that he did not have to constantly worry about being dragged into some ill conceived, spontaneous life threatening caper thought up on the spur of the moment by Sam. Although the Uprising continued with further incidents throughout the day and night, Sam and Alan played no further part in them.

Ansett started recruiting immediately. He remembered that the boys had recommended the services of Sergeant Jock MacDonald. He also remembered that the boys had said that MacDonald had killed a wounded German on what they referred to as their own 'Private Guy Fawkes Party' on the evening prior to 'Bloody Wednesday.' They had also told him that MacDonald had won a Military Cross during the Great War whilst serving in the Ross shire Highlanders. He sounded like a useful man to have around.

Ansett approached him at home and matter of factly asked him whether he would like to join. He couldn't see the point of beating around the bush. When MacDonald asked Ansett how he could prove that his offer was genuine Ansett replied that he should choose a message that Ansett would arrange to have played on the B.B.C MacDonald chose "Campbelltown Loch I wish you were whiskey."

The message was played on the B.B.C. at 9 p.m. the following evening. Ansett returned to visit MacDonald the next morning. They sealed the deal with a manly bone crunching handshake, a dram of whiskey and a toast to the King. It was the 21st of February. Approximately eight weeks until the visit. Ansett asked MacDonald to recruit one more member of the group. He would return in two weeks time to confirm that MacDonald had carried out his orders.

"So the arrangement is that the Army is responsible for the security of Reichsstatthalter Scheimann and Prime Minister Mosley for the duration of their journey between London and Hereward. However, as soon as the convoy reaches Hereward it becomes the responsibility of the S.S." Von Schnakenberg explained to the assembled officers of his brigade packed together in Hereward Cathedral Hall. "General Fruenkel's Division is responsible for the security of the convoy between London and Cambridge." He pointed with a captured British Army Officer's swagger stick at a giant map pinned to a blackboard. "Our Brigade is responsible for the security of the convoy between Cambridge and Hereward. Brigadefuhreur Schuster's Brigade is responsible for security within Hereward itself. Any questions, gentlemen?" Von Schnakenberg asked the crowd.

A dozen hands went up at once.

"Hauptmann Alfonin?" Alfonin had been recently promoted to fill the dead man's shoes of his company commander who had been killed during a weekend visit to London.

"Why aren't we sharing responsibility with the S.S. for security in Hereward?" Alfonin asked. "Why is everything split up?"

"The Reichsstatthalter felt that one of the factors that contributed to the 'Remembrance Day Massacre' was the fact that security had been split between the S.S. the Luftwaffe and the Army. He felt that it would be more effective both from an administrative and security point of view if one service was given a specific area of responsibility."

Muttering and murmuring swept through the Hall. Everyone knew that Reichsstatthalter Scheimann was a serving S.S. officer and it had not escaped anyone's notice that the 'one service' in question was, not surprisingly, the S.S. It was common knowledge that Scheimann, Himmler, Schuster and Hitler himself were all old party comrades from the Munich Beer Hall Putsch days. This was an example of cronyism and nepotism at its worse.

Another question from the floor.

"Why are they visiting Hereward, sir?"

"Another good question, Hauptmann. It has probably not escaped your notice that there has been rather a lot of building work going on in Hereward recently, particularly within the grounds of St. John's Academy. Does anyone here know why?"

It was obvious from the lack of response that they did not.

"As you know," von Schnakenberg continued, "the Fuhrer has only visited England once, when he came to London shortly after our forces reached the Scottish Border in October last year..." Von Schnakenberg paused for dramatic effect. He wanted to let the tension build. He knew that the audience was on tenterhooks. "The Fuhrer decided a long time ago, months before the Invasion took place, possibly years before the War actually started, that if we ever went to war against England and, God willing, won then he would want an official residence somewhere in the country." He paused again. Von Schnakenberg was enjoying his role. "He has chosen a place for his official residence. The Fuhrer has chosen Hereward!"

Conversation flowed across the congregation like a

Mexican wave from the front of the crowded hall to the rear and back again.

"The Reichsstatthalter and Prime Minister Mosley will inspect the Fuhrer's Official Residence in England at St. John's Academy on April 23rd, St. George's Day."

Chatter dramatically increased throughout the Hall, rebounding off the walls as the assembled officers digested the news and let it sink in.

Von Schnakenberg ploughed on. He knew that what he was about to say would blow the assembled Officers away. "The Fuhrer himself will visit Hereward on September 27th, the anniversary of Operation Sealion."

During the next week Ansett approached and recruited a second man to the fighting group, David Mair, an ex-Physics teacher at St. John's and also a former Officer in the Royal Signals who had served during the Great War. Mair had been a Captain in Hook's Home Guard Battalion, but had been bed ridden with a severe migraine attack when the Fusiliers had marched out of Hereward. Ansett had found him only too keen to volunteer for further hazardous duties. Like other men who had watched their friends and comrades die, Mair experienced a strange feeling of guilt that he had survived whilst others had perished. Ansett could almost see the weight lift from Mair's shoulders as he cheerfully volunteered to once again risk life and limb. As with MacDonald, Ansett asked Mair to recruit another member of the group. Ansett would return in one week's time, on March 7th to confirm that Mair had carried out his orders.

Chapter Nineteen

Von Schnakenberg allocated the three units under his command three specific areas of responsibility to be covered during the convoy's journey from Cambridge to Hereward. Oberstleutnant Dahrendorf's motorcycle Battalion was responsible for providing motorcycle, A.P.C. and truck borne troops to escort the convoy. Oberstleutnant Rohm's Potsdam Grenadiers were responsible for guarding villages and towns along the route and supplementing and reinforcing the garrisons that were already there. Oberleutnant Todt's Oberschutzen Jaeger Regiment was responsible for guarding isolated houses and pubs, farms and hamlets and the general countryside along the route.

Dahrendorf remarked that it was a shame that Schuster and the S.S. would get all of the credit if the visit was a success. Rohm pointed out that Schuster and the S.S. would also get all of the blame if the visit was a failure. Von Schnakenberg wasn't willing to put any money on it, but he was pretty sure that Rohm had had a mischievous glint in his eye as he had made that observation. It seemed that von Schnakenberg was not the only one who wanted to rain on Schuster's parade.

On March 7th Ansett returned to visit MacDonald. He informed Ansett that he had successfully recruited another member for the fighting group. Before he could continue, Ansett interrupted him and told MacDonald that he didn't want to know who the new recruit was. MacDonald cottoned on pretty quickly. He realized that he would have to think in a completely new way. His every thought and action would have to be governed by one word-security. Ansett told him that he and the other group member should stand by for further orders.

Ansett then went to see Mair. He told Ansett that he had not managed to recruit the person whom he had wanted to. Ansett told him that he would return in one week's time on the 14th of March. If Mair had not managed to recruit another member by that date then Ansett would have to do so himself. Ansett was aware of the risk of Mair being forced to work with someone who might be a complete stranger to him, but he was also conscious of the fact that he was rapidly running out of time. It was only six weeks until the St. Georges Day visit on April 23rd.

"What's happening within Hereward itself on the day of the visit?" Alan asked.

"There will be a platform built in front of the Town Hall where Reichsstatthalter Scheimann and Mosley will sit..." Ansett began.

"They're going to build a platform right where they built the gallows in January?" Sam asked incredulously.

"Christ!" Alan exclaimed. "That's in damn bad taste."

"The Germans have never been noted for their sensitivity, lads," Robinson remarked dryly.

The boys both turned to look at Robinson. They were

surprised at what he had said. In fact, they were surprised that he had spoken at all. Robinson was a man of few words and Alan and Sam had had very little contact with him since the 'Remembrance Day Massacre,' despite the fact that he was the School Janitor. Never the less, the boys were glad to have Robinson along. He was loyal, dependable and completely and utterly ruthless. Plus, there was safety in numbers. Robinson had proved his worth through his high body count in November.

"Scheimann and Mosley will inspect an Honour Guard made up of a company of S.S. a company of Police and a company of Specials. There will then be a Medal ceremony, a General Salute and a march past complete with an S.S. Military Band." Ansett explained.

"Should be quite a parade," Alan commented.

"Sergeant MacDonald," Ansett continued, "Alan and your good self, Sam, are going to be presented with medals for the part that you played in the ferocious shoot out between the terrorists and your gallant comrades in the S.S. on the evening prior to Bloody Wednesday.

Sam seemed to grow an extra couple of inches. "About bloody time," Sam said as he puffed out his chest like a peacock. "It's about bloody time that they showed a bit of appreciation around here."

"Poor young Bill Lindsdell will also be presented with a posthumous medal," Ansett added.

"The Jerries are really milking this incident for propaganda purposes," Alan observed.

"Both of you boys will command a platoon of Specials during the parade," Ansett continued. "MacDonald will command a small section of policemen who will act as Mosley's bodyguard on the platform."

"What are our orders regarding Scheimann and Mosley?" Alan asked.

"Kill them all."

Mason was eating lunch when he saw the familiar figure approaching. Several of the boys and girls stopped to chat to him as he walked through the school gates. David Mair had been a popular and well respected teacher and many a tear had been shed when he had announced his retirement. He had taught at St. John's for nearly twenty years and he was like a piece of the woodwork. No one was more disappointed that Mair was retiring than Mason. Mair had taken him under his wing when Mason had first joined the school ten years before. Mair had been his mentor and Mason remembered with fondness the many times that he had been invited to join David, his wife, Sarah and their daughter, Anne, for picnics, lunches and dinners.

So it was with genuine pleasure that he opened the door and waited for Mair to arrive.

"Afternoon, David," Mason said as he stretched out his hand in welcome. "This is a pleasant surprise."

"Hallo, Paul," Mair replied as he shook Mason's hand and entered his house.

"To what do I owe this unexpected visit?"

"I'm afraid that this is not a social call," Mair said grimly. "I think that you'd better sit down."

The rifle butts smashed against the front door. The door crumpled under the relentless barrage and splintered into a thousand pieces onto the wooden floor. A section of soldiers swept through the ground floor room like a troupe of whirling dervishes whilst another section raced upstairs. A half section stood guard outside the front door in the garden whilst another half section waited outside the back door incase anyone tried to escape.

Mair woke with a start as the door disintegrated.

"David! What is it?" Sarah shouted as she clutched her bedclothes against her.

A scream pierced through the night. "Anna!" Mair leapt off his bed and raced out of the door. A rifle butt slammed straight into his face. He collapsed to the floor and lay in a groaning and bloody heap. Sarah screamed. Four soldiers stepped over Mair's inert form and entered the bedroom. They were led by a young officer.

"Pick him up," the officer ordered curtly. Two of the soldiers did so whilst the other two covered Mair and his distraught wife with their weapons.

"Mr. Mair?" The officer asked in well spoken English.

"Yes," Mair groaned through broken teeth and bleeding gums.

"We're taking you into protective custody. If you don't resist then no harm will come to your wife and daughter."

Anne burst through the door, brushed past the soldiers and ran straight into the arms of her father. "Dad, what's going on?" she asked through tear and fear filled eyes.

"Don't worry, darling," Mair replied as he stroked her hair and tried to soothe her. "Everything will be alright."

"Take him away," the officer ordered. Two of the soldiers supported the still groggy Mair under the shoulders as they dragged him out of the room. He left a trail of crimson red blood in his wake. The officer looked at his watch. It was just after three. The whole operation had taken less than five minutes.

Zorn parked his captured British Army Staff Car outside the front steps of the Police station. Zorn mounted the steps two at a time to the Police station and barely acknowledged the salute of the Police Sergeant on duty at the front desk. Ulrich followed hot on his heels.

The Duty Sergeant took them to the cell where the suspect was being held.

"Obersturmfuhrer Halder. How is the prisoner?" Zorn asked the S.S. officer who had arrested him the night before.

"We left the suspect in the cells to sweat it out as you instructed, sir," Halder answered. "We haven't touched him since last night."

Zorn gave Halder a withering look. "I expressly ordered you not to touch him."

Halder came to a position of attention. "He tried to resist arrest, sir. He might have a few broken teeth, but nothing more."

"I hope so, Halder. For your sake," Zorn said menacingly. "Heaven help you if he's too injured to be interrogated. 'A few broken teeth' will be the least of your worries," he threatened. "Open the door," Zorn ordered.

The door opened to reveal an inert form lying on the floor. "You know what to do, Halder."

Halder nodded.

"Carry on."

Halder saluted. "On your feet, you English scum!" He yelled. "Strip and stand in the center of the cell with your arms fully stretched out above your head."

The prisoner tried to carry out Halder's instructions as quickly as he could, but his hands were shaking so much with the mid-March cold and trembling so much with fear that he could only move at half speed. He was absolutely petrified at the thought of what was to come.

"Send in the animals, sir?" Halder suggested.

Zorn nodded. "One minute only." He looked at his watch.

Halder saluted.

Four S.S. musclemen dressed in standard issue physical training uniform charged screaming into the cell.

"Why aren't they wearing their uniforms?" Ulrich asked.

Zorn raised a finger to his lips and smiled.

Halder closed the door as he reentered the cell. Zorn and Ulrich watched through the spy hole as the prisoner collapsed beneath an avalanche of kicks, punches and pickaxe handles.

"Are you sure that this is absolutely necessary?" Ulrich asked Zorn with wide and bulging eyes.

"This is nothing, Ulrich. This is just part of the softening up process. Wait until the Gestapo turn up with their pliers and blow torches."

Ulrich was violently sick in the corridor.

Zorn looked at his watch again. Precisely one minute after the musclemen had entered the cell they reemerged. Their P.T. uniforms were completely saturated in blood.

The suspect lay in a bruised and bloodied heap in the center of the cell. Ulrich involuntarily wretched at the odour of faeces, urine and vomit that assaulted his senses. He upchucked again in the corridor. The prisoner had lost control of his bodily functions and lay in a rank pool of his own mess.

"Ulrich. Pull yourself together," Zorn said to him in disgust. "It's our turn now. Listen to me, Ulrich. You will translate everything that I say, word for word. Understand?"

Ulrich nodded as he wiped the last few globules of sick on his sleeve.

Zorn asked a guard for two chairs, a dish of warm water, a couple of pillows, as many bandages as he could lay his hands on and an S.S. medical orderly. When the chairs appeared Zorn and Ulrich sat down. Zorn beckoned the orderly inside the cell and told him to attend to the suspect's wounds. The medic's hands were shaking as he cleaned the prisoner's injuries. He had never seen the horrific injuries which were the result of a man being tortured before.

"Don't be afraid, Mr....?" Zorn said gently.

The suspect remained silent. Ulrich could hear him painfully suck in air through his damaged lungs.

"No matter...introductions can come later." Zorn said. "Who is responsible for inflicting these terrible wounds?"

"You know fine well who's responsible..." the prisoner rasped through bruised and broken ribs. "Your...your animals..." The orderly began to gently remove the man's bloody rags.

"My 'animals?'" Zorn's eyebrows raised in mock surprise. "You mean Obersturmfuhrer Halder?"

The suspect nodded. The medic began to wash his wounds.

"Halder!" Zorn bellowed. "Get in here at the double!"

Halder appeared at the cell door.

"Is this the man responsible for hurting you?" Zorn asked as he pointed at Halder.

The prisoner nodded.

"Obersturmfuhrer Halder!" Zorn barked. "We are soldiers, not savages!"

Halder came to attention. "Yes, sir."

"We are members of the most civilized and highly developed race on the surface of the planet."

"Yes, sir."

"This barbaric treatment will cease immediately. You will report to me tomorrow morning for punishment. Dismissed!"

Halder saluted, about turned and marched away.

"Thank... thank you," the suspect said through lacerated lips.

"You're very welcome." Zorn bowed graciously. "Now. Where were we, Mr...?"

"Mair. David Mair." The orderly continued to clean his wounds with the warm water.

"You understand that in order for me to help you, you will have to help me." Zorn was the very voice of reason.

Mair nodded. The medic started to wrap his wounds in clean bandages.

"I'm going to ask you a few simple, straight forward questions. All I ask of you is to give me simple, straight forward answers."

Mair nodded.

"Are you now or have you ever been a member of the terrorist organization known as the British Resistance?" Zorn asked.

"No."

"Do you know anyone who is presently or has ever been a member of the British Resistance?"

"No."

"Has anyone ever contacted you with the express purpose of recruiting you for the Resistance?"

"No."

Ulrich waited to translate Zorn's next question. But it never came. The orderly continued to dress Mair's injuries. He was treating him with the same care as he would treat a German.

At length Zorn sighed and stood up. "I'm sorry, Mr.Mair." He shook his head and tutted with feigned disappointment. "I've tried to help you, but you haven't tried to help me. You haven't tried to help yourself. You've given me nothing." Zorn walked over to the dish of now tepid water which the medic had been using and began to wash his hands like Pontius Pilot before Jesus.

"There's nothing more that I can do for you, Mr. Mair."

222

Zorn said with resignation. "Hauptsturmfuhrer Ulrich? Rottenfuhrer?" he addressed the orderly. "Come on. We're leaving."

The medic looked up at Zorn with a half unrolled bandage in his hand. "But I'm not finished yet, sir," he protested.

"You might not be, but he is," Zorn said as he left the cell. "Obersturmfuhrer Halder?"

"Yes, sir?" Halder had been standing outside the cell the whole time.

"Send in the animals again. Two minutes this time."

The interrogation continued throughout the morning and into the afternoon. Halder and Zorn alternating their questioning of Mair. However, Mair said nothing.

"I don't think that your 'Good cop, Bad cop' routine is working, Sturmbannfuhrer," Ulrich said.

Zorn detected a hint of smugness in Ulrich's tone, but he decided to ignore it. There was more than one way to skin a goat. "I hate to admit it, Ulrich. But you may be right," he admitted.

"What if he doesn't know anything?" Ulrich was desperate for the torture to stop.

"My dear Ulrich. Some people may find your youthful naivety an endearing feature of your character. I merely find it annoying. If Mair truly did not know anything then he would've given us a name just to stop the torture."

"So what next?" Ulrich asked rhetorically. He already knew the answer: the torture would continue.

Zorn tapped the side of his nose with his finger. "I've got one more trick up my sleeve." He grinned. "If this doesn't work then I'll resign my commission and join the Vienna Boys' Choir."

Ansett sat back on a chair in the underground bunker. He was stunned. He was speechless. He was flabbergasted. He had just decoded the latest message from Edinburgh. He could not believe the instructions that he had been given. As if their original mission had not been hard enough. He had passed on the information that he had been given the night before to Edinburgh and he had eagerly awaited their response. But never in his wildest dreams or more accurately, never in his wildest nightmares had he envisaged such a response. Not only was he uncertain about how he felt about the new orders, but also he was not sure how he and his two fighting groups would be able to achieve them. That was if he actually managed to organize two fighting groups in time. He was due to meet Mair tomorrow. Mair only had one day to recruit the fourth member. If he had failed to do so, considering the new orders, Ansett didn't know what he would do. The St. George's Day Visit was rapidly turning from a mission improbable into a mission impossible.

"Mr. Mair, can you hear me?" Zorn asked. "Mr. Mair?" Zorn shook Mair by the shoulder. For the first time he was concerned about the extent of Mair's injuries. There was a very real possibility that the beatings that he had suffered might have rendered him deaf, if not both deaf and dumb. Zorn wiped his blood-soiled hand on Mair's rag covered shoulder. "Christ!" He swore. "Don't tell me that those mindless muscle bound brutes have killed him!"

Mair groaned. He was slowly coming to. He had no idea where he was or what day it was. He couldn't remember why he had been captured and tortured. He probably couldn't even remember his name.

"Mr. Mair," he heard the voice say, "There are two people here who would like to speak to you."

"Daddy!"

"Oh my God! What have they done to you?"

Mair recognized the two voices. Then he identified them. Jesus Christ, he said to himself, what have I done? Why did I want to be a hero?

Soldiers formed a human barricade at the door and prevented Anne and Sarah from entering the cell.

Zorn knelt down beside Mair and whispered in his ear. "Mr. Mair, I told you that if you helped me than I would help you...Obersturmfuhrer Halder has your wife and daughter. I've done everything that I can to help you... but if you don't help me now then I'll have no choice but to hand Anne and Sarah over to Halder and his friends."

"You...you bastard!" Mair spat out a globule of blood and teeth.

"Give me something...anything," Zorn urged. "Give me two names. Give me two names and you will join your wife and daughter."

Mair started to cry. He had done enough. He had done his best. He was willing to risk all for the cause. Give up his life if necessary. But not the life of his wife and daughter. Not Sarah and Anne.

Chapter Twenty

The man was walking down the High Street to the Town Square when they took him. An S.S. Staff car screeched to a halt in front of the man and another one skidded to a stop behind him effectively trapping him and blocking off any escape route. The arrest took place on the High Street in full view of the public. There was no attempt to disguise it. On the contrary, the S.S. wanted the good townsfolk of Hereward to know that they were not safe. They could be arrested at anytime and anywhere. Nowhere was unreachable. No one was untouchable. The S.S. snatched the man on the High Street to put the fear of God into anyone who was unlucky enough to witness. Word of the arrest would spread as would the fear of arrest.

Zorn and Halder put the man through exactly the same routine as they put Mair. Halder and his men were particularly keen to take out their frustration on being denied the fruits of their prior interrogation. Zorn and Halder carried on with their 'good cop, bad cop' routine.

The man grit his teeth through the pain. During a brief respite he tried to think. Who had betrayed him? MacDonald? No. He had recruited him more than two weeks ago. MacDonald had had ample time to betray him. He would have done it by now. Anyway, the boys had vouched for him and MacDonald himself had lied and put his neck on the line to protect them. What about the man whom MacDonald had recruited? No. He had recruited him more than one week ago and for the S.S. to get to Ansett then they would've had to get to MacDonald first. But he had seen MacDonald on duty when the S.S. had dragged him in that evening. And he was very much alive and kicking. So it wasn't MacDonald or the man whom he had recruited. So it had to be Mair. But he had also been recruited more than two weeks ago. He also had had ample time to betray him. So it wasn't Mair. Who was it? Where was I going when they arrested me? He gritted his teeth and tried to think clearly through the clouds of pain that circled his head. I can't remember. Christ, they were coming for him again…

"What can we use against him?" Zorn asked himself as he scratched his chin.

Mair. I was going to see Mair. He was going to tell me whether or not he had recruited the fourth member of the group.

Mair had not betrayed him. The fourth man had betrayed him, just as the fourth man had betrayed Mair. Mair had been captured. He had been tortured until he confessed. Mair was probably in the cells right now. Or dead. Yes, Ansett decided. He was probably dead. The S.S. would've had no use for Mair once they'd squeezed all of the information out of him.

Halder appeared later that evening.

"Mr. Ansett, you have some visitors…" Zorn ushered Ansett's guests into the cell.

227

"Mr. Ansett...is that you?"

Ansett recognized the voice. Charlie Bratten...eight years old...the youngest boy in Cromwell Boarding House.

"Mr. Ansett, what have they done to you?" George Hemphill asked. At nine years old, he was the second youngest boarder.

"You ...you bastards!" Ansett growled.

"Give me what I want, Mr. Ansett," Zorn said as he crouched down beside him.

"Mair...Mair...David Mair," Ansett groaned. I'll give you him because you have him already.

"Good." Zorn stood up with a smile on his face. "Now, we're getting somewhere." He turned to face Ulrich. "We have Ansett." He pointed at his prisoner with an unlit cigar. "We have Mair." He lit up, "and we also have the other man that Mair named, Mason." Zorn was not worried about naming names in front of Ansett. Ansett would never have the opportunity to reveal those names. The only way which he would be leaving the Police station would be in a body bag.

Ansett jerked at the mention of the third name, but neither Zorn nor Ulrich noticed. They were too busy playing detective.

"The Resistance operates in four man cells. So we're looking for one other name..." Zorn was thinking aloud.

"Cut a deal, Zorn," Ulrich urged. "You have two boys here. He's given you one name. Release the youngest boy as a gesture of goodwill."

Zorn bit down on his cigar. "I hate to admit it, Ulrich, but that's not a bad idea." He extracted the cigar from his mouth and pointed it at Halder. "Obersturmfuhrer Halder?"

"Yes, sir?"

"Drive young Charlie Bratten back to Cromwell and then return."

Halder saluted and left.

Zorn turned back towards his prisoner. "Mr. Ansett, I'll offer you a deal. One name per child. Charlie Bratten is already on his way home."

Ansett did not reply.

"Mr. Ansett?"

No response.

Zorn was seized by a sudden feeling of panic. Don't tell me that he's dead. Don't tell me that we've killed him. And we were doing so well.

"Medic! Shake him awake!"

The medic shook the crumpled heap lying on the floor. He shook his head. "It's no use, sir. He's unconscious. He's passed out."

"Verdamnt!" Zorn swore. He stood up from his chair. "Alright. What's the time?" He looked at his wristwatch. "Eight o'clock. I'm starving." Zorn patted his belly. "Medic, when Obersturmfuhrer Halder returns kindly tell him that Hauptsturmfuhrer Ulrich and I have nipped out for a bite to eat, a shower and a change of clothes. Tell him that we'll return sometime after 10 p.m. He's not to touch him whilst we're away. Understand?"

"Very good, sir," the Medic replied.

"And one more thing…"

"Yes, sir?"

"Clean Ansett up. He's absolutely filthy. He looks like something that the cat dragged in. I don't want to get any of his blood on my nice, clean, shiny uniform."

Ansett watched Zorn and Ulrich leave the cell through a blood encrusted eyelid which could barely open. He slowly let out a breath of relief. His desperate effort to feign unconsciousness had worked. Ansett was certain that he had been aided and abetted by the medic who had helped him to deceive his torturers. He was sure that the S.S. orderly would have been able to tell whether or not he was faking. For whatever reason, the German had decided to give him a rest rather than to blow the whistle on him. Ansett was certain that Halder and his bullyboys would have hurt him twice as badly if they knew that he was faking.

Mason, you bastard, Ansett said to himself. You're the traitor. You're the betrayer. I should have thought of you sooner. First Hook, then Mair and then me. What do we all have in common? We all are, or all were, teachers at St. John's. Hook didn't enter the school gates to walk through the school grounds enroute to somewhere else. He entered the school gates to walk to your house. The deputy rector's house within the school grounds. Ansett clenched and unclenched his fist in frustration. Because I didn't put two and two together I'm in this S.S. torture chamber. Because I didn't figure it out Mair is dead. And if I don't get out of here then Zorn will squeeze the name of the surviving members of the Resistance out of me. Robinson. MacDonald. The boys. The boys. I can't give him their names. Robinson and MacDonald. They were both soldiers. They know the risks and they'll take their chances. But the boys. They're only children. This is still a game to them. I won't give them to Zorn. I'll kill myself before I let that happen.

"Alice, what on earth is going on?" Sam asked.

"The S.S. arrested Mr. Mair, your Physics teacher yesterday," Alice answered "They tortured him to death."

"Jesus Christ!" Sam's eyes widened with shock.

"And Alan…" she gripped her friend's forearm. "They arrested Mr. Ansett."

"When?" Alan asked.

"Early this evening. About five o'clock."

"How do you know?"

"Mrs. Mair told me when she arrived here with Anne. They're both upstairs now having a rest," Alice answered. "They were leaving the Police station as Ansett was being brought in."

Alan looked at his watch. "It's just past seven. They've had him for nearly two hours."

"He could've talked," Sam said grimly.

"Which means that they could be after us by now," Alan said.

"But if he had talked then the S.S. would've been waiting for us," Sam said.

"They could still be waiting for us. They could be waiting for us right now. Hiding in the houses around us." Alan pointed out of the window. "They might be waiting to see what we do. Whether we try to warn other members of the Resistance." He was thinking aloud.

"They're waiting for us to lead them to Robinson. Christ..." Sam shook his head.

"Alright. Let's give Ansett the benefit of the doubt. Let's say that they haven't broken him yet." Alan meant that in a literal as well as a literary sense. "But they will break him sooner or later. He will talk and give us up unless..."

"Unless we get him out," Sam said firmly.

At 9.05 p.m. an S.S.sturmbannfuhrer and two S.S. troopers walked up the steps to the Police station. The sturmbannfuhrer approached the desk. "My name is Sturmbannfuhrer Schmitt. You are to transfer one of your prisoners, Mr. Ansett, into my custody." The sturmbannfuhrer handed over his orders.

Duty Sergeant Russ Dickson looked at Schmitt's orders and scanned the page. The words were written in German and were completely incomprehensible, but he recognized two names, "Peter Ansett" at the top of the page and he saw Brigadefuhreur Schuster's name and signature at the bottom of the page. "Very well, Sturmbannfuhrer." Dickson bowed slightly. "Everything seems to be in order. If you'd care to follow me." He walked out from behind his desk.

Dickson grabbed a large set of keys from the wall behind his desk and led Schmitt and the two young S.S. troopers down the corridor towards the cells. "Here he is." He stopped outside a cell. "Peter Ansett."

Halder heard the jangling of the keys in the lock. He looked at his watch. Only 9.10 p.m. My God, Zorn and Ulrich were keen. He and the boys had barely had enough time to grab something to eat. Zorn and Ulrich had eaten dinner, had gone to the barracks, showered , changed into a fresh set of uniform and had returned to the Police station within slightly over one hour.

"Hallo, Obersturmfuhrer. You must be enjoying your rest after all of your hard work today," Dickson said good-naturedly.

"What going on here?" Halder asked in halting English as he fastened his belt and holster. An S.S. sturmbannfuhrer was standing behind the Police sergeant. The door to Ansett's cell was open.

"Everything is perfectly in order, Obersturmfuhrer," Dickson answered. "The sturmbannfuhrer here has orders to take Mr. Ansett to hospital." Dickson looked over his shoulder.

Schmitt was surprised to see the sergeant wink.

"Who are you?" Halder asked the sturmbannfuhrer.

"How dare you address a senior officer without standing at attention!" Schmitt exploded. Spittle flew across the room.

Halder automatically braced, clicked his heels and saluted.

"Sturmbannfuhrer Zorn felt unwell after dinner and he asked me to come down here to transfer the prisoner to the hospital." Schmitt's S.S. troopers had an arm each around Ansett's waist and they were carrying him out of the cell.

"Very well, sir." Halder said, his ears still stinging form the fury of Schmitt's ferocious rebuke.

"Herr Obersturmfuhrer! Is everything alright out there?" A voice from the guardroom asked.

"Yes, Raeder. Everything's fine." Halder saluted, about turned and returned to the guardroom. The sturmbannfuhrer spoke rather good English and even appeared to have picked up a Cambridge shire accent. He must've been here since the Invasion way back in September. Or even before September…a long time before September…

My God!

"Scharfuhrer Raeder! Grab the men, grab your weapons and follow me!" Halder ran down the corridor towards the entrance and leaped down the front steps of the Police station.

Dickson heard Raeder and his three men thunder down the corridor following their leader. They emerged in the foyer frantically buckling their belts and making ready their weapons. Dickson waited for the last soldier to run past him.

Halder peered into the darkness. "No one! Where the hell are they? I can't see a damn thing." He swore in frustration. The Square was empty except…there. Four figures. One being helped to walk by two others. Halder jumped when he heard the shots being fired from behind him. However, Raeder's shots had missed; the figures had speeded up and had disappeared into the shadows. Halder turned around and raced back up the stairs. "Raeder, you bloody idiot! I want them alive, not dead!"

Two rounds tore a ragged hole in Halder's stomach and he crumpled up and lay on the cold floor clutching his fatal wound through blood soaked fingers. Dickson slowly walked towards Halder holding a revolver in his right hand and stood over him. His left arm hung loosely by his side. Blood dripped from his fingertips onto the floor.

"This is from David Mair." Dickson shot him again in the stomach.

"This is from Peter Ansett." He shot him in the chest.

"And this is from me." Dickson shot him right between the eyes. He looked up as he heard someone running up the stairs. Dickson raised his revolver and pointed it at the door. Too late, he realized that he had run out of rounds.

"Sergeant Dickson. Are you alright?" Sturmbannfuhrer Schmitt asked.

"I'm alright." Dickson smiled weakly. "It's just a flesh wound." He tried to move his left arm. It stayed still. It felt as he someone had strapped it tightly to his side.

"What are you going to do?" Schmitt asked.

"I…I don't know." Dickson looked at the five bodies lying sprawled on the floor.

"I've got an idea." Schmitt walked over to Halder and fired a burst of three bullets into his chest. The gunfire echoed around the room. He then walked up to each corpse in turn and fired a few rounds into each body making sure that no two cadavers had the same wounds. Schmitt stopped and changed his empty magazine for a full one.

Dickson smiled and looked at Schmitt. His vision was beginning to fog over and his eyelids were starting to close, but he understood what Schmitt was doing.

Chapter Twenty One

Zorn and Ulrich pulled up outside the Police station at exactly 10p.m. Zorn whistled the Horst Wessel, the S.S. anthem, as he mounted the steps two at a time. Ulrich smelled the sickly sweet smell of blood before Zorn and drew, cocked and switched off the safety catch of his Luger in one swift and fluid movement.

"What the hell happened here?" Zorn asked. The foyer of the Police station looked like the abattoir of a slaughter house. Six bodies lay sprawled on the floor. Blood had pumped out to form a huge sticky crimson lake that was already congealing. "Scharfuhrer Maier!" Zorn shouted over his shoulder. "Bring the men in at the double!" Zorn had brought another four soldiers and a medic to replace Halder's interrogation team.

"My God!" One of Maier's men was immediately sick when he saw the grisly sight that greeted him. His vomit added to the mess.

"Check the wounded!" Maier ordered. He cursed and cajoled his stunned and shell shocked men into action.

"Come on, Ulrich," Zorn said as he checked that the magazine of his pistol was full, "Let's check the cells."

Sam and Alan watched as Zorn's staff car and a lorry arrived at the Police station. The boys emerged from the shadows of the main door of the Cathedral and brazenly walked straight across the cobblestones of the Town Square as if they owned the place and had every reason in the world to be there. No one would have any reason to challenge two S.S. troopers lawfully going about their business.

Alan and Sam approached the staff car and lorry from behind. Zorn had not left anyone to guard the vehicles. Sam ducked underneath the front wheels of Zorn's car.

Sam finished what he was doing, stood up, nodded and gestured with an outstretched hand for Alan to go first. They silently climbed the stairs together. They stopped at the top. Ready? Sam's mouth asked the silent question. Alan nodded. Safety catches off.

The boys burst through the door. Four S.S. troopers and a medic were tending the dead and wounded. Maier turned around. Too late. The arc of bullets cut through the Germans sending them flying in all directions to sprawl over the bodies of their fallen comrades.

"Dickson! There! Look!" Alan pointed at the Police sergeant.

Sam jumped over the corpses to Dickson. "Zorn!" Sam shook the sergeant's uninjured shoulder. "Where is he?"

"What the-?" Zorn exclaimed. The machine gun fire echoed throughout the station.

"Partisan attack!" Ulrich shouted above the sound off the shooting.

"What weapons do you have?" Zorn asked desperately. Ulrich held up his Luger.

"Shit."

Sam cautiously came up to the corner where the corridor to the cells began.

"Be careful," Alan warned.

Sam fired a burst down the hall. "Zorn, you bastard!" He shouted. "We're coming to get you! Ready or not!" Sam looked over at Alan. "Cover me!"

Alan fired a burst down the corridor. "Go!" He shouted.

Sam ran down the passageway to the next corner. He fired a burst around the corner. "Go!" He ordered.

Alan ran down the hall and came to a halt beside his friend. "Where are they?" Alan asked.

"They must be in the guardroom at the end of the corridor." Sam pointed.

"Where are they?" Zorn asked.

"At the end of the corridor," Ulrich answered. He fired three rounds down the passageway. "Christ!" Ulrich hurriedly slammed the door.

The grenade exploded against the guardroom door.

"Have you got another one?" Sam asked.

"Here." Alan handed it over. "Be my guest."

"Don't mind if I do." Sam grinned like a berserker.

The second grenade blew the heavy metal door off its hinges. The blast sent metal splinters hurtling into the room catching Ulrich in the face and the chest. The explosion threw him across the room. Zorn and Ulrich were sprawled flat on their backs, shocked and concussed by the explosion. They were choking and spluttering for air like fish out of water.

"My God..." Ulrich groaned. "We're finished..." His

face was a mess of blood, cuts and bruises and his tunic was shredded and smoking.

"Never…say…die, Ulrich." Zorn moaned through broken and bleeding gums. He gritted his teeth and pointed his pistol at the door.

"Can you hear them?" Alan asked.

"Yes," Sam answered. "Police sirens. It won't be long before they get here." He walked up to the door with the Schmeisser butt tucked in tight against his right shoulder at the ready. "We better make this snappy." He turned towards Alan. "Are you ready?"

"I was born ready." Alan grinned.

"Come on," Zorn said. "Get it over with."

"What are they waiting for?" Ulrich asked through blood-encrusted teeth.

Ulrich's question was answered almost before he could finish the sentence. A grenade cart wheeled through the air and landed slap bang in the middle of the room between the two men. The grenade exploded but most of the shrapnel sailed harmlessly over the Germans lying on the floor.

Sam and Alan both fired a burst of machine gun fire as they leapt into the room. Zorn fired his Luger at Sam but the grenade explosion had ruptured his eardrums and had affected his aim. His shots were wide and to the right. Zorn's rounds drilled holes in the wall above Sam's head and caused the boy to duck automatically. Sam instinctively fired a burst of bullets at Zorn, punching into his chest and leaving bleeding gaping holes.

"Let's make this quick," Alan said. The boys could both hear the Police sirens approaching in the background.

"Alright," Sam said wiping his cordite and sweat-soiled brow on the filthy sleeve of his tunic. Zorn looked as if someone had thrown a bucket of blood over him. Sam's bullets had chewed up the floor leaving splinters and broken floorboards. Zorn was still alive. Sam could hear his breath rasping out through a desert dry throat and lungs desperately fighting for air. "This is for Mair and Ansett and the other good men that you've murdered." Sam spat on Zorn's forehead and watched the spittle dribble into the German's eye. "And this is for me." He emptied the remainder of his magazine into Zorn's chest.

"What about him?" Alan asked before Zorn's body had stopped twitching. He pointed with his Schmeisser at Ulrich.

Sam walked over to the last German. Ulrich lay on his back. His knees were bent and his tunic was torn and smoldering. Shredded by shrapnel. His face was a mess of cuts and bruises and the blood was already drying. His arms were bent at the elbows and his fingers were curled up like talons on a claw. Ulrich's breathing was shallow and uneven. It seemed to take an intense effort to inhale and exhale.

The partisan stood over Ulrich and looked into his eyes. The German had never felt such intense hatred before. How ironic, Ulrich thought to himself. He couldn't help smiling as he recognized the terrorist. Sam Roberts. His girlfriend's brother. It seemed that Fate was not without a sense of humour. This was divine retribution, he thought grimly.

Sam looked at the wounded German lying on the floor. He applied first pressure, lightly squeezing the trigger. Sam remembered the first time that he had met Ulrich. At the New Year Eve Party in the Cathedral Hall. When he had learned that Alice was a Hun whore. But MacDonald had told him how Ulrich had begged and pleaded for Mrs. Mair and her daughter, Anne, to be spared when Zorn had wanted them to be thrown to the wolves. He had risked his life to prevent Anne and Sarah Mair from being given to the S.S. torturers to be raped and murdered. What did many people say-the only good German is a good German?

Sam released the pressure on the trigger and knelt down. He lowered his mouth to Ulrich's ear. "Ulrich," he whispered, "I want you to remember this moment." Sam stood up.

"What the hell do you think you're doing?" Alan was completely flabbergasted. "Kill him and let's get out of here."

"No. Let's go." Sam turned to walk towards the door.

Alan swore dismissively and raised his Schmeisser to his shoulder but as he pulled the trigger Sam knocked the barrel out of the way sending the bullets thudding into the back wall.

"No," Sam said sternly, pushing Alan's machine gun towards the floor. "For Alice," he whispered in his friend's ear.

"Alright," Alan turned on his safety catch. "For Alice. I hope that your act of mercy doesn't come back to haunt us. I just hope that you know what you're doing."

So do I, Sam thought to himself. He nodded his head. "Come on. The Police are here. Let's go." He walked over to Zorn and bent down.

"What are you doing?"

Sam straightened up. He had dipped his fingers in Zorn's blood.

"They're friends. It's alright." Mason called to his men. "They're Germans." The Specials responded by blowing out a collective sigh of relief, uncocking their revolvers and switching on their safety catches.

Mason was sheltering behind Zorn's staff car. Two German soldiers staggered out with their hands and weapons raised above their heads. Mason couldn't help grimacing at the sight of them. They looked a bloody mess. Their faces, uniforms and hands were smeared with blood, gunpowder, soot and dirt.

"What happened?" Mason asked as the soldiers staggered down the stairs.

"Terrorist attack," one of the Germans answered. "There are dead and wounded men inside."

The soldiers lurched past Mason. "Sergeant Anderson!"

"Sir?"

"Call the hospital. Get some ambulances here immediately."

"Yes, sir!"

"Come on." Mason cocked his revolver, switched off the safety catch and led his men in at the double.

"Bloody hell!" One of the Specials swore as they entered the reception area. The room resembled the inside of an abattoir. It looked as if a mad artist had splashed buckets of blood all over the walls. The Specials had to tread carefully in order to avoid stepping on the writhing and wriggling bodies.

"Sergeant Dickson!" Mason rushed over to the injured policeman lying in the corner. An S.S. medic lay sprawled across the sergeant's legs. Mason pushed the dead German off and knelt down beside him. He gently shook Dickson's shoulder. Dickson's eyelids slowly flickered open.

"What happened?" Mason gently asked.

"Terrorist attack…" Dickson croaked.

"Who were they? Did you recognize any of them?"

Dickson remembered the last words of Schmitt, the S.S. sturmbannfuhrer who spoke English uncannily well. "Dressed as German soldiers…"

"'Dressed as German soldiers?'" Mason repeated

241

incredulously. He rocked back on his heels as if he had been slapped across the face. He raced to the entrance and jumped down the steps. But the soldiers were nowhere to be seen. They had disappeared into the darkness.

"Walker!" Mason shouted to a Special standing beside a Police car. "Did you see where those Jerries went?"

"No, sir." Walker shook his head.

Mason saw an S.S. Staff car approaching. 'Real' Germans this time. He recognized the pennants fluttering from the aerial as the car pulled up to a stop beside him. Mason snapped to attention and saluted as the passenger emerged.

"Good evening, Inspector Mason." Brigadefuhrer Schuster returned the salute and shook Mason's hand.

"Good evening, sir."

"What's going on here?"

"Terrorist attack, sir."

"Casualties?"

"All of the dead are German, sir. S.S. Another S.S. trooper is wounded and also a policeman."

"My God," Schuster said as he watched a pair of stretcher bearing Specials carry out a torn and tattered body. "What a mess."

"Yes, sir. My men are bringing out the wounded now." Mason looked toward the Police station steps. Two of his men were helping Dickson to walk down the steps.

"Where's my man?" Schuster asked.

"Still inside, sir. They'll be bringing him out next."

Schuster nodded grimly. He watched as the injured policeman walked down the steps with his colleagues supporting him. Come on, where's my man? He asked himself. I must remind Mason to bring out German wounded and dead first and then British. He idly glanced at another car, which was parked at the bottom of the steps.

At first he had thought that it was a Police car, but then he had noticed the solitary pennant hanging limply from the aerial. S.S. And the car itself. A captured British Army staff car. He recognized the number plate. My God. Zorn. My evil apprentice. What the hell was he doing here? Up to no good, I suspect. Best to keep a lid on it whatever it is. The less people who know the better. "Inspector Mason. Please leave my man. We'll take over now."

"As you wish," Mason said curtly with a slight bow.

Schuster turned to his aide-de-camp. "Sturmbannfuhrer Hassell, Sturmbannfuhrer Zorn may well be one of the casualties. We can't afford to wait for the ambulances. Please take him to the hospital yourself."

"Yes, sir." Hassell started bellowing orders.

Two policemen emerged from the main entrance carrying a wounded man on a stretcher.

"There he is," Hassell said. Two S.S. troopers exchanged places with the policemen "Wait a minute," Hassell ordered. He pulled back a piece of material that had been draped over the injured man's face. He turned around to face Schuster. "It's not Zorn, sir. It's Hauptsturmfuhrer Ulrich."

Schuster slowly nodded. "Get him in the car, anyway. Where is Zorn?" "

The explosion lifted Zorn's car a metre off the ground and sent shrapnel, splinters of hot metal and glass flying in all directions. Schuster was thrown forwards onto his front as a tidal wave of heat hit him in the back. One of the S.S. stretcher-bearers fell to the ground and wriggled and writhed as he clutched his throat, vainly trying to stem a stream of blood that flowed out between his fingers. The other stretcher-bearer lay curled up on his side in the foetal position holding his stomach as he tried to stop his intestines from spilling out onto the pavement. All that remained of

Hassell was a smoking and smouldering hunk of burnt meat covered in the tattered and torn remains of a uniform.

Schuster slowly raised his left hand to the back of his head. His ears were ringing and he was finding it difficult to focus properly. His hand touched skin. The blast must have burnt off some of his hair. His flesh was raw and tender. He brought his hand round to his face. The back of his hand was bleeding. Schuster slowly pushed himself up onto his knees and gradually stood up. He felt like a tired and crippled old man. Stricken with arthritis. He turned around. Zorn's car was a burning wreck. A simmering rag covered corpse lay where Hassell had been standing. One of his S.S. troopers lay on his back with arms and legs spread akimbo like a crucified starfish. The other stretcher-bearer had stopped struggling. His steaming entrails lay coiled beside him like a pile of wet and sticky rope. Moans and groans came from all around. Schuster was surrounded by a sea of dead and dying police, Specials and S.S.

Schuster unbuttoned his holster with trembling hands of shock and hatred. He slowly drew out and cocked his Luger. He switched off the safety catch with shaking fingers and raised his arm until his pistol was pointing at the sky. Schuster howled at the moon like a wolf and squeezed and squeezed the trigger until he had run out of ammunition. The shots echoed around the Town Square, rebounding from wall to wall until the echoes eventually faded into the night.

"Jack... Jack, is that you?" Ansett asked weakly.

"Yes, Peter," Robinson answered as he carefully rewrapped Ansett's fingers in clean bandages. "You're safe now," he said gently.

"Where am I?"

"You're in the bunker. You're in the Crypt."

"What happened?"

"What do you mean 'what happened?'" Robinson stopped bandaging Ansett's fingers. "You were captured and tortured by the Germans."

"I… I don't remember."

"What do you remember?" Robinson was starting to become worried. It was vital that Ansett remembered what he had told and what he had not told the Germans so that they could begin to limit the damage. Had he told them of their secret hiding place? Were the Germans surrounding and sealing off the Cathedral as they spoke?

"I remember being arrested in the High Street…" Ansett started, "… and I remember waking up with the sensation of extreme pain… of hearing agonized screaming." Ansett abruptly stopped talking.

"And then?"

"I realized that the screaming was my own."

Robinson thought for a moment. "Do you remember what they asked you?"

Ansett shook his head.

"Do you remember what you told them?"

"I…don't remember a thing."

"What was the last thing that you do remember?"

"You and the boys coming to get me…that's all.

Robinson looked at his friend with concern. Ansett seemed to have forgotten or to have blocked out most, if not all, of the last four hours of his life from the time of his arrest at approximately five p.m. until his rescue at nine o'clock. Robinson tried to jog Ansett's memory. "Peter," he said gently, "David Mair was arrested and murdered by the Jerries." He didn't have to spell out that he was tortured to death. Ansett would have suffered the same fate if he had not been rescued.

"Oh my God," Ansett moaned. "I killed him…"

he buried his face in his hands. "I recruited him for the Resistance."

Robinson grabbed his friend by both shoulders. "Listen to me, Peter. You didn't kill him-the Huns killed him."

"I also recruited Jock MacDonald."

"We know. Jock told the boys that you had been arrested."

"Things are going to have to change, Jack." Ansett said. Some of the old steel was returning to his voice. "We can't do this on our own anymore. I'm going to be useless to you for at least a couple of weeks…" he held up his bloody fingers.

"Here come the boys," Robinson said. He turned around and picked up his Schmeisser. He cocked the weapon and pointed the machine gun at the trap door in the ceiling. He heard the first whistled bars to "I'll take the low road and you'll take the high road…"

"Hallo, boy," Ansett croaked as Alan started to climb down the ladder.

"Mr. Ansett." Alan reached the bottom. "How do you feel?"

"I feel like someone who's just had his fingernails pulled out." He managed a weak smile as held up blood stained bandaged wrapped hands.

The boys laughed. They were reassured to learn that Ansett had not lost his dark sense of humour.

"What happened to your face?" Ansett pointed at Sam.

"It's nothing…

"I know." Ansett said. "It's not your blood."

Everyone chuckled.

Sam walked over to Ansett. He gently placed a hand on Ansett's shoulder. "How are you?"

Ansett was touched by Sam's concern.

"I'm alright." Ansett placed his own hand on top of Sam's and squeezed. "All things considered."

"We killed Zorn," Sam stated simply.

But we let Ulrich live, Alan almost added.

"Good." Ansett nodded. "I'm glad that he's dead. He was a nasty piece of work. Even for a German. I'd dance on his grave if I could. But I won't be doing any dancing for a while." He looked down sadly at the ruined nailless wrecks that used to be his feet.

"What now?" Alan asked.

"On April 23rd, St. George's Day, Reichsstatthalter Scheimann and Mosley will be visiting Hereward…" Ansett started.

"But someone else is joining them?" Robinson asked.

"Correct." Ansett confirmed. "The King is joining them."

"The King!" Sam stood up with shock.

"The King. Edward is coming here?" Alan asked.

"Yes. Together with Queen Wallis." Ansett answered.

"My God. Kaiser Eddie himself." Sam collapsed back into his chair. His legs felt as if they were made of rubber. All strength seemed to have left them.

"What are our orders?" Alan asked.

Chapter Twenty-Two

The sudden sound of many engines revving shattered the calm of the Sunday morning.

"What is it, Bishop Rathdowne?"

"I'm sure that it's nothing, Mrs. Haves." Bishop Ben Rathdowne patted the hand of the elderly lady standing beside him on the top step at the entrance to Hereward Cathedral. "There's no need to worry."

But he was worried.

Lorries suddenly entered the Town Square from all four corners and drove towards the War Memorial where they screeched to a halt. The tailgates were immediately lowered and Germen soldiers started piling out with their weapons at the ready.

"What's going on?" Mrs. Haves asked.

Rathdowne didn't answer. He quickly walked down the steps of the Cathedral and started heading towards the memorial where a group of German officers had gathered. Soldiers had sealed off all of the exits from the Square and they were preventing anyone from entering or leaving. More S.S. troopers had surrounded Rathdowne's congregation and they were busily shepherding them towards the Town Hall like so many sheep dogs.

"Standartenfuhrer, I demand an explanation." Rathdowne interrupted the officers in fluent German. Rathdowne looked with alarm at the storm troopers setting up machine guns at the exits to the Square and at the bottom of the steps leading up to the Town Hall.

"Ah, Bishop Rathdowne, I presume?" The S.S. standartenfuhrer said. "I don't believe that I've had the pleasure. My dear Bishop, you are of course familiar with the Books of the Old Testament?" Standartenfuhrer Lowe looked Rathdowne up and down as he spoke. He was sizing him up. Trying to anticipate his reaction. "You are familiar with the idea of 'an eye for an eye and a tooth for a tooth?'"

"Yes, of course I am." Rathdowne answered with growing impatience. He could feel a bead of sweat running down his back. "What do you mean?" Rathdowne could see soldiers wading into his parishioners and pulling out men and women. They seemed to be working without rhyme or reason. There didn't seem to be any plan. The storm troopers appeared to be picking on people indiscriminately. Anyone who resisted was clubbed unconscious to the ground under a barrage of rifle butts. The comatose victim was then dragged to the foot of the Town Hall steps and unceremoniously dumped in a rapidly growing pile of unconscious congregation members.

"There's your answer, Rathdowne," Lowe replied grimly. He pointed at the Police station at the opposite end of the Square. Rathdowne could see the dark brown stains of blood that had dried on the cobblestones following the partisan attack from the night before.

"My God..." the hair on the back of Rathdownes' neck

stood on end and the strength seeped from his legs as he sagged onto the bonnet of Lowe's staff car.

Lowe walked up close to the Bishop and spat on the ground at his feet. "Twenty of your teeth for one of mine," he sneered into Rathdowne's ear. "Twenty of your eyes for one of mine," he continued.

Rathdowne tried to stand up. Two of Lowe's soldiers grabbed him by the shoulders and forced him to turn around to face the Town Hall. Ten of his parishioners appeared on the balcony. Two S.S. troopers stood behind each one.

"Watch, Holy Man!" Lowe's sauerkraut breath assaulted Rathdowne's nostrils. "Pray for your God to save your people." A storm trooper grabbed Rathdowne's hair and wrenched his head back, forcing him to watch.

Lowe raised his right arm, stuck out his thumb and pointed it towards the ground. Soldiers immediately grabbed the men and women, pushed them up to fence and threw them over in one fluid movement. The parisioners' cries were immediately cut off as the ropes stretched taut and snapped their necks. Rathdowne felt the tears well up in his eyes and flow down his cheeks in a flood. He tried to break free, but Lowe's bullyboys held on fast. Another ten members of Rathdowne's congregation followed. And then another ten and another. The screaming, protests and pleading of those about to die filled the Square as the death toll mounted. A father and son managed to break through the cordon of S.S. troopers. They started running towards one of the exits. Too late they realized that a machine gun squad blocked their path. The machine gun opened fire and knocked them to the ground almost cutting them in half. More victims followed the path to the balcony until there were so many men and women hanging there that it was impossible to tell where one person ended and another one began.

Lowe turned around and gave orders to another of

his officers. S.S. storm troopers hung the last ten men and women from the veranda and then ran down the stairs and headed back to Lowe at the War Memorial in the center of the Square. Other soldiers standing at the entrance to the Town Hall ran down the sides of the Square and also headed towards Lowe. "Form another line." Lowe ordered. The S.S. troopers formed a double line behind the storm troopers who were still herding the parishioners towards the Town Hall.

The obersturmfuhrer in charge of the double line marched towards Lowe, halted and saluted. "What about the children, sir?" He asked.

Lowe shrugged indifferently. "Kill them all. Nits breed lice." Lowe raised his right hand to his neck and drew his right forefinger rapidly across his throat from ear to ear.

The storm troopers poured bullet after bullet into the remaining members of Rathdowne's cowering congregation. The sound of the soldiers' gunfire mingled with the sound of the parishioners screaming and dying and echoed around the four walls of the Square. The men, women and children collapsed and lay twitching on the cold and bloody cobblestones in heaps and mounds. The storm troopers didn't stop firing until their magazines were empty.

"Cease fire! Cease fire!" The obersturmfuhrer shouted. He turned towards Lowe. "What about him, sir?"

"Leave him." Lowe's voice dripped with contempt. "He's no use to his people. He's no use to anyone."

The S.S. troopers let go off Rathdowne's shoulders. He slumped to the ground and vomited onto the cobblestones. He wiped his lips with the sleeve of his Bishop's cassock and he watched the storm troopers wander amongst the dead and the dying. Rathdowne leant against the War Memorial and watched through tear filled eyes as the soldiers slaughtered the last of those still living and left in their lorries.

251

"My God…" Alan stood still, his mouth hung open with shock and disbelief." What have they done?"

Alice held her hand to her mouth, her eyes brimming with tears. Limp, lifeless bodies hung from the Town Hall balcony. Their hands tied tightly behind their backs, their thick blue black tongues protruding from half open lips, eyeballs bulging from their sockets already turning black. Pyramids of people lay by the steps to the Town Hall and blood ran like a river between the cobblestones. Ambulances had parked haphazardly in the center of the Square. Stretcher-bearers were hurrying from the ambulances to the bodies and bearing away anyone who showed signs of life. Doctors, nurses and passerbys crouched beside the corpses administering first aid to the wounded. Several patrolling policemen and Specials had torn off their lapels, armbands and jackets in disgust and had thrown them amongst the bloody bodies, refusing to be associated with the Occupation Forces any longer. Other Specials and policemen had formed a loose cordon at the steps leading up to the Town Hall and were preventing an angry crowd from running up the steps into Schuster's S.S. headquarters. A mob of hysterical people was gathering at the bottom of the steps and they were baying for blood shouting "Butchers!" and "murderers!" The solid oak double doors at the entrance to the Town Hall swung open to reveal a grim faced machine gun crew crouching behind an MG 42. The crowd automatically took a few faltering steps backwards. The policemen knew that if anyone broke through the Police line the machine gun crew would cut them down like so many chaffs of wheat. More townspeople looked up and they saw another MG 42 crew appear on the balcony.

Alan and Sam raced amongst the bodies frantically

searching for Sam's parents who had attended church that morning. They searched through pile after pile of bodies until their clothes, hands and face were covered in blood and gore.

"They're not here, Alan…they're not here," Sam muttered and mumbled to himself. "Maybe they got away. Maybe they escaped." He was thinking aloud. He was not really talking to Alan. Sam's eyes were wide open and his hair was matted together with sweat and blood. He looked like a madman.

A scream suddenly split the air.

"Alice!" Sam shouted. He dodged between weeping women and mourning men grieving for their relatives and raced towards the source of the sounds.

"Sam…" Alice sobbed. She looked upwards towards the balcony and collapsed into Sam's arms as he reached her.

Sam looked up. Alex Roberts' wide-open eyes stared into the distance towards an indeterminate point. Michelle Roberts hung beside him. Mercifully, her eyes were shut.

"Those bastards…" Sam hissed. "You'll pay for this!" He turned towards the balcony. "You'll pay for this, you murdering Hun bastards!" He screamed at the top of his voice.

A figure appeared on the balcony. Schuster. Sam tried to force his way through the press of people forming at the base of the stairs. "Schuster!" He screamed. Schuster turned towards the source of the sound. "You bastard! I'll get you! You'll pay for this! You're a dead man!"

"What the hell is he doing here?" Sam demanded angrily as he climbed down the ladder to the bunker. He glared at the person sitting beside Ansett.

"He's with us, Sam." Ansett replied calmly.

"Since when?" Sam asked in disbelief. "He's a bloody

traitor!" He lunged at the man. His fingers were curled like claws as he stretched towards his eyes.

Robinson blocked his path and grabbed Sam's wrists. He held them in a vice like grip. "Sam! Sit down!" Robinson physically forced him into a chair. "Sam. Listen. I know that this is difficult for you, but you've got to listen."

"You're damn right it's difficult: I've just found my mum and dad hanging from a balcony!" Tears flowed freely down Sam's cheek, carving a path through blood, filth and gore. "How is it that he survived?" Sam pointed an accusing finger at the figure.

"Sam. You more than anyone deserve an explanation," Ansett replied reasonably. He swung himself painfully from a lying to a sitting position on the bed on which he had been resting. "And so do you, Alan." Ansett paused. "Do you remember when you first joined I told you that Jack and I were members of a four person Resistance cell?"

The boys nodded.

"You said that one of you had been killed during the Invasion." Alan said.

"That's right." Ansett nodded. "But I never told you the identity of the third member of our group. You're looking at him."

Ben Rathdowne, Bishop of Hereward, stood up.

The five figures emerged from the shadows and mounted the steps to the Town Hall. The two S.S. sentries on duty at the door snapped to attention. The S.S.sturmbannfuhrer returned the salute. His four companions followed him through the entrance to S.S. Headquarters.

"Any movement?" The sturmbannfuhrer asked the rottenfuhrer in command of the machine gun crew at the door.

"No, sir," the rottenfuhrer replied. "It's as quiet as a church out there…excuse the pun, sturmbannfuhrer." It was common knowledge that the executed civilians were members of the Cathedral congregation.

The sturmbannfuhrer laughed. "Keep up the good work, Rottenfuhrer." He patted the soldier on the back as he walked by.

The sturmbannfuhrer raged inside. He had never felt such hate before in his life. He squeezed his fingers into a fist as tightly as he could in a desperate attempt to stop himself from screaming at the top of his voice. Screaming for justice. Screaming for vengeance.

The sturmbannfuhrer breathed a sigh of relief as he and his men walked up to the fourth floor. At last. Schuster's office. And with three S.S. Staff cars outside there was a good chance that Schuster and all of the commanding officers of all three of Schuster's S.S. regiments, including Lowe would be inside.

"Ready?" The sturmbannfuhrer whispered over his shoulder as they approached the two S.S. sentries guarding the door.

His team members behind him nodded.

"Are they inside?" The sturmbannfuhrer asked authoritatively.

"Yes, Sturmbannfuhrer." One of the two storm troopers answered.

"Good."

Two team members stepped out from behind the sturmbannfuhrer and they each fired two shots. The rounds from the silencer equipped pistols ripped into the storm trooper's stomachs. They collapsed into the arms of the other two team members who caught them as they fell. The sturmbannfuhrer looked down the stairs. No sign of movement. He looked down the corridor to his left and his right. No noise apart from the continuous chatter of a typewriter. No one had raised the alarm

"Bring them inside," the sturmbannfuhrer ordered. He knocked on Schuster's door and entered. The officers were gathered around Schuster's desk.

One of the men looked up. "What the-?" he fumbled for his pistol. The sturmbannfuhrer's shots sliced into his stomach and the man collapsed in a heap to the ground. He curled up in the foetal position and lay moaning and groaning.

"Hands up!"

The Germans quickly raised their hands.

"Where's Schuster?"

No one answered.

The sturmbannfuhrer fired.

Another officer crumpled to the ground.

"I won't ask you again. If I don't get an answer then I'll execute the whole bloody lot of you."

"He's gone. He's left," another officer answered. "You just missed him."

"That's better."

"You're too late," Lowe said smugly. "Your mission to kill the Brigadefuhreur has failed."

"Au contraire, Standartenfuhrer Lowe."

The colour drained from Lowe's face: the assassin knew his name.

"Schuster is not the target: you are."

The officers standing beside Lowe began to back away from him until he was completely isolated.

"Standartenfuhrer, you are of course familiar with the Books of the Old Testament?"

Alarm bells started ringing in Lowe's head as he broke out in a cold sweat.

"Before the cock crows today, you will deny me three times."

"Bishop...Bishop Rathdowne?" Lowe asked in disbelief.

"Yes, Lowe." Rathdowne smiled. "Luke Chapter twenty two verse sixty one. Peter denies Christ. See how your 'friends' desert you?" Rathdowne pointed to Lowe's companions. They had completely abandoned Lowe and they were backing away from him at a rapid rate of knots as if he was a leper.

"Business first," Rathdowne said. "Gentlemen?"

MacDonald and Smith, a newly recruited Resistance member, fired their silencer pistols at the three remaining S.S. officers. They fell backwards and collapsed in a heap to the floor. Smith and MacDonald exchanged their empty magazines for full ones and turned to face Lowe. Sam and Alan kept guard at the door. Sam covered Lowe with his Schmeisser. Alan kept the door to Schuster's office slightly open so that he could see along the corridor that ran either side of the door. He could also see up and down the stairs.

"Then pleasure." Rathdowne said. He turned with a wolfish grin towards Lowe.

Smith and MacDonald quickly tied Lowe's hands behind his back and slipped a noose over his head. They propelled him through the open windows onto the balcony where they picked him up and dumped him on top of the balcony fence. Rathdowne leaned close to Lowe until they were eyeball to eyeball. He was so close that he could feel the German's rancid breath on his face and smell his urine soaked trousers.

"Pray for your Fuhrer to save you, Lowe. He's no use to you and you're no use to anyone."

"But...but I'm a German officer," Lowe pleaded.

"I demand to be treated according to the Geneva Convention."

"You were a German officer, Lowe and this is what I think of the Geneva Convention." Rathdowne spat once between Lowe's eyes and then shoved him over the side.

Chapter Twenty-Three

The sentries stood gaping and gawping at the sight of the hanging man swaying gently above them. They heard a loud bang and an explosion. A light burned bright red in the black night sky and floated lazily towards the ground.

"A flare." The rottnefuhrer said. "What the hells going-?"

The rottnefuhrer didn't get the chance to finish his question.

A machine gun opened up and cut down the rottenfuhrer, the sentries and the MG 42 crew where they stood.

The soldiers in the guardroom on the ground floor tumbled out of their beds and their chairs.

"Quick!" The obersturmfuhrer in charge of the guard commanded. "Grab your weapons! We're under attack! Everyone outside on the double!" He ran outside the room, frantically buckling on his webbing belt and drawing and cocking his Luger. His men piled out after him in a mad panic, scrambling to load and make ready their weapons.

"Where's the machine gun crew?" The obersturmfuhrer asked. "Christ! They're outside!" He saw the mound of murdered men lying at the top of the steps. Steam was rising from their still warm bodies.

The machine gun rounds raced through the open double doors and drilled a neat line of holes from the center of the obersturmfuhrer's forehead to his groin, nearly tearing him in half.

The scharfuhrer, who was second-in-command, arrived on the scene just in time to see his platoon commander cut down. "Get down!" He bawled. "Keep away from the door!" his men didn't need to be told twice. They huddled behind the scharfuhrer at the side of the door. They were scared but they knew that as long as they kept out of sight of the machine gunner outside they would be safe.

"Scharfuhrer, what's going on here?"

The voice startled the scharfuhrer. He turned towards the source of the sound and saw a sturmbannfuhrer and a small group of officers and men hurrying down the stairs. "Partisan attack, sir," the scharfuhrer answered. "They killed the sentries, wiped out the machine gun crew and shot the obersturmfuhrer." He pointed to the mangled mess of blood and bones that used to be living breathing men.

"I see," the sturmbannfuhrer answered.

"Thank God that we're in here, sir." The scharfuhrer took off his helmet and wiped the sweat from his forehead. "We're safe inside."

Rathdowne and his Resistance group cut the scharfuhrer and his storm troopers down. The S.S. guards didn't stand a chance. Most of them had their backs towards their attackers and they collapsed onto their fronts and lay side by side in a tangled mess of arms and legs.

Rathdowne fired his Verey signal pistol out of the door straight up into the air. Alan watched as the flare exploded in the air, sending bright green sparks flying through the sky.

"Alright. Let's go," Rathdowne said. He stepped out of the door with his arms stretched out in a horizontal position. No machine gun rounds greeted his appearance. Rathdowne let out a sigh of relief. "Alright," he said over his shoulder. "The coast is clear. Follow me." He stepped over the pile of dead storm troopers outside the door and started walking down the stairs. Rathdowne's Resistance group followed him outside and disappeared into the night.

Schuster arrived in time to watch a medic being bodily blown out of his fourth floor office balcony. The man only stopped screaming when he impacted rather heavily with the ground. His body left an ugly red smear on the cobblestones. Schuster issued urgent orders that no one was to check the bodies. They would wait for the Bomb Disposal Team to arrive from Cambridge.

When the Bomb Squad arrived they cut the rope holding the hanging body. Everyone took shelter inside the building before the body was sent hurtling to the ground. Schuster examined the body. It was Lowe, as he had feared. He was the only one of his regimental commanders who had not been accounted for. All of his other standartenfuhrers had been shot. Their corpses had then been shredded by grenade booby traps attached to their bodies. Schuster ripped off the message tied to Lowe's tunic with trembling hands. It was written in English. He asked for another officer to translate. The message read: 'an eye for an eye. A tooth for a tooth.'

During the confusion following the partisan attack no one noticed that the plans which the standartenfuhrers had prepared concerning the forthcoming royal visit which they were going to use to brief Schuster had disappeared. In fact, no one knew of the plans at all, since the men who had devised them were dead and the men who had taken them were not likely to inform Schuster that they had captured them.

In response to the partisan attack on headquarters and to the previous attack on the Police station, Schuster asked Reichsstatthalter Scheimann for permission to equip the Police and Specials with Infantry weapons since it would be the Police and Specials who would largely be responsible for guarding Mosley and the Royals during their visit to Hereward. A few days after the event that became known, not very originally, as "Bloody Sunday" Sam and Alan reported for duty to be issued with Schmeisser machine guns. The boys could not stop smiling at the irony of the situation as they already had their own Schmeissers. In fact, they had several and an MG 42 as well. Schuster tried to convince himself that the tooling up of the Police and the Specials compensated for the fact that members of both Forces were resigning in droves. Some were not resigning, they were simply disappearing. Vanishing into the Fens countryside, complete with their weapons and uniforms, to join the swelling ranks of the Resistance. Schuster rationalized that he was better off without them, the fence sitters and the fair weather Fascists. What remained was a hard-core group of committed collaborators, traitors and pro-New Order British Nazis who knew which side their bread was buttered on. The Winning Side.

Hauptsturmfuhrer Ulrich reported back for duty at the beginning of April. He had been in hospital for two weeks where he had received treatment for a punctured lung, broken ribs and severe lacerations to his legs, stomach, chest and face. The doctors told him that he was lucky not to have lost an eye. Or both eyes. He was lucky not to have lost his life. When Ulrich finally had the chance to look at himself in the mirror he gave himself a fright. He didn't recognize himself. A stranger stared back at him. And an ugly stranger at that. His face was a mosaic of deep purple, dull yellow, bright red and pale white. Scars criss crossed his face like railway tracks on a map. When Schuster had seen him, he had laughed. He had assured Ulrich that he would be a hit with the girls. The ladies liked war wounds, he said. Schuster also told Ulrich that following the recent attack on headquarters and the Police station several vacancies had arisen for senior officers in the Triple S Brigade and it was his pleasure and privilege to promote Ulrich to sturmbannfuhrer. Not only was he officially the youngest sturmbannfuhrer in the S.S. but Reichsstatthalter Scheimann would also present sturmbannfuhrer Ulrich with an Iron Cross on St. George's Day.

"Will your men be ready?" Brigadier Daylesford sat on a rock at the water's edge on the banks of Loch Torridon. The Alligin Hotel, temporary training centre for the Special Operations Executive, appeared in the background through a break in the fog.

The captain sidestepped the question. "You haven't given us much time," he protested.

"I know," Daylesford admitted. "But unfortunately, it couldn't be helped."

"How is the shopping going?"

"They're doing alright. They should have everything that you want by the time that you arrive."

"Bon," the captain grunted. "Then my men will be ready."

"What's this? Roadblock?" The driver of the lorry saw the soldier standing beside the motorcycle combination. He was waving for the lorry to pull over at the side of the road beside another lorry. "Bloody S.S." The oberleutnant in the passenger seat swore. "I don't need this. We're late enough as it is."

The lorry slowed down and parked just beyond the other lorry. The driver could see that it was a Police lorry. Two policemen sat in the cab. It was obviously a joint S.S.-Police patrol.

A hand slapped the side of the oberleutnant's door. "Alright, Oberleutnant. Everybody out. Identification check," the voice said. "Get your men out of the lorry at the double," The S.S. sturmbannfuhrer ordered.

"Yes, sir!" The oberleutnant saluted, opened the door and jumped down from the cab. He quick marched to the back of the lorry. "Alright, men. Everybody out!"

There were muffled moans and groans of protest. Most of the men had been sleeping after wasting yet another unsuccessful day hunting partisans in the Cambridge shire countryside.

"Line them up, side-by-side facing the road, Oberleutnant," the sturmbannfuhrer ordered.

"Very good, sir."

The tailgate banged open and the tired and hungry soldiers piled out of the lorry. The oberleutnant and the platoon scharfuhrer chivvied their charges like shepherds herding their flock. At last the physically and emotionally exhausted soldiers stood in an approximately straight line facing the sturmbannfuhrer.

The oberleutnant snapped to attention. "All present and correct, sir."

"Take out your Pay Books ready for inspection," the sturmbannfuhrer ordered.

Several of the soldiers unslinged their weapons, took them off their shoulders and placed them on the ground beside their boots in order to allow them easier access to their Pay Books which were buried deep within their inside tunic pockets.

The sturmbannfuhrer took off his hat and rubbed his itchy scalp.

The machine guns tore into the Germans bowling them over like tenpins. MacDonald, Smith and Robinson appeared beside Rathdowne and also poured their Schmeisser rounds into the dead and dying soldiers.

"Cease fire!" Rathdowne ordered.

Sam and Alan appeared from further down the road and started walking towards them. Sam was holding the MG 42 that he had looted after the attack on headquarters. Alan followed carrying an ammunition box.

Rathdowne turned to face the others. "Jock and Grant, finish off the wounded. Right lads," he turned back to Alan and Sam. "Let's strip the Jerries of any uniforms and weapons that we can use and pile them into the back of the Hun lorry."

Chapter Twenty-Four

"I don't like it, sir." The S.S. scharfuhrer leaned down from the main compartment of the Sd Kfz 251 armoured personnel carrier and spoke to his platoon commander.

"Why, Heinz?" The obersturmfuhrer asked.

"Think about it, sir," Scharfuhrer Heinz Hirschfeld replied. "We took two of their half tracks, now they want to take two of ours." He pointed with his thumb over his shoulder to the second A.P.C. traveling in convoy behind them. "The Army thinks that it's payback time."

"That's if they are Army," Obersturmfuhrer Kaltenbranner said.

The Army oberleutnant lowered his binoculars to his chest. "Feldwebel Johst?" Oberleutnant Warlimont said over his shoulder.

"Yes, sir?"

"The A.P.C. s aren't going to stop. They're going to try and ram through the roadblock. Action stations. Get the boys ready. Tell them that we're going to let these bastards now whose boss. We're going to stop them."

"Here we go." Kaltenbranner tightened his helmet chinstrap. "Gunner. Heinz, tell the men: open fire on my command."

"Now, Beck!" Warlimont ordered. A soldier quickly drove the platoon's lorry onto the road and swung it around until it completely blocked the road through to Hereward.

"Obersturmfuhrer?" The half-track driver said nervously.

"Straight through, Schlageter! Straight through! Don't stop!" Kaltenbranner ordered. "Heinz! Prepare to open fire!"

"They're not stopping, sir!" Johst said.

"Open fire!" Warlimont ordered.

Rounds raced from the weapons of the Army platoon hiding in concealed positions amongst the trees and bushes that ran along both sides of the road. Most of the bullets ricocheted off the A.P.C.'s armour plating and failed to find their targets. Many of the occupants of the half-tracks wisely kept their heads down and contrary to their platoon commander's orders did not return fire, believing that discretion was the better part of valour. Kaltenbranner's A.P.C. hit the rear left wheel or the lorry and battered it to the side. The half-track skidded across the road until Schlagater, the driver, regained control.

"Keep going!" Kaltenbranner screamed in Schlagater's ear as the A.P.C. screeched past the lorry. Hirschfeld popped up, grabbed hold of the rear MG 42 and poured half a belt of 7.92 millimeter rounds into Warlimont's platoon headquarters group. Feldwebel Johst and the platoon radio operator were killed outright. Warlimont collapsed onto the road as the second half-track screamed past. Soldiers leapt out from the bushes at the sight of their platoon commander being cut down and ran onto the road. Some kept firing at the A.P.C.s as the half-tracks disappeared over the horizon whilst others raced towards the mortally wounded Warlimont.

He clutched his stomach and forced the words out through pain clenched teeth. "Tell headquarters…half tracks heading towards Hereward…partisans."

"Ulrich! Get the Quick Reaction Company ready!" Schuster barked down the phone. "We've just intercepted a contact report from an Army patrol. They've exchanged fire with partisans who are traveling in two captured half-tracks towards Hereward. If we're fast then we can set up a road block before the Army and claim the credit for killing or capturing the partisans."

"Yes, sir." Ulrich slammed down the phone. He ran out of his office, grabbing his Schmeisser and helmet on the way out.

Ulrich raised his binoculars and peered over the top of the hastily erected roadblock. There. Two half-tracks. Heading this way. And what could he hear? He wasn't sure. But it sounded like singing. Yes, Ulrich said to himself. Singing. Definitely. By Christ, these partisans were cocky bastards. Singing at the tops of their voices as if they owned the place.

"Right. We'll see about that. We'll wipe their grins off their faces. Ready?" Ulrich asked.

"Yes, sir!" The obersturmfuhrer in command of the two 75 millimeter IeIG Infantry artillery guns answered.

"Fire at will."

The first 75 millimeter shell tore through the cab of Kaltenbranner's A.P.C. and exploded in the main passenger compartment, blowing the obersturmfuhrer, Scharfuhrer Hirschfeld and Schlageter, the driver, and the rest of the crew into a thousand bloody bits.

The driver of the second half-track swerved to the right and narrowly missed ploughing into the burning wreck in front of him. The rottenfuhrer in charge took a second to react before he opened fire with the forward machine gun.

The rounds whistled over Ulrich's head causing him to duck. Two of the 75 millimeter gun crew were not so lucky and were thrown backwards like bloody rag dolls.

The second 75 millimeter gun opened fire. The cabin disappeared in a shower of smoke and shrapnel as the second burning A.P.C. stuttered to a shuddering stop, carried forward by its own momentum, the driver dead in his seat, burnt to a blackened crisp. Several of the storm troopers leapt over the side of the half-track in a futile attempt to escape. They were all on fire and their screams cut through the night air. The massed machine guns of Ulrich's Quick Reaction Company mercifully ended their tortured cries.

"Still no sign of the missing men?"

"No, sir."

Ulrich stood at attention in front of Schuster's desk in his fourth floor office. Schuster sat in his customary position with his back to the balcony with a lit cigar dangling out of a corner of his mouth and a glass full of the amber liquid in his right hand.

"Let's not beat about the bush," Schuster said. "You know, I know and the Brigade knows that the 'Lost Patrol' are not going to turn up this side of Judgment Day, don't we, Ulrich?"

"No, sir," Ulrich replied. That's because Obersturmfuhrer Kaltenbranner and the charred remains of the rest of his platoon had been towed in their still smoking half-tracks to a forest and had been unceremoniously dumped like burnt trash amongst the trees. Kaltenbranner's Company Commander had informed headquarters that the patrol was missing. It had not taken long for H.Q. to put two and two together and realize that either partisans had destroyed Kaltenbranner's platoon and had hijacked the two A.P.C.s or Ulrich's Quick Reaction Company had blown Kaltenbranner to kingdom come with their cannons. Publicly, everyone preferred to give the incident the benefit of doubt. Privately, everyone realized that this was another example of Germans killing Germans. In Hereward's case, however, these Friendly Fire incidents seemed to be the norm rather than the exception. Official S.S. records would show that Obersturmfuhrer Kaltenbranner and his men were missing, presumed killed by partisans, and not killed by fellow S.S. storm troopers.

It was time. Rathdowne took his torch out of his pocket and flashed the Morse code signal into the sky. All's clear. No Jerries around. It was safe to land.

He heard a whoosh as the glider headed towards him. In the darkness he could sense rather than see its shape. Rathdowne rapidly leapt out of the way as the glider made contact with the ground like a flat stone skimming across the surface of a lake. The glider ploughed up the ground in front of it digging giant furrows into the earth before it finally came to a shuddering halt.

Rathdowne ran towards the glider as shadowy shapes emerged. A soldier ran towards him.

"Welcome to England." Rathdowne stretched out his hand. "Merlin."

"Napoleon." Berreud shook his hand, cradling his Schmeisser in the crook of his left hand. He and his men were all armed with German weapons to make resupply of ammunition easier. Berreud turned to watch the sky. "Here comes the second glider."

Rathdowne and Berreud ducked instinctively as the glider swooped down low over them. "Mon Dieu, he's coming in too fast!" Berreud exclaimed. Berrued's commandos and Rathdowne's Resistance watched with open mouths filled with horror as the glider plummeted towards the ground like a stone.

"Pull up!" Rathdowne screamed.

"He's coming in too steep!" Berreud shouted.

The nose of the giant Hamilcar glider impacted with the ground and the whole glider immediately flipped tail over cockpit and cart wheeled across the field. A massive explosion tore through the air as the glider exploded. Dirt and debris fell to the ground like giant snowflakes.

"What was she carrying?" Rathdowne asked as he got to his feet.

"A six pounder anti-tank gun and towing vehicle," Berreud answered as he brushed clumps of dirt from his paratrooper smock.

"And the crew?"

Berreud sadly shook his head. "Pilot and co-Pilot. What a terrible waste. There's no way that they will have survived that. What now?"

"Get your men onto the two lorries. The Huns may be here any minute."

"The S.S. maintains that Oberleutnant Warlimont and his men were killed by partisans who had already

271

killed the members of an S.S. platoon, stolen their uniforms and hijacked their half tracks." There was no need for von Schnakenberg to mention the name of the S.S. platoon commander. Everyone in Hereward knew of Obersturmfuhrer Kaltenbranner and the infamous friendly fire incident when S.S. artillery had opened up and destroyed S.S. A.P.C.s. It went some way towards relieving the bitterness that the men of Erich Warlimont's company and regiment, the Potsdam Grenadiers, felt at the murder of their comrade. Some way towards relieving the bitterness, but not all of the way. Kaltenbranner's death would not make up for Warlimont's murder.

A murmur of discontent swept through the packed ranks of the assembled officers of von Schnakenberg's Brigade like rolling thunder.

"Gentlemen, gentlemen," von Schnakenberg said. "I understand your frustrations, but this is not the time or the place to discuss these issues. Let's get back to the matter in hand. Let's concentrate on the Royal Visit in three day's time."

The mumbling gradually died out, but von Schnakenberg could tell that his officers were far from satisfied. The oberstleutnants in charge of the three regiments under von Schnakenberg's command had already informed him that they were barely managing to keep the lid on the bubbling and boiling sense of anger and frustration that their men were feeling. Anger at the S.S. for the injustices that they had suffered and frustration at the Army's impotency and the Army's perceived inability to act in response to S.S. depredations and provocations. The feeling had spread throughout the ranks like an epidemic and had even infected the officer corps as von Schnakenberg had witnessed. The soldiers were like caged dogs and the senior officers were barely managing to keep hold of their leashes. The leashes were becoming increasingly stretched and stressed. The oberstleutnants admitted to von Schnakenberg that they didn't know what to do.

The briefing continued, the words echoed around the vast interior of Hereward Cathedral Hall. Von Schnakenberg finally finished and dismissed the men. As the officers stood up and gathered their pencils and notepads, von Schnakenberg shook the hands of his senior officers.

"Colonel Dahrendorf," von Schnakenberg addressed the commanding officer of the Motorcycle Battalion, the regiment responsible for escorting the convoy. "A word in your ear, if I may."

"Certainly, sir." Dahrendorf moved towards him.

Von Schnakenberg waited until everyone was out of earshot.

"Kurt, I understand that you're a Classics man."

"Yes, sir." Dahrendorf smiled. "I studied Ancient Greek and Latin at the University of Dusseldorf before I joined the Army. Why?"

"Who are they?" The gunner asked the armoured car commander.

"Police," the commander answered.

"Not Army or S.S.?" The gunner asked nervously. It was common knowledge that the Resistance often disguised themselves as German soldiers.

"No." The commander shook his head. "They're definitely Police. They appear to have crashed into a ditch."

The gunner looked through his vision slit. He could see a Police lorry with a few policemen standing beside it. The front of the lorry had rolled into a ditch running parallel to the road. It looked genuine and innocent enough.

"Where the hell's Hoepner?" The commander asked.

"He should be right behind us," the gunner said.

"Well, he's bloody well not." The commander huffed.

"They probably stopped for a piss."

"Geiger," The commander shouted to the driver, "pull in at the back of the lorry."

Geiger drove the armoured car to the other side of the road and pulled in about five meters beyond the back of the lorry.

"Alright, lads. Everybody out. Let's see if we can give the Tommies a hand."

"But Scharfuhrer Schillendorf," Geiger said. "What about the new Standing Orders that we should be extra vigilant, sir. Military Police Units are only permitted to examine the identification documents of one half of a unit at any one time. This allows the other half of the unit to keep guard and react if the M.P.s turn out to be Resistance."

"Well, they aren't Military Police, Geiger." Schillendorf hauled himself out of the turret. "They're not German soldiers or even Tommies dressed as German soldiers, they're English policemen, pure and simple." He continued talking as he jumped to the ground. "Honestly, Geiger, my grandmother has bigger balls than you. Stop sounding like an old woman," Schillendorf joked good-naturedly. "Get your scrawny ass out here and bring some rope and the tool box."

"Yes, Scharfuhrer." But Geiger was not convinced.

"Here they come," Sam whispered to MacDonald. "It's working."

"Don't count your chickens yet," MacDonald warned.

The armoured car crew started to walk towards them.

"Good morning, Officers. What seems to be the problem?"

The German's words caught MacDonald and the boys

274

off guard. They had not expected any of the Germans to speak such good English. MacDonald's personal radar began to pick up danger signals: how loudly had he and Sam been speaking? Could the German have over heard the conversation?

"We crashed into this ditch, Scharfuhrer," MacDonald replied. "I wonder if it would be possible for you and your men to give us a hand."

"We'd be delighted, Sergeant," Schillendorf said.

"You speak very good English, Scharfuhrer," MacDonald said.

"Thank you." Schillendorf bowed his head. "I worked as a waiter on a North Sea Ferry before the War." He was pleased that the Police officer had complimented him on his English. Schillendorf relished the opportunity to practice his English and spoke it as often as he could. In fact, he was an Anglophile and considered it a tragedy that Britain and Germany were at war. He switched back to German. "Geiger! Attach that rope to the back of their lorry and then attach it to the rear of ours."

Machine gun rounds rudely interrupted Geiger's actions. He turned in time to see Schillendorf being shot. The next burst of bullets hammered into his chest. "I told you so…" he said bitterly. They were the last thoughts to pass through Geiger's head before his vision clouded over.

MacDonald stood over Geiger and looked into his lifeless staring eyes.

"A job well done." Sam walked up to stand beside him.

Grant Smith appeared beside them cradling the MG 42 in his arms that he had used to cut down the Germans. "Like taking sweets from a–"

A burst of machine gun fire tore through the air. The

rounds punched into MacDonald's chest and lifted him bodily into the air sending him flying five feet backwards to land in a crumpled heap on the road.

"Half track!" Sam shouted. "Take cover!" He and Smith dived to the side as more bullets zipped through the air like angry hornets. "Where did that come from?"

"I don't know," Smith answered as an A.P.C. bore down on them. German soldiers were hanging out of the sides pouring out a wall of rounds.

"Where's Al?" Sudden panic seized Sam and he felt his chest tighten as he realized that he hadn't seen his friend since MacDonald was hit.

A large bang made Sam jump as the captured armoured car's barrel boomed flame and smoke. The cannon round narrowly missed the half-track and exploded behind it.

"Al!" Sam smiled.

But the A.P.C. kept coming. Sam realized that he was not alone. Napoleon and his men had come along for the ride to stretch their legs and to see how the Resistance ran things around here. Now several of the commandos lay beside him and were pumping bullets towards the Germans.

Another explosion. This time on target. The burning wreckage of the half-track burst through a cloud of smoke and gradually rolled to a stop. Several charcoal bodies lay draped lifelessly over the side. There were no survivors. Sam slowly stood to his feet and brushed the dirt and grass from his uniform.

"Christ, Sam. That was a close call." Alan's head peered from the armoured car turret.

"Good shooting, old boy," Sam said.

"Thank you." Alan smiled as he jumped to the ground. "Beginner's luck."

"Grant. Did you see Al's shooting?" Sam asked. But

Smith didn't answer. He would never answer another question again. He lay on top of his machine gun without moving. He looked so peaceful. As if he was taking a nap. But he would never wake up again.

Chapter Twenty Five

Mason shivered. The morgue was absolutely freezing. Or was it something else that made him shiver. Fear? He looked at the two naked and bloody, bullet-ridden bodies lying on the slabs. So it had come to this, he thought. The Resistance had actually started to deliberately target policemen. Britons had begun to kill Britons. The Resistance executing policemen as traitors. Mason sighed. The fratricide had begun. A new civil war. And this one promised to be as long and as bitter as the last one three hundred years before.

An S.S. patrol had found MacDonald and Smith lying beside the road. Their lorry was missing. No doubt it had been hijacked. The Germans had themselves been searching for an armoured car and half-track patrol which had failed to report in. They had found the dead policemen with a note underneath MacDonald's body. It simply said: 'Traitor.' The S.S. had found the burnt out wreck of the A.P.C. south of Hereward. It contained the charred remains of its crew. There was still no sign of the missing armoured car. This was not a good omen. Especially the day before the Royal Visit.

"Are we all set?"

"Yes, we are.," Rathdowne replied. "The convoy will leave London at 9 a.m. and it's due to arrive in Hereward at 12.30 p.m. the parade and medal ceremony will take half an hour and then lunch will be served at one o'clock. The King and Queen, Reichsstatthalter Schweimann and Mosley will have lunch with Brigadefuhreur Schuster and his senior officers, Superintendent Brown, Chief Inspector Mason and senior Police and Specials Officers in the Cathedral Hall."

"Good," Captain Berreud said. "So, no changes to the plan."

"As far as we know," Rathdowne confirmed.

Berreud nodded. "We'll hit them between Ely and Hereward between noon and half past twelve." He patted the bonnet of his recently captured armoured car. Berreud looked at his commandos making final preparations in the barn. They were ready. Berreud and his men had spent the last few days planning and preparing in a barn on the grounds of Rathdowne's Family Estate, 'Woodend.'

Berreud turned to look at Rathdowne. "If anything goes wrong, we'll try and make it back here. Woodend will be the rendezvous point."

"Yes," Rathdowne said. "Contact Arthur on the radio. He'll get word to me." He stood up to leave. "You should get a good night's sleep. It will be a big day tomorrow."

"Yes," Berreud agreed. "For all of us." He thrust out his hand. "Thanks for everything, Merlin."

"Avec pleasir, mon Capitaine," Rathdowne said. "Bon chance et vive la France!"

Berreud saluted. "Good luck to you, my friend and God save the King."

King Edward VIII, formerly the Duke of Windsor, sat in the back of the Rolls Royce with his wife, Queen Wallis.

"Don't worry, darling," she pat Edward's hand, "we're doing the right thing. You'll see. Just think, a year ago you were the Governor of Bermuda and look at you now? The true and rightful King of England! We're back where we belong!"

Edward smiled bitterly. "Perhaps I was foolish and naive. I wanted to do an important job so I allowed Churchill to convince me that my appointment as Governor of Bermuda WAS an important job. But now I know the truth." Edward shook his head sadly.

"Churchill never gave you permission to leave Bermuda to carry out your role as a link between the U.K. and the U.S. I see the hand of your dear brother, George, behind Churchill's decisions, my love."

"I only wanted to help, my dear, but the powers that be wouldn't let me. They have blocked my wishes on every occasion," Edward said as he punched his thigh with his fist in frustration. His eyes filled with tears as he remembered the faces of friends and family who were buried in Flanders fields. He thought of his sister-in-law Queen Elizabeth, the "other" Queen, whose brother, Fergus, was killed in the Battle of Loos. Edward envied him. "All I've ever wanted is to serve my country on the field of battle and die with honour if necessary."

"The powers that be decided that you could not marry me and continue to be king. Your countrymen turned their backs on you, darling. After all that you had done for them. After all of your attempts to help your people during the Depression." Wallis spoke to Edward in the same tone that mothers use to speak to their young children. "After all of your attempts to avert war."

"If there are enough men of good will on both sides

then it should always be possible to come to some sort of a compromise," Edward said reasonably. "I was banished to Bermuda because I dared to speak my mind," he continued bitterly.

"You were the only man in England with the courage to do so, my love," Wallis interrupted.

"The Fuhrer built Germany brick by brick, from the ashes. The New Germany was like a Phoenix reborn." Edward said with admiration. "Herr Hitler assured me that he displayed no hostile intentions towards the British Empire. On the contrary, he saw the Empire as a force for stability. 'Leave us Europe and we'll leave you the rest of the world,' he had offered. What could be fairer than that? The Fuhrer was confident that we could smooth over any potential areas of conflict or friction."

Edward was debating the endless motion: that the ends justify the means. The end being the preservation of the Empire. Wallis knew that a misguided minority of her husband's countrymen considered Edward's 'means' to be nothing less than bare faced treason. They called him the Anti-King, the Puppet King, the German King, Kaiser Eddie. She knew that if the words hurt her, then the slurs and accusations, the insults and the cruel nicknames were tearing Edward apart.

"I know in my heart of hearts that we are doing the right thing, my dear. Britain has to seek and ensure her rightful place in the sun beside Germany in the front rank of the New Order. We have to follow the example of France, under the benevolent leadership of Marshal Petain. Britain has to take the defeat square on the chin and learn from her mistakes," Edward continued. "Unlike the Jew Shylock, Hitler has not demanded his pound of flesh. Britain has to demonstrate her gratitude by joining Germany and France in the coming Crusade against Bolshevik Russia." Edward stated the Government of National Unity's party line, "Everyone agrees that a final showdown with the Soviet Union is inevitable and we have to be in it to show our commitment and support for the New Order and that is why it is of vital importance to our national interest that we raise a British S.S. St. George Division to fight alongside our German brothers in the coming conflict."

Wallis looked up at her husband with eyes tear stained with pride and emotion. It was exhilarating to hear the steel and conviction return to Edward's voice.

"Yes, my dear," Edward said with new found vitality in his voice. "We are doing the right thing. We're doing the right thing for Britain; we're doing the right thing for the Empire and the right thing for the world. In the spring, we will invade Scotland. We will deal with Churchill, our misguided Celtic brethren and the rest of his warmongering Jewish-Bolshevik clique. And George, my dear brother, I will deal with you as well, for we both know that, as Genghis Khan said, there can be only one sun in the sky."

"Armoured car and half track approaching, sir," the A.P.C. driver said.

"Army?" The half-track commander asked.

"No, sir, S.S."

"S.S?" The commander said. "What the hell is the S.S. doing here? This is an Army operation. They don't take over until we get to Hereward." He looked at the vehicles behind and in front of him traveling in convoy. "Hippel, get the S.S. armoured car on the radio."

"Yes, sir," Hippel, the radio operator replied. "Sir?"

"Yes, what is it?" The commander asked impatiently. The S.S. armoured car was fast approaching.

"We don't have the S.S. frequency, sir."

"Oh, for Christ's sake!" The commander swore. "What a bloody balls up! Get me Standartenfuhrer Dahrendorf!"

"Sir, Hauptsturmfuhrer von Pfuhlstein on the radio." The radio operator passed the headset to Standartenfuhrer Dahrendorf.

"Hallo Eagle two, this is Eagle one. Message, over," von Pfuhlstein said.

"Eagle one, this is Eagle two. Send, over." Dahrendorf replied.

"Eagle two, unidentified S.S. armoured car and half track approaching. What are your orders, over?"

"Eagle one, establish contact. Verify identification and find out purpose of mission. S.S. frequency is as follows…"

"Sir, you're on the S.S. frequency." The radio operator handed the head set to von Pfuhlstein.

"Hallo, unidentified S.S. armoured car, this is Eagle one. Message, over."

"Hallo Eagle one, this is Josephine one. Send, over."

"Josephine one, explain purpose of your mission, over."

"Eagle one, we are the Hereward Welcoming Committee, over."

Von Pfuhlstein smiled and breathed out a sigh of relief. Who said that the S.S. did not have a sense of humour! A welcoming committee indeed! There was something else, though. Josephine one's accent. He spoke German strangely. From Alsace-Lorraine, perhaps. Von Pfuhlstein's brows furrowed. Something was niggling him, but he couldn't figure out what it was. Not Alsace-Lorraine, France! Von Pfuhlstein grabbed the headset.

The cannon shell ripped the turret from the Army armoured car at the front of the convoy.

Von Pfuhlstein dropped the head set as his half-track crashed into the back of the armoured car wreck. He fell forwards as the lorry traveling behind him ploughed into his A.P.C.'s rear. My God, he thought. We're trapped. "Everybody out!" he bellowed. Von Pfuhlstein looked down into the driver's cab. The driver was dead. He lay slumped over his steering wheel. Von Pfuhlstein and his men piled over the sides of the half-track.

The S.S. armoured car gunner lined up his cannon on the group of German soldiers leaping over the sides of the A.P.C. The gunner pressed the trigger. Bullets leapt out of the barrel of his machine gun and cut down the debussing troops.

"What the hell's going on?" The gunner of the armoured car at the rear of the convoy asked.

"We're under attack! Spaeter! Contact Dahrendorf!" The armoured car commander ordered. "Kriegsheim! Get us out from behind this half track so that we can find out what's happening!"

Kriegsheim drove the armoured car out from behind the A.P.C. in front of it.

"Armoured car, twelve o'clock, two hundred yards, fire!" The S.S. Armoured car commander screamed.

"S.S. armoured car to the front-!" Those were the Army armoured car commander's last words. The S.S. shell hit them straight on and sent deadly slivers of steel shrapnel whizzing around the inside of the crew compartment cutting everyone down before she blew up from the inside out.

"Direct hit, Captain!" The S.S. armoured car gunner announced triumphantly.

"Well done, Hemphill, but don't get cocky. There are plenty more Boche to take care of," Berreud said. "Now. Where are the King and Queen?"

"What's happening?" Dahrendorf demanded.

"Eagle one is under attack, sir," his radio operator replied.

"Get me the Stuka squadron at Cambridge," Dahrendorf ordered.

"There they are!" Berreud pointed. "Get the first Staff car! We're too close! Back up! Back up!"

The driver reversed the armoured car so that Hemphill, the gunner, could get a clearer shot.

Berreud was aware of the armoured car reversing over the bodies of dead and dying Germans. "Fire at will!"

Hemphill squeezed the trigger. The first Staff car disintegrated into a million pieces. "One down, two to go, sir."

"Five minutes until the Stukas reach the ambush site, sir."

"Five minutes? They could all be dead in five minutes. Christ!" Dahrendorf swore. "Get the convoy to close up with the Advance Guard."

Berreud watched as the doors of the second and third Staff cars burst open. What the hell was going on? German soldiers piled out of both cars. Where were the King and Queen? Mon Dieu. A trap! "Hemphill!" He screamed.

"I can't see them! We're too close!" Hemphill couldn't swivel his turret around fast enough to aim at the soldiers.

A German combat engineer dived for cover behind the wreckage of a burning lorry. He crawled on all fours until he was right behind the S.S. armoured car. He counted to ten and caught his breath before leaping out and attaching a lump of plastic explosive to the turret.

"Where are they?" Hemphill shouted.

"I don't know!" I can't see them!" Berreud screamed. German soldiers were everywhere. They were nowhere. He couldn't see anyone from his turret. They had all gone to ground.

The explosion made the whole armoured car shake. Berreud was blown out of the armoured car like a cork popping out of a champagne bottle and landed in a crumpled heap on the ground beside the road. A second explosion blew the armoured car inside out as the first blast triggered off the ammunition.

"Hemphill!" Berreud croaked through a bloody mouth full of broken teeth.

The combat engineer who had successfully destroyed the armoured car spotted Berreud crouching on the ground like a helpless kitten. "Time to finish the job," he said grimly. He leveled his Schmeisser.

The machine gun burst made Berreud jump. He watched the combat engineer topple sideways with a surprised look of shock on his face.

Robinson appeared beside Berreud. "Come on, Napoleon. We've got to get out of here."

"They're not here, Lancelot," Berreud mumbled through his shredded gums. "The King and Queen aren't here…"

"I know." Robinson pulled Berreud to his feet. "Come on…"

"Hemphill...my men...they're all dead..."

"And we will be too unless we get out of here." Robinson dragged Berreud towards their remaining half-track. Berreud could see his commandos firing the twin MG 42s from the passenger compartment.

"Lewis!" Berreud shouted at the A.P.C. driver. "We're getting out of here! Drive back to the rendezvous point at Woodend!"

"Yes, sir!" Lewis replied.

The explosion sent Berreud and Robinson flying backwards. They slowly lifted themselves up off their backs onto their knees and looked at their half-track. It was a burning wreck.

"My God!" Robinson exclaimed. "What was that?"

Berreud pointed towards the convoy. An Army armoured car was heading towards them at a rapid pace of knots. He watched as its machine gun barrel belched out a burst of bullets that cut down the surviving commandoes from his A.P.C. Realization suddenly hit Berreud like a thunderbolt between his shoulder blades. The vehicles that he and his men had attacked were not part of the main convoy. The vehicles were the Advance Guard. They were a decoy. He and his men had walked into a trap. The King and Queen were a million miles from here.

"Come on. We've got to get out of here." Berreud tried to shake off his concussion. His head felt as if it had been hit with a giant hammer and he was aware that blood was trickling from his ears. His ears felt as if they had been stuffed with cotton wool. He couldn't hear properly and he was finding it difficult to focus. Berreud lurched towards the front of the convoy with Robinson staggering unsteadily behind him.

"How are we going to get out of here?" Berreud asked.

"There. Look." Robinson pointed at a motorcycle

combination that had crashed into a ditch. Berreud and Robinson dragged the dead German passengers to the side and manhandled the motorbike onto the road.

"Can you drive this thing?" Robinson asked.

"I can drive anything with a pack of Boche on my tail baying for blood!"

"Blast! Look!" Robinson pointed from his position in the pillion. An armoured car and half-track were charging towards them. Berreud looked to his left and to his right. A thick forest ran parallel to the road, blocking of all potential escape routes.

"What are we going to do?" Robinson asked.

Berreud thought quickly. They could turn around and try to outrun the armoured car. They might well succeed in outrunning the armoured car, but they would not succeed in outrunning its bullets or artillery shells. "Get your head down and pretend that you're wounded and unconscious." Berreud slowed down as the Germans rapidly approached.

A head popped out of the turret. "What happened?" The armoured car commander asked.

"Thank God that you're here, Feldwebel! Partisans disguised as German soldiers have attacked the convoy!" Berreud replied. "I only just managed to escape! They're hot on my heels in a captured armoured car and half-track. I'm going to brief headquarters on the situation and I'm taking my comrade here" he pointed to Robinson "to hospital. It's vital that I reach H.Q. I want you and your men to destroy the partisans who are chasing us. "

The commander saluted. "Yes, sir!"

Berreud returned the salute and sped away.

"You what!" Dahrendorf shouted. "You let them get away?" He said incredulously.

"I ...I didn't know, sir. He told me that you were the partisans," the armoured car commander answered.

Dahrendorf had seen a motorcycle combination stop and talk to an armoured car and an A.P.C. in the distance. He had not known that the motorcycle combination contained two of the fugitives whom he was searching for. The next thing he knew, the half-track traveling in front of him blew up in a ball of flames. The armoured car traveling behind him instinctively returned fire and destroyed an enemy A.P.C. After much frantic shouting and screeching Dahrendorf managed to arrange a cease fire with the opposing armoured car commander.

"They were partisans, you idiot!" Dahrendorf screamed at the young armoured car commander.

The young feldwebel turned crimson with anger. He had just lost more than a dozen of his men. And they had been killed by fellow Germans. This had not been a good day and it was about to get worse. And now he had been called an idiot by this geriatric fool.

Dahrendorf seemed completely oblivious to this volcano brewing and turned to his second-in-command. "Major Lorenz, where's the map?" He demanded impatiently. Lorenz handed it over. "Two men on a motorcycle. Where can they go?" His eyes roamed over the map with practiced ease searching for potential hiding places. Where would I hide? He asked himself. "They won't go towards Hereward. It's crawling with S.S." He was thinking aloud. "There can't be too many places around here that they can hide. Feldwebel?"

"Yes, sir?" The armoured car commander replied.

"I'm placing you under Major Lorenz's command. Major, I want you to take command of the Rear Guard and carry out an extensive search of the surrounding countryside. I don't want you to stop until you've found them. Understand?"

"Yes, sir." Lorenz saluted.

"And Feldwebel?" If you succeed without killing any more of my men I may forget about dragging your sorry carcass before a court martial enquiry."

risked their lives to save him. Now he would risk his life to save them. He stopped at the bottom of the stairs and looked in the mirror. He brushed a piece of fluff from his tunic, adjusted his peaked officer's cap to a jaunty angle, opened the door and stepped outside.

"Hallo Wolf one, this is Eagle two. Message, over." Dahrendorf said as the convoy raced towards Hereward. They were late and he hoped to make up for lost time. They had been forced to wait whilst his men attended to the wounded and cleared the wreckage and bodies from the road.

"Hallo Eagle two, this is Wolf one. Send, over." Von Schnakenberg replied.

"Wolf one, the partisans are dead, the King and Queen are alive and the convoy is heading towards Hereward. Estimated time of arrival: thirteen hundred hours, over." Half an hour late. It couldn't be helped.

"Eagle two, roger so far, over."

"Wolf one, Bishop Rathdowne is a partisan. Advise arrest immediately, over."

"Eagle two, say again, over."

"Wolf one, I say again: Rathdowne is a partisan, over."

"Eagle STATIC say STATIC…"

"Wolf one, I say again…" but all Dahrendorf could hear was whistles and pops from the other end. "Christ! What's the use?" He threw the headphones at the radio operator in frustration. If only they were in time, he thought.

Von Schnakenberg smiled to himself. So. Rathdowne was a partisan. That wily old fox. So that was why he had invited him and his men to the New Year's Eve Party. That was why he offered the use of the Cathedral Hall as a venue for his Welcome Back Dinner. That was why he allowed

Chapter Twenty-Six

"Sir, Stuka Squadron commander," the radio operator said. "He's sighted the partisans on a motorbike. What are your orders?"

Dahrendorf thought for a moment.

"Kill them?"

"No." Dahrendorf waved his finger. "Follow them and find out where they're going."

Robinson sat at the radio. "Lancelot calling Arthur, Lancelot calling Arthur. This is Lancelot. Come in Arthur, over."

"Hallo Lancelot, this is Arthur. Send message, over."

"Arthur, Holy Grail still at large. Knights dead... Napoleon and myself only survivors, over." Robinson looked over at Berreud. He lay slumped on his side on a bale of hay. He must have been wounded back at the ambush, Robinson thought.

There was a pregnant pause at the other end as Arthur digested the news of the disaster.

"Lancelot, get yourself to Percy, over."

"Arthur, message received and understood!"

Ansett jumped as he heard the burst of machine gun fire.

Major Lorenz stepped over the body of the partisan. It would've been better if they had been captured alive, but… his men were pumped up and full of adrenalin. Dahrendorf would be disappointed, but it couldn't be helped.

"They're both dead, sir." A soldier nudged the body of the partisan who had been shot as he lay on a bale of hay. His smashed and shattered, smoking radio sat on top of the table in front of him.

Lorenz looked at the walls of the barn. "Get on the radio and tell Generalmajor von Schnakenberg that Bishop Rathdowne is with the partisans."

Ansett took off the radio headphones and stood up. He leaned on the table and shook his head. Robinson dead. Berreud dead and all of his commandos. What a bloody disaster. What had gone wrong? He walked with difficulty towards the wardrobe in the corner of the room. There was plenty of time for a post mortem later. If any of them came through this day alive. He selected a uniform. An S.S.sturmbannfuhrer's. He hurriedly changed into the outfit, wincing when his bandaged fingertips brushed against the material. He buckled on his officer's belt and he made sure that his Luger pistol was loaded with a full magazine. He jammed as many spare magazines into his ammunition pouch as he possibly could. It looked like he was going to need them. Ansett looked out of the window of his room. He could hear the S.S. military band playing in the center of the Square. He walked down the stairs. He had to warn Rathdowne because the Germans would know now that he was a partisan. They would arrest and torture him and force him to give up the names of the boys. Sam and Alan had

293

von Schnakenberg to use the hall to brief his men about the Royal Visit. Rathdowne must have been listening the whole time. That was how he discovered the details of the visit. Von Schnakenberg liked the Bishop and he was glad that he had turned out to be a patriot instead of a traitor. Thank God for the Trojan Horse Plan.

As for the other secrets which Rathdowne had over heard. The Bishop would take them to the grave with him. But first things first. Von Schnakenberg saw an ideal opportunity to kill two birds with one stone. Yes. It could work. If he played his cards close to his chest and the gods were smiling.

Chief Inspector Mason was standing on the steps of the Police station tapping his right foot impatiently. The whole parade had been stood down for some inexplicable reason.

He absent-mindedly glanced across the Square. An S.S. officer was weaving in and out of the crowd. He was walking awkwardly. He had a limp. Possibly wounded in recent anti-partisan operations, Mason thought. He was heading towards the podium where Schuster, Rathdowne, the Mayor and the other V.I.P.s were standing. There was something familiar about him…Mason rocked backwards on his heels as if someone had slapped him. Ansett! My God! What was he doing here?

What to do? He couldn't exactly march over and arrest Ansett in public. He was dressed as an S.S.Sturmbannfuhrer. The Jerries had itchy trigger fingers and they would probably shoot him instead of Ansett. They would think that Mason's arrest of the S.S. officer was yet another example of British treachery. O perfidious Albion! What to do?

He needed time to think. What was the connection? Hook, Mair, Ansett. But the Resistance worked in four men cells. What was the link? They were all teachers…

Mason swore under his breath as he walked through the corridors of the Police station. Correction. The Resistance worked in four person cells, not necessarily four men cells. Rebecca Templar. Rebecca Templar must have been an ex-teacher at the school, or possibly an ex-student. Who ever she was, she must have been there before his time, because he had never heard of her. She must still live in Hereward. Who would know about her? Perhaps she had left school a long time ago or she could even have left school shortly before he had arrived ten years ago. Who would know? He was the only teacher in the Specials so he couldn't ask a colleague. Mason walked through the station, chewing the problem over in his head, until he came to the rear courtyard. His men were standing in ranks of three.

"Sir, what's going on?"

Sam. Sam Roberts. He would know. His three elder brothers had all been at St. John's, as had their late father before them. Members of the Roberts family had been going to the school since St. John's had been first established in the sixteenth century. Maybe Sam had heard of her. "Sam," Mason blurted out, "Rebecca Templar. Ever heard of her?"

Sam grabbed his chest. He suddenly found it difficult to breath. Blood rushed into his brain like a tidal wave.

"Sam. Are you alright?" Mason asked with concern.

Sam shrugged off the hand that Mason had placed on his shoulder as if it was made of red hot metal. "I'm alright," Sam answered, rubbing his chest. "It's my chest. This bloody uniform is too tight. I can't breathe properly."

"Well, when this is all over, get down to the stores and they'll give you a new one," Mason said. He was puzzled by Sam's strange behaviour.

"Thank you, sir," Sam said. "I better go, sir."

"Yes, you're right, Sam. You'd best be on your way."

Sam saluted and walked off.

Mason returned the salute. He watched as Sam walked away to join one of the three platoons that made up the Specials Honour Guard. The boy had found his mother and father hanging from the balcony of the Town Hall, for Christ's sake, Mason said to himself. It was hardly surprising that he was not his usual chirpy, cheery self. Sam was holding up remarkably well, considering.

Schuster noticed Rathdowne walking down the podium stairs. What the hell did the bishop think he was playing at? The convoy would be here any minute. And who was that S.S.sturmbannfuhrer that he was talking to? In fact, Schuster had never seen him before in his life.

"Sir!" Schuster's Adjutant said. "Convoy's coming."

Chief Superintendent Brown announced the award of the Police Gallantry Medal to the recently promoted Inspector Dickson in recognition of the courage that he showed during the terrorist attack on Police headquarters.

Sam watched out of the corner of his eye. Dickson now. He would be next. But this time it would be King Edward and Queen Wallis who would pin the medal on his chest. That would be his chance. His only chance to make amends.

Alan looked across at his friend. He was worried. Sam had that familiar mad Berserker one-way-ticket-to-Valhalla look in his eyes that he always had just before he did something crazy. Sam had told him about Mason just before they went on parade. Alan had tried to convince Sam that they would deal with him later. But news had already spread like wild fire about the unsuccessful attack on the Royal convoy. The plan to kill the King and Queen had failed. Robinson, Napoleon and the commandos were probably all dead. Alan knew only too well that he and Sam were the Resistance's only hope.

The explosion ripped Dickson, Brown, Prime Minister Mosley and Major-General Fuller to pieces. Bits of bodies flew through the air and covered the nearest Policemen in a bloody shower.

Sam lay flat on his back and raised his hands to his eyes. He couldn't open his eyes and for a heart stopping moment he thought that he must have been blinded. But then his fingers pulled away a thick layer of goo, guts and gore from his eyelids and his face and his vision was restored. He raised himself onto his elbows. The scene was one of complete and utter chaos. Policemen, Specials and S.S. troopers were running around like headless chickens whilst their officers flapped in a futile attempt to restore order.

"Save the King! Save the King!" A lone voice was shouting. Not Brown. Brown was dead. He had been too close to Mosley for his own health.

Mason stood next to the King with his revolver drawn. He was panting heavily as if he had just run a race. "Your Majesty, are you alright?" He asked.

"Yes, Chief Inspector." Edward answered. "I'm fine." In fact, he was a lot more than fine. He was happy. He was excited. He was exhilarated. He was pumped full of adrenalin. Full of life. He had never felt more alive in his life. He had walked through the Shadow of the Valley of Death and he had survived. Twice. Terrorists had tried to kill him on two occasions and he had survived both attempts. He had beaten them. He was invincible. He was indestructible.

Alan ran at a crouch over to Sam. "Sam, are you alright?"

"Yes, I am."

"Are you ready to do it now?"

"Yes. Let's do it."

Sam and Alan ran towards the podium with their pistols drawn. Sam shot Mason twice in the chest and he fell backwards with a surprised look of shock on his face.

Rathdowne mounted the stairs, reached under his cassock, drew out a pistol and shot Schuster in the back; the bullets exited through his chest and left bloody gaping holes. Scheimann tried to escape, but Ansett shot him before he had taken two steps.

Alan and Sam wiped out the rest of Schuster's dazed and confused bodyguard before they had a chance to react. Rathdowne and Ansett took care of Schuster's regimental commanders and second-in-commands. Edward and Wallis stood aghast as the terrorists disposed of their German hosts.

"Have you...have you come to rescue us?" Wallis asked excitedly.

Edward's face suddenly drained of all colour. He said nothing. He knew why they had come.

Sam shook his head. He aimed at the King's chest and pulled the trigger twice. Edward VIII, the Anti-King, the Puppet King, Kaiser Eddie fell to the floor of the podium. Alan fired two shots at the Queen's chest and she collapsed to the ground beside her husband. The two boys fired the entire contents of the rest of their magazines into the bodies at point blank range to make sure that they were dead and then swiftly replaced their empty magazines with full ones.

"Come on," Ansett said. "Let's go."

"Damn," Rathdowne said. "The S.S. is sealing off the exits." There was a mob of men, women and children desperately trying to force their way through the stormtroopers guarding the four main roads leading from the Square. "We need a diversion," Rathdowne said.

Sam turned and squeezed off a full magazine of rounds at a group of S.S. troopers milling around on the Square. "There's your diversion," he said simply.

"Where the hell did those shots come from?" an S.S. scharfuhrer asked as he sheltered behind the corpse of a comrade.

"From over there." Another stormtrooper taking cover pointed vaguely in Sam's direction. "The Specials."

"The Specials?" The scharfuhrer pointed towards the Square.

"Yes."

The scharfuhrer fired a burst of machine gun bullets at a group of Specials malingering around on the Square. Half a dozen Specials fell to the ground in agony. But the survivors reacted swiftly. They started firing back and several S.S. troopers were hit.

"I love your work," Alan said admiringly as a Battle Royale erupted in the Square.

"What happened in the Square?" Ansett asked

"Inspector Dickson blew himself up," Alan answered.

"He must've taken some grenades from the Police Armoury. He was the quartermaster," Sam added.

"His wife and son were killed on Bloody Sunday," Rathdowne said. "They were two of my parishioners," he said sadly.

"I didn't know that," Ansett said somberly.

"Inspector Dickson tipped Jock off that the Police station was lightly guarded..." Sam said.

"So that we were able to rescue you," Alan interrupted. "Where are we going now?" He asked.

"Percival's," Ansett answered.

Von Schnakenberg stood next to Dahrendorf in the center of the Square. The scene was one of utter death and destruction. Straight out of Dante's 'Inferno', he thought to himself. Specials, policemen and stormtroopers lay in piles and mounds scattered all over the Square. The Police and Specials had presented two platoons of sixty men in total on parade, where as the S.S. had only presented one platoon. The Britons had almost succeeded in wiping out the S.S., but the stormtroopers had been saved by the timely arrival of Dahrendorf's Convoy Guard who were hastily recalled from their barracks. Following the partisan attack on the convoy Dahrendorf's men were in no mood to take prisoners. They had killed all the Police and Specials, including those who had begged for mercy. Dahrendorf's men had also wiped out a renegade S.S. section that was firing at their fellow storm troopers.

"Well, I suppose that we'll never find out what really happened here," von Schnakenberg remarked.

"The S.S. says that the Specials started it," Dahrendorf said.

Von Schnakenberg guffawed. "They would say that though, wouldn't they? The S.S. doesn't want to take the blame for starting this." He spread his arms and slowly twirled around in a circle.

Dahrendorf gazed over the Square and shook his head. "What a bloody disaster..."

"What a bloody S.S. disaster, Kurt," von Schnakenberg emphasized. "We delivered the King and Queen safe and sound, but the S.S. screwed up and got them killed. Just remember this. None of this will stick to us. We'll come out of this clean."

"I hope so."

So do I, von Schnakenberg said to himself. "By the way," he said, "what was the message that you tried to give to me on the radio?"

"Ah yes, sir," Dahrendorf replied. "Bishop Rathdowne is a member of the Resistance."

"Ben Rathdowne?" Von Schnakenberg exclaimed incredulously. "I don't believe it," he chuckled. "In a way, I'm glad," he continued. "I'm glad that Ben turned out to be a patriot and not a traitor."

Dahrendorf came to a position of attention. "Your orders, sir?"

"I want the Bishop dead or alive."

The A.P.C. appeared on the brow of the hill. Rathdowne, Ansett and the boys looked to their left and their right. There were no roads that led off the one that they were walking on for a hundred yards in front of them and behind them. Eight feet walls ran alongside either side of the road. Anyway, Ansett was hardly in a fit state to walk, never mind scale eight feet walls. Alan and Sam reached for their holsters.

Rathdowne put his hand on Sam's arm. "It's no use, boys. We can't fight them."

The A.P.C. ground to a halt less than a dozen yards from the partisans. They found themselves staring down the barrel of an MG 42 machine gun at point blank range.

S.S. Obersturmfuhrer Stein examined the group. He recognized Bishop Rathdowne from the New Year's Eve Party. He had not seen the S.S.sturmbannfuhrer or the two young Specials before. "Hands up!" Stein ordered. The men obeyed. "Perhaps you would be so kind as to tell me exactly what's going on here, gentlemen?"

A figure watched the encounter from a first floor window. Percival had been alerted by the earlier outbreak of shooting in the Square and had prepared for the possible arrival of Ansett and his companions.

"One moment please, Bishop." Stein held up a finger. He switched to German. "Headquarters, Schultze."
The radio operator passed Stein the headphones.

Christ, Sam thought. It hasn't worked. They're going to kill us. He turned to Alan. He nodded. They both reached for their Lugers.

Stein understood. "Wolf One, message received and understood. Out."

The machine gun burst shattered the tense silence. The MG 42 gunner was thrown forwards over his weapon. Stein was shot in the back and fell to the deck of the half-track. A grenade sailed through the air and exploded in the A.P.C. sending two Germans flying over the side. Ansett and Rathdowne strode up to the wounded men and each of them fired twice. Sam and Alan ran up to the halftrack and fired through the vision slit at the driver. The whole episode was finished in a few seconds.

Percy appeared outside the house with a Schmeisser still smoking in her hands. Outside the house. Outside Sam's house.
"Alice?" Sam's mouth was open wide like a goldfish.

"Yes, Sam. Meet Percy." Ansett walked up to Alice and wrapped an arm around her shoulder. He enjoyed watching the look of shocked surprise on Sam's face.

"But I-but I thought that Percy was a man," Sam said.

"Most men do," Alice said.

"How long have you been in the Resistance?" Sam asked.

"Since the beginning. Since the War started."

Sam was speechless. He was completely gob smacked.

"Look. We haven't got time to waste. Huns will be here any minute." She rapidly took charge of the situation. "Ben. What size are your shoes?"

Chapter Twenty-Seven

"They found Stein and his men, sir," Oberleutnant Alfonin reported to von Schnakenberg. "Dead in their half track."

"And Bishop Rathdowne?"

"Dead as well, sir. Together with an S.S.sturmbannfuhrer and two Specials."

"Did you manage to identify them, Nicky?"

Alfonin shook his head. "Impossible, sir. The A.P.C. was a smoking and smouldering wreck when one of our patrols found it. The bodies of Stein and his men were burnt beyond recognition. It's difficult to even tell how many men were in the half-track. Rathdowne and the rest were shot in the back of the head at point blank range. The rounds nearly knocked their heads off. Their own mothers weren't recognize them."

Von Schnakenberg grimaced at the image that Alfonin's words conjured. He knew all too well the terrible damage that a bullet could do to a person's face at a close distance. "Were they executed?"

"It appears that they might well have been, sir."

"By Stein?"

"Or by the Resistance. God knows the bastards have been busy today, sir."

Von Schnakenberg nodded. "I guess that we'll never know." He shrugged his shoulders with resignation.. "Was it a routine patrol which found them?"

"No, sir. Someone contacted headquarters anonymously."

"How very public spirited and how convenient." Von Schnakenberg leant over and picked up a cigar from Brigadefuhreur Schuster's desk. Neither Schuster nor his brigade were fit for purpose at this precise moment in time and von Schnakenberg saw this as an ideal opportunity to arrange a change of ownership of the Town Hall where he had now established his tactical H.Q. He swung his legs onto the former occupant's giant oak desk. I could get used to this very easily, he said to himself as he puffed on Schuster's cigar and helped himself to a glass of Schuster's Chivas Regal Malt whiskey. He offered Alfonin a seat, a cigar and a glass of whiskey. "Alright then, Nicky. Who's now in command of the Schuster Brigade?"

Alfonin looked at a list in his hand. "A Sturmbannfuhrer Ulrich, sir."

Von Schnakenberg spat out his cigar. "A sturm-bannfuhrer?" He asked incredulously. "A sturmbannfuhrer is the most senior officer in the brigade?"

"Yes, sir," Alfonin smiled. "Brigadefuhrer Schuster and all of his senior officers are casualties…"

"And Sturmbannfuhrer Ulrich?" von Schnakenberg interrupted.

"He was not on the podium and survived, sir. Without a scratch." Alfonin laughed. "In fact, sir, he's known through out the brigade as 'The Cat.'"

"Why?"

"Because he has nine lives, sir. He's survived countless scraps with the partisans."

Von Schnakenberg was less than impressed. He would have liked to have got rid of the whole bloody lot of them. "Well, inform 'The Cat' that as the highest ranking S.S. officer in Hereward he is now the acting commanding officer of the Triple S Brigade effective immediately." he said dryly.

"Very good, sir." Alfonin stood up to leave.

"And Nicky. Ask him what he wants us to do with the dead S.S. sturmbannfuhrer."

"Cause of death, sir?"

Von Schnakenberg shrugged without concern. "The usual reason: partisan attack."

"Alice...what? How? When?" Sam shook his head. "So many questions..."

"Sam." Alice put her hand on top of her brother's. "All in good time. I was recruited a long time ago. Before the Invasion. Before you and Al joined the Home Guard. In fact, before the War began."

Sam was stunned. Alice. His own sister. A secret agent from before the War. A real live Mata Hari.

"I was part of an Intelligence cell. We supplied information to headquarters during the Invasion and after the Occupation began. After the Jerries established control over Hereward, Edinburgh ordered us to link up with a Fighting cell."

"What happened to the Communications cell?" Alan asked.

Alice shrugged. "Wiped out? Captured? Given up? For all that we know, they may still be functioning. Or they may simply be lying low. Maybe they haven't been ordered to link up with any survivors. Who knows?"

"And then what happened?" Sam asked.

"Our role changed. We were ordered to go deep cover

at Christmas. We were ordered to become an Infiltration cell..."

"At Christmas?" Sam interrupted. "When you broke up with Danny Edwards?"

Alice nodded. "Our cell was called a 'Delilah' Unit. I imagine that there were many more groups formed up and down the country. Our mission was to seduce and sleep with, if necessary, members of the German Armed Forces for the purpose of gathering information."

"Norbert Ulrich?" Alan asked.

Alice nodded. "It was too much for one of the girls-she quit. The other two girls and I kept each other going."

"How are they?" Alan asked the question for Sam.

"One of the other Delilah's is alive, the other one is dead. She was killed in the firebomb attacks."

Sam began to cry. He started slowly and gradually built up until his face was covered in tears and his entire body was wracked with convulsions. He was shaking and sobbing and hugging himself with his arms as he rocked backwards and forwards on his heels. He repeated the same words over and over again "I'm sorry...I'm so sorry..."

The Lysander slowed to a halt in the field. Rathdowne helped Ansett to walk to the aeroplane.

Alice, Sam and Alan stood beside the bonfire that burned fiercely as a beacon.

"Remember," Ansett shouted above the noise of the propeller. "Keep a low profile until we return!"

"Don't worry!" Sam shouted back. "You can depend on me to keep these two impudent young pups in line. You know what a stickler I am for following orders!"

Ansett smiled and gave Sam the finger.

Sam reciprocated.

"We'll be back!"

The group watched as the Lysander gathered speed and took off narrowly missing the top of the trees at the end of the improvised runway.

Ansett turned around in his narrow seat and peered down at the ground. There was no sight of Sam, Alice and Alan. It was if the darkness had swallowed them up.

THE END

2607232R00159

Printed in Great Britain
by Amazon.co.uk, Ltd.,
Marston Gate.